OUTCAST Ops: The Poseidon Initiative

Rick Chesler

Cover art by J. Kent Holloway

10 9 8 7 6 5 4 3 2 1

PROLOGUE

1999: Scheveningen Beach, Netherlands

The surf was high that day, a day budding marine biologist Jasmijn Rotmensen would never forget. Breaking right on the sand, the waves exploded into a fine mist of sparkling water droplets that filled the air, delighting hundreds of beachgoers along the packed shoreline that hot Summer day as they ran and splashed and basked in the sun.

The twenty-year old stood on the edge of the sand, her backpack slung on one shoulder as she glanced at the pier to her right. She cursed the fact that she'd been up all night studying and slept in. Now she'd be lucky to find a patch of sand large enough to accommodate her towel, and it would be far back from the water's edge. Such is life, she thought, as she tip-toed across the scorching beach. All she wanted to do, anyway, was to read a few s from her biochemistry text and get outside for a little while. No big deal.

Threading her way between people's blankets and dodging tossed frisbees and balls, Jasmijn reached a relatively open spot of sand and stood there, gauging her chances of getting any closer to the water. It didn't look good. *This will have to do if I want to get some reading done anytime soon.* Shielding her eyes with a hand, she glanced longingly at the ocean directly in front of the beach, just beyond the breaking waves. A frown formed over her delicate features. She blew a wisp of her blonde hair away from her eye as she studied a discolored mass just beyond the waves.

What's that?

A shapeless, reddish-brown patch lay in the water, stretching roughly parallel to the beach in both directions as far as her eyes could see. An onshore breeze cropped up, causing her to blow another strand of hair off her face, and also, she noted, to push the discolored mass of water toward the breaking surf where dozens of kids and a few adults frolicked. She thought back to one of her biology books, her quick mind associating the physical thing in front of her with a passage of text she'd read a year earlier.

Red tide!

She couldn't recall all of the details, but Jasmijn knew that a red tide was a massive bloom of algae—microscopic plants in the water—that could be dangerous to fish because they depleted the surrounding water of all oxygen. Neither plants nor animals, they belonged to a classification of living creatures known as Protists.

She was trying to remember more when she heard the first screams.

"Help!" First one voice, then many more. "Help me!"

Others stood around her and Jasmijn had to crane her neck to look at the water's edge, where clusters of bathing-suit clad people knelt on the wet sand.

"He can't breathe!"

Up and down the beach the cries were repeated. A mass exodus of swimmers swarmed up the beach, trampling those who didn't bother to get up to see what the commotion was about.

Shouts went up about making emergency calls.

Jasmijn squinted, looking past the throng of bodies now lying in the sand to the water beyond. The waves were red in color now, and when they crashed, a thick plume of red mist rose into the air where the onshore wind caught it and sprayed it over the beach crowd like a mister fan. Jasmijn stopped trying to make her way to the water as she dredged up a little more of what she knew about red tides from her memory banks.

Red tides are caused by dinoflagellates. They produce a powerful toxin that is accumulated by shellfish. People who eat shellfish that have been exposed to red tides sometimes contract Paralytic Shellfish Poisoning.

But that was through eating them. Even people who swam through a red tide weren't known to get sick from it. As far as she knew, it only happened from eating shellfish, which accumulated the red tide toxins in their flesh. When cooked, that toxin failed to break down. Could it be that these people were breathing the red tide organisms in through the wave plumes and concentrating the toxins in their bloodstream that way?

Jasmijn watched another wave smash on the sand, sending another plume to waft out over the crowd of people which had swelled with those arriving to help.

Within an hour, the death toll would rise to nearly three hundred people.

ONE

Present day

Royal Netherlands Institute for Sea Research, Den Hoorn, Netherlands

Dr. Jasmijn Rotmensen looked up from a microscope and rubbed her tired eyes. The hour was late. Looking out the single lab window, she could see only a couple of dim lights on in the neighboring buildings. She was the only one crazy enough to work weekends. Then she quickly bent to the 'scope again as if things might have changed in the last few seconds. Tanks full of saltwater bubbled on the lab bench around her. To a glance they appeared empty, but Jasmijn had carefully stocked them with dinoflagellates. She looked at the slide again and sighed, brushing a strand of hair—still blond but no longer the platinum it used to be—out of her eyes.

“Didn't work?” Jasmijn's research assistant, Nicolaas Aarens asked. Nicolaas was a second-year master's degree student who had pestered Jasmijn for over a year in order for the chance to work with her. Yes, her reputation in the scientific community was unmatched after over a decade of hard work, but she suspected it was also a bit more than that. She often caught him looking at her a little too long. He produced quality work, though, and so she was willing to ignore it, at least for now. She looked up from the scope to return his gaze, his white lab coat one size too large for his slender frame, his bulbous nose anchoring a face full of freckles.

"Oh it worked all right," she said with a sarcastic laugh, turning her attention to a cage nestled amidst the water tanks. She pointed inside to a still rat.

"The cancer's dead. Trouble is, so's Oliver."

"Rest in peace, Ollie. You were my fave lab rat!"

"This STX derivative kills everything I throw at it within minutes."

"Who would have thought that applying the red tide toxin that causes paralytic shellfish poisoning in this way would be *too* effective?"

"Yeah, I was just having a look at a cross-section of cells from the injection site to see if I could make sense of this, when—"

Suddenly the door to the lab burst open and in ran two armed men wearing combat fatigues and ski masks. Bursts of sound suppressed automatic weapons fire sprayed the lab. Glassware shattered, overhead lights blinked out.

"Freeze!" said the first.

"Don't shoot the tanks! We all die if they break!" Jasmijn pointed at the row of bubbling water tanks plastered with hazardous materials warning labels. The special acrylic material was thick enough to handle an accidental drop to the floor, but wasn't designed with stopping bullets in mind.

"Hands in the air!" shouted the second, eyes scanning the array of tanks. Jasmijn complied.

Then a third man entered the room, this one wheeling a hand truck supporting a tall, white plastic vat. He set the cart by the lab bench with the tanks and then said nothing while he roved about the lab, making certain no one else was here. He crouched and turned until he had scouted the entire room. He gave a hand signal to the other two, who then relaxed a bit before focusing on Jasmijn. One of the intruders, the taller of the two, stepped forward.

"Dr. Rotmensen," the gunman said in Dutch. "Tell me. Why are you so concerned about the tanks?" He waved his gun at the row of bubbling rectangles.

"They contain an isolate of STX—Saxitoxin—it's the chemical compound that comes from red tides."

"It's what gives people paralytic shellfish poisoning," Nicolaas added, ever helpful. Jasmijn scowled at him.

"I'm using it to develop a cancer cure."

In response, the third man, dressed head to toe in black, unscrewed a lid from his plastic vat and removed from it a coil of hose. He then brought the hose over to the nearest of the water tanks, where he examined the lids. They were sealed tightly shut, each retained with a heavy-duty combination padlock. He addressed Jasmijn.

"What is the combination?"

At this, Jasmijn balked. These men knew exactly what they were looking for. And that was what scared her most of all. This wasn't a random break-in. The specific STX variant she had developed in her lab was a thousand times more potent than what occurred naturally. She had only recently made this breakthrough, however, and had then applied to her university for heightened security, so how did they know...

Damn it!

Jasmijn balled her fingers into fists with her realization even as she held them in the air. The security application! It was filed online with a university intranet system. Probably run by student assistants and not difficult at all to hack into.

Could this be from where the breach had come? Her eyes tracked over to Nicolaas. His hands shook as he held them high. He attempted to turn his head like an owl as the sounds of one of the gunman's footfalls echoed on the tile floor somewhere behind him while he circled the two scientists with his gun. The other shooter remained stationary, his snub-nosed automatic weapon aimed casually in Jasmijn's direction from the waist.

"Dr. Rotmensen!" The masked man at the vat shook the padlock on the tank.

The circling gunman squeezed his trigger and chips of porcelain sprayed Jasmjin's lower legs as the floor tiles broke up around her, a warning.

"The combination!"

Jasmijn blew another lock of hair off her face. "I can't give it to you. Besides, I'm sure you could dismantle the locks or the tanks themselves if you really wanted. The locks are just to prevent people who don't know any better from getting hurt. That's not a protection I'd like to afford the likes of you."

The gunman talking to Jasmijn nodded to one of his associates, who promptly walked up to Nicolaas and grabbed him by pulling his elbows sharply behind his back. He yelped with the sudden pain.

"Then I guess we'll have to see if we can smash them open with your friend's face, here." The gunman started to drag Nicolaas toward one of the tanks.

"You don't understand." Jasmijn did her best to keep her pleading from sounding too much like outright begging. "If you bust even one of those tanks open and that water spills out onto the floor, the invisible SPX molecules it contains will aerosolize—that means they'll become suspended in the air—we'll breathe at least a few of them in, and we will die an excruciating death within minutes." She paused to let this sink in, the only sound in the lab the bubbling of the tanks and the hum of their air pumps.

“Is that what you want?”

The one who did the talking for the group spoke up again, having produced a small pistol fitted with a sound suppressor in contrast to the submachine guns favored by his associates. Jasmijn was correct in her assumption that this made the man no less lethal, however, and he pointed his weapon at Nicolaas’ temple.

“You will unlock each of the tanks or I kill your friend, here.”

“He's not my friend. He's a just a lab assistant who works for me.” Jasmijn felt bad for a second when she saw the pain on Nicolaas’ face, pain that became evident even over his existing mask of stress at having a gun pointed at his head. But she knew that to reveal feelings for him would be a weakness that would be used against them.

“You do not believe me?” The pistol-wielding assailant raised his voice. “Perhaps this will convince you.” He lowered the gun sight until it aimed at Nicolaas’ right foot and pulled the trigger. They heard a quiet *pffft* and then saw a neat red circle appear on Nicolaas' white Adidas. He dropped to the floor, hands clutching his ruined foot. The shooter raised his voice over the lab worker's howling.

"The locks, Dr. Rotmensen! Every time I have to repeat myself, your assistant will receive another piece of lead."

Jasmijn's inner turmoil was so great that she almost collapsed, so devoted was her brain to sorting out her thoughts that it could no longer control her muscles. She could not bear to see Nicolaas—or anyone, for that matter—suffer. On the other hand, knowing what these men could do with her SPX product made her cringe for the sake of humanity. The amount of death that could be caused...She started to curse herself for proceeding too quickly with her work, without pausing to let the administration catch up with security protocols, but stopped herself. There was no time for that now.

"Too late!"

The intruder's silenced weapon spat once more, and Nicolaas had a matching set of tennis shoes with red circles on the toes. The young man curled into a fetal position on the floor, crying softly.

“Next I go to the knees,” the tormentor said, moving in a slow circle around his victim as he tested his aim.

Jasmijn could take no more. She rationalized that she didn't know exactly what these men were going to do with her dangerous concoction born of the sea. Or to herself. That was part of it, wasn't it? She asked herself the question as she looked at Nicolaas’ crumpled form, fat smears of blood now arced across the floor where he flailed his feet in agony. *Maybe they're from a competing lab and they want to beat me to publication so they're stealing my modified SPX stock?* She laughed aloud at the absurdity of it.

“You laugh at us?” The shootist aimed his deadly pistol at her breasts, first the left, then the right, then back again.

Jasmijn was so deep in thought she hadn't realized her laugh was not only in her head.

“No. I'm just nervous. That's what I do when I'm nervous. I laugh. All right. I'll open the locks. Please, no more violence.”

“Move slowly!” All three gun barrels in the room tracked Jasmijn as she walked to the nearest of the six tanks. She put her fingers on the lock and paused, giggling out of nervousness.

“I'm sorry. I forgot the combination.”

“Do not toy with us!” The leader pointed his pistol at Nicolaas’ knee.

“No! I'm just...tired and stressed. I know it. I know it...” She stood there thinking for a second and closed her eyes. She pictured herself standing on a tranquil beach, gulls in the air, dolphins jumping in waves that were free of red tides...When the series of numbers alighted in her brain she bent once more to the lock and opened it.

The gunman motioned her out of the way with his pistol and one of his henchmen wheeled the dolly over. This man paid out a plastic tube and dropped it into the unlocked aquarium. Then he flipped a switch, starting a pump that began to suck the water from the tank into the vat on the dolly. Jasmijn noted that the vat was a properly equipped vessel to deal with hazardous liquids. The opening had a narrow, fluted neck to prevent splashes. The container was labeled with poison and biohazard warnings.

"Next!" the gunman warned.

Jasmijn repeated the process for the rest of the aquaria, the vat becoming more full with each emptied tank. It also bothered her that they were nearly exactly correct in their estimation of how much capacity their vat would need in order to hold all of her product. How did they know this?

She would have plenty of time to ponder it, but right now the men were on the move, one of them wheeling the vat toward the lab door while the other two kept their weapons trained on their victims as they backed out.

"Good night, Dr. Rotmensen. The world will thank you for your good work!" He laughed as he walked to the lab door. Then he turned around to face her in the doorway.

"Perhaps you wonder why we are leaving you with your life?"

The words chilled Jasmijn. Now that she thought of it, what good reason was there not to kill her? They were presumably stealing her ultra-toxic lab product to exterminate as many people as they could, or to sell to someone else who had that goal. She said nothing.

"We want for you to continue your good work. In particular, we'd like you to focus on an antidote to STX. You don't have one yet, do you?"

She shook her head. "I only just developed the STX product."

“We would like an antidote. We will pay you a visit again in seven day's time. Perhaps here. Perhaps at your house. Perhaps somewhere else. Have the antidote ready or you will be truly sorry.”

Jasmijn turned red with anger despite her inner voice telling her it would be best to let these thugs leave with no further interaction. “I have no idea if that's even possible!”

The terrorist turned around to the vat on the dolly and produced something that looked like a fancy squirt gun. When he turned around again he was wearing a gas mask of some sort over his balaclava. His two associates put one on as well. He tossed an identical one to Jasmijn. “Put it on.”

He did not offer Nicolaas a mask. He shook the pressurized squirt device and strode back into the lab until he stood over the fallen research assistant, now in a sitting position clutching both feet.

“What are you doing?” Jasmijn shrieked. “Do not play around with this substance!”

He shook his head as one of the terrorists aimed his automatic weapon at her.

“This is not play. Perhaps you are lying to me and you already have an antidote.” The man with the squirt gun thing aimed its fat nozzle at Nicolaas’ head. Nicolaas put his hands up in protest, sputtering nonsensical syllables.

“I don't have an antidote!”

“Then this should incentivize you to develop one within the next few minutes.”

The masked terrorist pulled back on a plunger attached to the device and a plume of fine mist was ejected from the nozzle onto Nicolaas’ face.

TWO

Bethesda, Maryland

Tanner Wilson picked up the secure line in the second-floor study of his modest suburban house.

"Tanner here."

"I couldn't do it, Tanner. I couldn't do it..." He was just able to recognize the female voice on the other end of the line before it broke into uncontrolled sobbing. His expressive eyes—one white and the other black due to a condition called heterochromia—took on an intense glint as he flashed on good times years ago, then spoke into his handset.

"*Jasmijn*? Is that you?"

The reply was prefaced with sniffling. "Yes. I'm sorry, I know it's been years. I didn't know who else to call."

"What's going on? Are you okay?"

He didn't mean the question to come from a relationship standpoint, and hoped that wasn't what this was about. At the same time, she was once a close friend of his and he wanted to help.

“I'm...” She fell apart again. “I'm okay. But my lab assistant's dead.”

Tanner sat up straighter in his desk chair. “When? What happened? Where are you?”

“A couple of hours ago. I couldn't save him in time, Tanner. I tried...I tried so hard...It was so awful and horrible...”

“Jasmijn, where are you right now?”

“At my place in Netherlands.”

He'd never been there before, so he couldn't picture it. But he could envision her face, her soft skin, sparkling blue eyes and silky blond hair.

“Slow down and tell me what happened from the beginning. Take a deep breath. Okay?”

She did. First she told him about her cancer research with STX and how lethal the stuff was. And then she related to him the masked terrorists breaking into her lab. Tanner interrupted to ask how many of them there were. He slid a notepad in front of him and picked up a scrimshaw pen made from whale ivory that she had given him many years before. He took notes as Jasmijn continued to lay out what had happened to her. He broke in at one point to ask if she could see their skin color.

"They were clad head to toe in black. The skin around some of their eyes was dark, some light, but they all spoke Dutch."

Jasmijn went on as Tanner scratched on the pad. "The police came and took a standard report. They said they're looking for the men. Officials from my university stopped by but they only seemed concerned about liability. They told me how my elevated security request for working with the modified STX hadn't been approved yet."

But Tanner was having trouble focusing. *Dark skin, speak Dutch...terror...*The name *Hofstad* rode the nerve impulses through his brain.

Although he was no longer with the FBI, Tanner Wilson was a veteran Special Agent having served for a dozen years—two as a field agent and then a decade as a counter-terror specialist. Though not as well known as Al Qaida, Hofstad had been committing local level acts of deadly terrorism from their base near The Hague, Netherland's seat of government, for at least a decade. They had loose ties throughout Europe, and although the group was never at the top of Tanner's watch lists while working in the FBI's vaunted Counter-Terror division, they were usually on the list—somewhere near the bottom, perhaps even dropping off for a while, only to claw back up to the bottom rungs.

"Jasmijn, tell me more about STX. I'm not familiar with that. What is it?"

“Saxitoxin, a potent neurotoxin. It’s derived from marine microorganisms that cause paralytic shellfish poisoning. I was working with a genetically enhanced dinoflagellate population to influence the STX to target cancer cells, but it turns out all I really did was to make the toxin even more potent.” She told him about how all of her lab animals died from it.

“So how exactly did they kill your lab assistant with it?”

“They sprayed it on him from some kind of mister attached to the vat they transferred it to.”

The word *aerosolized* hopped on the neuron train in Tanner's brain.

“And tell me exactly what your assistant's symptoms were?” He immediately regretted the question as he heard her begin to cry softly.

“Never mind, that can wait if you—”

“No, it's okay. If anyone can help me it would be you. You see, Tanner, I haven't told you the worst of it yet. I didn't call you just to cry on your shoulder. I'm in trouble.”

“Go on.”

He heard her take a measured breath. “As soon as they left, I called 1-1-2—that's like 911 in your country—knowing it would do no good, since there is no known antidote for even naturally occurring STX, and mine is slightly modified. But I’ve been working off and on on an antidote—so as to understand this compound as thoroughly as possible, not to mention to create a safety factor for my own lab. As soon as they left I immediately set up my latest antidote samples—unproven samples that were simply the next iteration from the last batch that failed miserably. I had no other recourse. Even to set that up required almost twenty minutes and toward the end Nicolaas was convulsing on the floor, banging his feet, which had just been shot, into the lab benches. But I couldn't stop to help him, I had to prepare—”

She broke up into a crying jag. Tanner waited, consulting a device that displayed the security status of his home line as he did so.

Green light. So far so good.

“By the time I had the experimental antidote ready to administer, Nicolaas’ face was turning purple and he was unable to talk or move. I knew that he had mere seconds before his muscles were so paralyzed that he wouldn't even be able to breathe. I injected him with the antidote, and then...” She choked back a sob.

“He didn't make it,” Tanner finished for her.

“No! His eyes opened for a brief second and I thought, maybe—I—”

“You did your best.”

“The emergency responders arrived right after that. They tried to resuscitate him but it was no use.” She paused for a moment, composing herself, and then continued. “The terrorists said they'll be back for me, Tanner, and when they come if I don't have the working antidote ready, they'll kill me. Probably with my own STX."

"Jasmijn. Listen. This is very important. Did they say anything or give any kind of hints about what they were going to do with the STX?"

He heard snuffling sounds for a few seconds, and then, "No. Only that 'the world will thank me for my good work,' whatever that means."

Jasmijn continued before Tanner could respond. "Tanner, this is bad. I've been working with STX for a long time. Ever since I saw a natural instance of STX become aerosolized on a beach one time, I knew I had to know more about it. It's one of the most potent toxins in existence."

"I'm familiar with STX as a potential bioweapon, but to my knowledge it hasn't yet been able to be harnessed on a large scale. And I know lots of people get sick and even die from tainted shellfish that carry concentrated STX in their flesh."

“Right, but believe me, Tanner, this is much, much worse than that. First of all, the tanks of the stuff were concentrated a hundred-fold over what even the most tainted shellfish would have. Even if a shellfish lived for ten years inside a potent red tide, it wouldn't have nearly the concentration of STX that I was working with. And that was before I modified it in the lab. It killed Nicolaas in fourteen minutes, Tanner. Fourteen minutes. And I don't think I can make the antidote within the terrorists' timeframe. A week is not enough...”

“Forget about the antidote for now. You need to get to a safe place.”

He heard her sigh in frustration. “I was thinking of going to stay with my mother in the country, and then for some reason I decided to call you.”

“You did the right thing.” Tanner slid out a computer keyboard from his desk and tapped some keys. He brought up a file he had on Hofstad and started reading and viewing pictures of North African Muslims while he spoke. “But you won't be safe at your mother's.”

Silence greeted him from the other end of the line. “I...I don't know where else to go, Tanner.” She paused for a moment before adding, “I'm not seeing anyone. All I do is work, and now my work is not safe.”

“You could come to the States and stay with me for a while. You'll be safe here.” Tanner stared at the small bank of CCTV monitors on his wall that showed views of his front entrance, backyard and driveway.

“Oh, Tanner, I don't know, I—”

“It's no inconvenience at all. I'm not seeing anyone, either, so I've got plenty of room here. I've got a spare bedroom you can use, you can use my phone—yours might be compromised, but don't worry, I've got safeguards on my end that'll take care of that for this call. But don't use your phones—personal or lab—after this call.”

“Okay.”

“I'll make your flight arrangements.”

THREE

Sun Life Stadium, Miami, Florida

In the subterranean labyrinth of tunnels beneath the stadium, Pablo Guitierez sat inside the rear work area of a special production truck that contained equipment needed to put on the halftime show. He was testing an image projector when he heard footsteps approach the open back of the truck behind him. Fellow employee Alec Schmidt walked up to the ramp into the truck, which was dimly lit inside by banks of closed circuit monitors showing the football field, as well as blinking LEDs on various pieces of equipment.

Pablo turned around to acknowledge Alec before quickly resuming his work. It was way too close to showtime to be needing assistance, but Pablo did his best to keep his cool and give the guy a break. Alec was hired only a couple of months ago and was still learning the ropes. "What do you need, Alec?"

The newcomer looked about the truck, including through the thin window into the cab, which he could see was empty. Glancing once behind him, he pulled a three-inch Kershaw folding blade from his front right pocket and stepped up to Pablo, who was hunched over the projector.

“Is the projector working?” He leaned over him while he worked.

“Yeah, it's good to go, why?”

“I need to put a new slide set in.” The projected images that were used as part of the show were carefully curated and approved beforehand.

“Whoa, nobody told me about any new—”

Pablo never finished his sentence.

“Alec Schmidt” reached out and drew his blade across Pablo's undefended neck. He made a weird gasping noise that Alec could swear came from the open neck wound itself and not his mouth, and then began to flail in blind panic, far too late.

Alec held his victim's left arm down with his own, and then used the crook of his right elbow to smother Pablo's mouth, both to prevent his death cries from being heard and to hasten his demise by smothering the life from him. Once he was still, he released him and allowed his body to slump to the floor.

"Thanks, Pablo, I'll just swap the slides out myself." Alec removed a USB drive from the projector and inserted his own in its place. That piece of business concluded, he turned his attention to other matters.

In this same rear area of the truck was a tarp covered bundle he'd carefully hidden there the night before. He went to it and threw back the tarp.

Yes! Still there. He picked up a small metal container that looked a lot like a thermos, along with a respirator mask. He walked with them outside to the golf cart he'd been driving around the tunnels. On the back of the cart was a large plastic tank of water that was used to create mist for a special effect during the show that would allow for images to be projected onto a thin film of water droplets, so that they appeared to materialize from thin air.

Alec scanned his surroundings. When he determined no one was coming, he unfastened the tank's lid. Then he hurriedly donned the biohazard mask and carefully opened the container that looked like a thermos but was many times more sturdy, able to shield its contents from both great shocks as well as wide temperature swings. He poured the contents of the metal container in to the larger tank on the cart. He carefully screwed the thermos lid back in place and returned it to its place beneath the tarp in the truck. Then he refastened the lid on the water tank and got back behind the wheel of the cart.

#

“Alec! Hey Alec! Where are you going with that? That tank should be on the field already.” Stephanie Parrish trotted down a concrete tunnel beneath the stadium toward her employee. Her ponytail bobbed beneath a Miami Dolphins ball cap as she bounced along. Always full of energy, as the manager for the production company responsible for putting on the stadium's halftime show, she kept in shape and it showed in her short but toned figure.

The young man was driving an electric cart with a tank of liquid on the back. He greeted her with an enthusiastic wave. “Hi, boss. There was a problem with the tank for the mister—it had a crack in it after we set it up, so I told Antonio I'd be back quick with another one. This is it.”

Stephanie looked at her sports watch.. These type of problems were par for the course for her in the five years she'd been doing this job. She even took a second to glance at her pedometer reading *(9,500 steps so far today—even more than usual—I'll lose those five pounds in no time*!) before noting the time.

"Okay, Alec. Step on it, though. We're on air in less than five minutes!"

"Yes ma'am." Alec nodded and took off in the cart down the tunnel.

High above in the broadcast booth inside the stadium, a sportscaster ushered out the first half of the game. "And it looks to be another disappointing first half for the Dolphins, Bret, as we head in to halftime here on *Monday Night Football*. We'll be back after these words from our sponsor with first half highlights and the Sun Life halftime show."

On the field, a marching band and cheerleaders walked out in formation and started through a routine. A few minutes in and the overhead lights dimmed, casting the stadium into momentary blackness before a series of effects lights ringing the field blinked on. The band stopped and electronic music played through the stadium's PA system.

From an elevated platform in the center of the field, a commercial grade mister ejected an invisible plume of liquid droplets high into the air. A slight wind blew through the open air venue, which the operator compensated for by increasing the spray volume and nozzle direction.

As the music built to a crescendo a technician turned on the projector. A gigantic image of a Miami Dolphins football helmet rotated slowly in mid-air, seemingly appearing out of nothing. Its shape shifted slightly with gusts of wind, but quickly coalesced. The crowd cheered. Additional performers took the field and the show continued.

About four minutes into it, the first screams came from the sideline facing the oncoming wind. Confusion reigned initially, those within earshot of the wailing under the false impression that the drama might be part of the performance. When six cheerleaders fell to the ground in mid-routine, a lifeless tangled heap of skin, pom-poms and glitter, a public address request for medical personnel brayed over the show's audio track.

As a medic team drove out onto the field in a cart normally used to haul off injured players, the holographic image began to morph from the football helmet into something else. A new shape materialized, indistinct at first but solidifying by the second, until, unbelievably, a massive human figure stood at the fifty yard line, its head reaching halfway to the nosebleed seats.

More frantic shouting rent the air as more and more bodies dropped.

In the broadcast booth, the announcer went live on the air. "Well I don't know about you, Brett, but I think this is the first time in my career I've had to interrupt a halftime show. But...there seems to be some confusion in the stadium...I'm getting word that people have fallen ill. And what's this—this image forming now?"

Midfield, the 3D image had solidified to an unmistakable rendering of a man with a long, flowing beard, clutching a trident.

The other announcer chimed in. “If I didn't know any better, Brett—and I caution that I may not—I'd say that was the Greek god, Poseidon. God of the sea?”

There was a pause filled with terrified shouts as the co-announcer thought about this. “I would agree with you, Brett.”

“The Dolphins are from the sea and this is their God, is that it?” The co-anchor speculated.

“No idea, Fred, but right now I don't see why they aren't stopping the show. There are people seriously ill down there on the field—spectators, fans, players, cheerleaders.”

“Seems to be affecting those on the lower levels, and closest to mid-field.”

In the broadcast booth an employee rushed to shut the windows and vents.

Far below them in the tunnel system, no one paid any attention to production assistant Alec Schmidt as he drove his golf cart out of the stadium to a nondescript sedan.

FOUR

Bethesda, Maryland

Tanner Wilson had just sat down to a post-workout protein shake in front of the cable news in his kitchen when his door chime rang. He rose and walked to the door. Glancing at the small video monitor in the entrance hall wall, he smiled upon seeing all 5'2" of Dr. Jasmijn Rotmensen standing there on his doorstep, looking as natural as can be in a winter coat, scarf and leather boots. The blond-haired scientist captivated him now as she had all those years ago. He reminded himself that he was forcing her to stand out in the cold while he admired her from inside, and abandoned his cozy memories. He scanned the video feed for signs of a presence besides Jasmijn's. Seeing none, he opened the door.

Jasmijn beamed, flashing a mouth full of big, white teeth. She threw her arms around Tanner and pressed his body to hers, hard.

"It's *so* good to see you, Tanner," she breathed. "Thank you for inviting me."

"Not a problem. Let me get your things." She handed him a duffel bag and he took it, beckoning her to follow him into the house. After giving her a brief tour of his home and dropping her bag in the guest bedroom, Tanner led her back to the kitchen where he poured them both tall glasses of iced-tea. He could see the tension in her eyes as she sipped.

"Relax. You're safe here." But then her eyes seemed to grow even wider. At first Tanner thought she was directing her gaze at him—that she took what he said as nonsense—but he saw that she was staring over his shoulder at the television, where the news channel still played.

On screen was a shot of a football stadium at night with a banner crawling beneath: "Hundreds confirmed dead among *Monday Night Football* stadium crowd in Miami—terror group makes demands."

Tanner snatched up the remote and turned up the volume. A panic-stricken woman answered a reporter's question. “It started right after the mist. I saw the image of a Greek god appear in mid-air, and right after that people started dropping like flies.”

A replay from the halftime performance showed the holographic image of Poseidon, and then panned in for a close-up of a cheerleader clutching her throat before crumpling to the turf.

“That looks horrible!” Jasmijn's mouth dropped open. Tanner turned up the volume some more as the view changed to a full screen shot of a bearded, light-skinned man standing in front of a plain white sheet. Tanner judged him to be somewhere in his mid-thirties. He held an automatic rifle in one hand, butt on the floor, and stared unblinking at the camera as he spoke.

“Oh my God!” Jasmijn clutched Tanner's arm.

Tanner did his best to comfort her while the man addressed the camera in halting, accented English with Dutch subtitles.

"Our organization is called Hofstad." Tanner bristled with a disarming combination of recognition and fear.

"We carried out the attack at Sun Life Stadium in Miami last night and we take full responsibility for that attack."

The terrorist paused for effect while he stared like a snake at the lens, then continued.

> "Our demand is but one. It is very simple and easy to carry out. We want the United States embassy out of The Hague, Netherlands. I will say it once more: We demand that the United States embassy at Lange Voorhout 102, 2514 EJ Den Haag, Netherlands, be removed from service. We are allowing the U.S. government a grace period of forty-eight hours in which to comply with this demand,

beginning..." The terrorist looked at the plastic digital watch on his wrist..." now."

He stared impassively at the camera for a moment before continuing. "If the premises have not been vacated in forty-eight hours, more incidents such as the one in your football stadium will happen. There will be no warning. They will be more severe. Take more lives. We are prepared to carry out these attacks in any or all of your fifty states. There will be no negotiating, no bargaining, no delays of any kind for any reason."

He shouted his final words: "Forty! Eight! Hours!"

Then the terrorist camcorder zoomed to a small television sitting on the floor in a corner, playing news footage of the stadium attack.

Tanner looked away from the TV. Jasmijn had her head lying on her arm on the table, shaking.

Tanner tried to comfort her but it was no use. “It's my fault,” she mumbled over and over.

On screen, the news report shifted to a view of the White House, where the president stood at a podium emblazoned with the presidential seal. A forest of microphones bristled in front of him, an eager throng of reporters hungry for answers waiting just beyond. The President cleared his throat, received a go-ahead signal from an assistant off-screen, and leaned into the microphones.

“It is with great sadness and a heavy heart that I learned of the 768 persons killed in a terror attack last night at Sun Life Stadium during Monday Night Football—an event that is supposed to be a good time for all. I would like to commend our valiant first responders for their prompt reaction and highly professional handling of this horrific incident. To those responsible, let me assure you: you will be held accountable. The United States does not negotiate with terrorists nor does it give in to the demands of terrorists. We are working tenaciously to bring those responsible for this heinous act to justice. We have elevated our terror alert status to the maximum alert possible until further notice. That is all for now."

The president started to step down from the podium.

"President Carmichael?" a female reporter called out. "What about the Hofstad video? Will you close the embassy in The Hague?"

The President halted for a moment and then stepped back up to the podium. He shook his head emphatically as he looked at the reporter.

"We will not."

FIVE

Bethesda, Maryland

"This is all my fault." Jasmijn cradled her head in her hands. Tanner clicked the television off and looked at her. He put a hand on her arm.

"It's not your fault. It's the terrorists' fault. They're the ones doing this."

Jasmijn raised her head and rubbed her eyes. "The president just said they won't give in to Hofstad's demands. If they don't shut down the embassy..."

"Standard policy. They'll be working behind the scenes as we speak to take Hofstad down." But no sooner had the words escaped his lips than he questioned the validity of his own statement. His loyalty to his country was beyond reproach, but his trust in some sectors of the government itself had been compromised through his own experiences as a former FBI Special Agent in the Counter-terrorism Division (CTD). Well regarded for both his field acumen as well as his analytical capabilities, Tanner had been directly responsible for identifying, tracking, bringing to justice, and in some cases, killing—literally hundreds of terrorists. Indirectly , that count easily rose into the thousands. After a dozen years it seemed that nothing could derail his stellar career within the vaunted CTD.

But then came along a fiery administrative assistant by the name Caitlin White. He'd had a brief relationship with her and when he tried to call it off after realizing it wasn't meant to be, she refused to accept it. In retaliation, she claimed Tanner had harassed her on the job, filing a formal grievance. In the hyper-politically correct era of the time, the Bureau preferred to let a good man go rather than suffer the negative press of any kind of impropriety happening in D.C. And thus had ended his illustrious career with J. Edgar Hoover's storied organization. His pride wounded but his skill-set untouched, Tanner had withdrawn for a time, taking long walks on the beach alone, solo swims farther from shore than was prudent, meandering hiking trips into the mountains with minimal gear. When he emerged from these soul-searching activities nearly a year later, he was more convinced than ever that his country needed him even if it had cast him aside. He would not turn his back on the nation that had given him so much, even though it had spurned him. Each day's news headlines reminded him that America needed him. He could not stand to sit idly by and do nothing while he watched threat after threat to his beloved homeland materialize.

And so it was that Tanner Wilson had cast himself out from hiding in order to seek out like-minded individuals. For the irony was that although he had been branded an outcast, he knew that he was not the only one. Far from it. And he had been all too aware that while talented, he would require help. In the FBI he had enjoyed the support of a competent and motivated team. That would not be easy to replace, but at the same time he had been aware that it was just a matter of finding those in a similar situation as himself. And he had known where to look.

Tanner held Jasmijn's gaze with his own. “I have some familiarity with Hofstad from my FBI days. I may be able to help here. But first let me ask you a question.” Her quizzical expression said she wanted to hear it.

“Based on your estimation of how much STX they stole from your lab, how much of that do you think they already used in last night's attack?”

She answered with no hesitation. “Hardly any. Unless they spilled some during the transfer process. But from what I saw on television, perhaps two percent of what they took, if that.”

Tanner tried not to let his concern show on his face. He kept the conversation moving so as not to dwell on this disconcerting fact. “Do you think they have the ability to make more of it?”

Again, her response was decisive and swift. “No. The process is highly technical and requires specific source compounds. They did not press me for it. They probably knew that what they were taking was more than enough.” She shuddered.

“More than enough for what?” Tanner wasn't sure he wanted to hear the answer.

Jasmijn shrugged. “More than enough to kill...” Her eyes looked up and to the right as she mentally calculated...” Let's see, if last night's plume in the halftime show killed 700 people, then they probably have enough, if they don't waste or lose—or sell— any, to kill...millions.” She hung her head as she concluded her grim estimation.

“There's a group of people I'd like you to meet.” Tanner's words hung heavy in the air.

Jasmijn raised her head as though its weight was almost more than she could bear. “Who are they?”

“They're a team of special people I work with to handle situations like these.”

She raised an eyebrow. “*Special* people? Did they ride the short bus to school?”

Tanner blushed, close to embarrassment. He wasn't used to explaining his organization to outsiders. He pushed his chair back from the table and stood.

“I’m glad you haven’t lost your sense of humor. Listen, it'll be a lot easier for me to explain once we're in the meeting. Not to mention,” he said, glancing at his G-shock watch, “that we don't have a lot of time before Hofstad acts again.”

SIX

Bethesda, Maryland

Tanner led Jasmijn down a flight of stairs in his house.

"I thought your garage is outside on ground level?" she said, recalling the quick tour he'd given her.

"It is. We're meeting down here. I saved the best part of the tour for last." He opened a heavy steel door at the bottom of the staircase and flipped on a light switch. Jasmijn stared cautiously inside.

"Your group is down here already?" Understandably, the idea that a bunch of people were hanging out downstairs that Tanner had only just told her about made her somewhat uncomfortable. Tanner gave her a good natured laugh.

"In a manner of speaking. C'mon in..." He walked into the converted basement, waving an arm for her to follow. Jasmijn entered and then stood still, taking in the space that served as Tanner's office area and war room.

"Wow."

While the main house had more of a rustic, almost-but-not-quite farmhouse quality to it, with a lot of natural wood and unpolished stone, this underground space was a sleek, ultramodern affair. Lots of glass, LED lighting, LCD screens and thin blue carpet. A glass, rectangular conference table occupied the center of the room on a sunken floor. Ergonomic mesh desk chairs surrounded it. Two conference phones sat at either end of the table, and there were cables and outlets built in to the table in front of each chair to plug in laptops and other devices. Ceiling mounted video cameras pointed at the table from either end. A large whiteboard and a retractable projection screen occupied one wall, while a glass etched map of the world graced another.

"This is your private office?" Jasmijn looked around, confused.

“I think of it more as a command center, but yes. Please have a seat. “Tanner wheeled a chair out for her and she sat. He walked to a networking cabinet and flipped on some rack mounted machines before turning back around to address her.

“I'd like to have a videoconference with my associates to discuss the Hofstad situation. If you're okay with it, I'd like you to participate as a subject matter expert on STX, as well as a witness who has seen the terrorists firsthand.”

Jasmijn nodded, intrigued. “Anything I can do to help.”

Tanner pulled one of the phones to him and pressed some buttons. “I lead a group of former government agents called O.U.T.C.A.S.T. It stands for Operational Undertaking to Counteract Active Stateside Threats.”

“I'd say Hofstad qualifies as a threat to the states.” Jasmijn watched as the projection screen descended from the ceiling with a soft mechanical whir.

Tanner nodded. “That's why I decided to consult with my team. Let's see what we might be able to do.”

There was a series of clicks and chirps while connections were made. A male voice with a slight Persian accent came on the line. “Good morning, Tanner. Stephen here.” Tanner preferred not to divulge more of the Outcast Ops team members' information than necessary, even to a friend like Jasmijn, so first names only were used over communications channels. He knew that the man was Stephen Shah, a former CIA agent who was fired after bringing a discrimination lawsuit against the agency. The man was an expert in middle eastern affairs with two decades of experience as a field operative. Tanner's mind automatically placed a face of Middle-Eastern ethnicity to the voice. Despite his heritage and the fact that he spoke and wrote fluent Arabic, Tanner knew that the man was a practicing Catholic, a conundrum that illustrated the person himself rather well.

Tanner greeted him and then another voice, this one also male but younger sounding and without an accent. “Liam here. How's it, Tanner? I guess not that good if we're having a meeting, right?”

“It's good to hear your voice, Liam, but you're right. We've got a situation. Standby while the others sign on and authenticate.” He knew the casual sounding twenty-something was actually Liam Reilly, an ex-SEAL Team 6 special warfare operator who was dishonorably discharged from the Navy for writing a non-fiction book of his account of the raid that killed terrorist Osama bin Laden. At 6'3” with sizable chest and shoulders, Tanner had seen him train in American Kenpo and Aikido. There was no one Tanner was afraid to fight, but Liam wasn't someone he'd ever want to go up against.

Next they heard a female voice over the line. The woman behind it introduced herself as Danielle. Tanner knew her to be Danielle Sunderland, age 37, a former

National Security Agency analyst. Like all of the OUTCAST operators, she, too, had been let go from her long-time government position for reasons having nothing to do with her actual job performance. For her, the cause for her dismissal had been intensely personal. After going through a bitter divorce with her ex-husband, she woke up one morning to find her young daughter missing. After realizing she was nowhere to be found, she knew that her ex had taken the child. In order to locate her, she tapped the powerful database systems she had access to at the NSA. The information she gleaned did aid in the search for her daughter, but it came at a price. She was fired from the NSA for using agency resources to support a personal matter. After fourteen years of service as a computational forensics expert, Danielle Sunderland was cast aside for doing what any parent would. Tanner could picture her frumpy, nerd-girl looks, replete with Lennon-style glasses that seemed to focus the fierce intelligence that issued from the eyes behind them.

A second female voice chimed in on the line, this one slightly huskier. “Hello, Naomi,” Tanner greeted her. She was Naomi “Nay” Washington, ex- Bureau of Alcohol Tobacco and Firearms after thirteen years of experience investigating arson and explosives. Like her OUTCAST peers, she loved her country deeply and wanted to help it during its times of great need, but officially no longer had that opportunity. Yet unofficially, as a member of Tanner’s organization, she had been given a second chance to do just that. Tanner mentally pictured her long legs, slim waist and vaguely exotic looks.

“Waiting on one more.” Tanner eyed the speakerphone incessantly.

There was no small talk on the line while they waited. The team was far too disciplined to generate unnecessary signal traffic. There were those in powerful places—both abroad and here at home-who would love nothing better than to expose their identities, perhaps even take whatever actions might be necessary to put a stop to what some saw as a "ruthless rogue outfit."

Soon a new voice issued from the speaker. "Dante."

Dante Alvarez, thirty-two years of age. Ex-Secret Service agent. Eleven years Presidential Guard detail and international fraud investigation experience, all flushed down the drain when he was summarily dismissed without benefits for his alleged role in a prostitution scandal while in South America during the President's visit. He had kept the Chief Executive safe even though it had ended up costing his job. Tanner had been surprised when he first met him how competent of a fighter he was with his very tall but lean, wiry physique. But his ropy muscles had translated to jujitsu skills that were superior to Tanner's own.

“I'll get right to the point.” Tanner looked over at Jasmijn to gauge her reaction so far. She was watching him closely, alert, engaged. He went on. “If any of you are not aware of the news reports on last night's football halftime show, speak up.” He paused for three seconds during which there was only silence.

“Let me inform you that I have a guest here with me at headquarters. Her name is Dr. Jasmijn Rotmensen, and she is the scientist who developed the aerosolized neurotoxin known as STX used in last night's attack. That toxin was stolen from her lab at gunpoint by members of Hofstad only one day before the strike. She was in close proximity with the terrorists during her ordeal. She is here to provide us with information so as to assess if we may be able to neutralize the threat before more innocent lives are taken, in...” He glanced at his watch. “Thirty-four hours.”

He turned to Jasmijn and asked her to recap her work with STX as well as the lab break-in. She did so in meticulous, thorough detail, pausing at one point to hold back tears as she described Nicolaas' excruciating death from the STX sprayed in his face. She also added what she had told Tanner earlier about how the quantity of STX used during the game likely represented a very small percentage of what was taken. When she was done, Tanner asked the group if they had any questions.

Danielle's voice came through the speaker. "Dr. Rotmensen , have you informed authorities that the deadly agent used in the attack was the STX from your lab?"

"No, I haven't done that yet. I will do that immediately following this call. A formal police investigation has been launched in my country based on my lab incident, but they may not have made the connection to the football stadium attack. However, although I can at least inform authorities as to what killed those people, there will still be nothing they can do about it. There is no known antidote for paralytic shellfish poisoning, nor for my particular saxitoxin derivative."

"You said Hofstad threatened you if you didn't provide them with the antidote," Danielle pressed. Tanner saw Jasmijn flinch at the word 'said'—at the implication that what she claimed had transpired in her lab may possibly be different from the truth. But he knew that an operative was trained to think that way. Trust nothing or no one. Only believe what you observe yourself. Tanner nodded at Jasmijn to respond.

"They gave me seven days and said they could pay me a visit anywhere. Rather than stick around after what they did to my lab assistant to see if I might fare any better, I decided to flee." *Into Tanner's arms*, was the unspoken rest of the sentence that she was sure Danielle was thinking.

"Is there any way you can work on the antidote in Maryland? What equipment and supplies do you need?"

Danielle asked. Tanner looked at Jasmijn, awaiting her response. When she hesitated, Danielle pressed on.

"Because if we had an antidote, and could mass produce and distribute it, Hofstad's threats become impotent."

Stephen Shah's accented voice came over the line. "We know from what they told Jasmijn in her lab that the terrorists want an antidote for the STX. We have to assume this is to exert further control over the situation. They would then be able to essentially sell the antidote to their own victims. To me this is even more reason to come up with an antidote before they do."

Jasmijn nodded. "It just occurred to me that they might even have other people working on an STX antidote. I'm not the only scientist in the world, or even in Europe, capable of doing it."

Tanner looked across the table. "Jasmijn, make sure you call the CDC as soon as this call ends to let them know definitively that STX is the bio-agent used in last night's attack. That way they might be able to get other scientists working on the antidote. You have a big head start, but with the CDC's resources, they might be able to crowdsource a solution faster than what you could do independently."

"Agreed." Jasmijn said.

Tanner went on. "But we can't sit around waiting for some government agency to fix things. Our collective decades of government service have taught us that, if nothing else." Hearty guffaws from the team broke out over the line before Tanner got back to business.

"What do you think, Jasmijn? If I could set you up in a discreet, secure lab around here, could you continue working on that antidote?"

"Unfortunately, it's not simply a matter of equipment and a space to work. The samples I have already developed that I believe are the key to creating an antidote are in my

Netherlands lab. I suppose I could request they be air-freighted to me here under special refrigerated conditions, but —"

Dante Alvarez broke in for the first time. "Why don't we just provide you a security detail at your Netherlands lab and you can do the work there under escort and 24/7 guard detail?" As ex-Secret Service, he was an expert at providing guard detail and so naturally would prefer that solution.

Tanner looked impressed. Jasmijn appeared doubtful. He addressed her concern.

"You'd be safe. Trust me. If Hofstad does return to your lab, we might be able to end this that way, too, because we'll be waiting for them."

"So we all fly to my lab?"

"Half of us. Dante, Stephen and Nay: you three will escort Jasmijn to her lab and guard her while she develops the antidote. Danielle, Liam and myself will remain in country to track Hofstad from here and respond to any related domestic threats that may arise. "

The three of them indicated their assent.

"So I came all this way only to turn around and go back home."

"To go back home safely," Tanner corrected.

SEVEN

Netherlands airspace

The Gulfstream G650 banked into a turn high over the Dutch coast. On board, the trio of OUTCAST operatives and Jasmijn returned to their seats from the conference table where they'd been seated for most of the flight from Maryland. She had answered all of the questions Dante, Stephen and Naomi had asked regarding the layout of her lab, university security protocols, storage locations, methods for the key antidote components, and more. She had furnished them with photos of the lab and surrounding campus. At the end of it all, she had been taken aback when Stephen had handed her a Dutch passport.

"But I already have a passport."

"Use this instead. Hofstad may be able to track your movements through customs. If we are lucky they'll think you're still in the U.S."

“Clearly, I'm not lucky,” she had responded dourly.

“You're still alive,” Dante had interjected. “That's pretty lucky.”

It made Jasmijn nervous to be using a false document to enter her own country, as if she had done something wrong. But she trusted Tanner Wilson, and Tanner had promised her before she left (and kissed her lightly on the lips) that she could trust his operatives with her life.

When the plane landed and they disembarked onto the much less crowded private plane terminal, she walked up to the customs counter, smiled and handed the official her fake passport. *Zoe Booten, indeed.* She wondered if Tanner had come up with that cute little name for her. Although she was sure the customs agent could see through her jittery smile and was about to wave over an associate like she saw them do in the movies, after a cursory glance at her passport he simply waved her through. And that was it. Dante, Stephen and Naomi had passed through with equal ease.

#

Initially, Jasmijn had expected to introduce her OUTCAST escorts to the university security guards posted outside her lab door as well as the campus police officers patrolling the general area, but during her in-flight briefing, Stephen had told her that wouldn't be necessary. Dante and Naomi were microbiology colleagues (with verifiable, appropriate credentials, of course) and would accompany her into and out of the lab at will.

“And you?” she had asked. She couldn't help but see a deep...*something*...in Shah's eyes. It was like a level of sadness that never went away, put there from having seen too much of the human condition's dark underbelly.

“Do not worry about me. I will be nearby, yet invisible. I will be there when you and my team need me, I assure you.”

Inwardly, Jasmijn questioned this, but she had no choice other than to take his words at face value. At least she had the other two operatives literally at her side. That was comforting, though she wondered how well they'd be able to pull off the role-playing aspect of their assignment. From what she'd seen of them thus far, they were about the farthest thing from the geeky, introspective associates she'd typically worked with.

But they'd assured her not to worry and so here she was, strolling up to her laboratory door flanked by two undercover operatives as if it was just another day at the office. She had to admit, though, that Dante in his Dockers slacks and rumpled Oxford U. sweatshirt, and Naomi in a slightly more fashionable yet still suitable for business lab rat outfit of jeans and a fisherman's sweater (it was cold this time of year in Netherlands), dressed the part surprisingly well.

As expected, all three of them including Jasmijn were required by the pair of radio-toting security guards at the door to show ID. Also as expected, the guards questioned Jasmijn about her new associates. She explained that they were visiting colleagues she had requested to work with her, and then the guards opened the lab door for them.

Once inside with the lab door closed, Jasmijn turned to Dante and Naomi, whose eyes already scanned the room, comparing the layout to the photos they'd seen. They walked in opposite directions between the rows of lab benches while Jasmijn talked.

“I noticed that the security guards don't carry guns. The campus police officers do, but not security. How are they going to help me against these terrorists if they come back? I'm sure glad you guys are here,” she finished, watching as Naomi lifted her head to gaze over a lab bench to the floor beyond. She was taking nothing for granted, posted guards or not. Naomi replied while continuing to stalk the lab.

“We have to assume that everyone here is compromised, guns or no guns. Those guards at the door could *be* card carrying Hofstad members, for all we know. Don't trust anyone except us.”

Jasmijn watched as she reached a large, metal square door with a curved handle. “Cold storage, right?”

“Right.”

“Walk-in or just racks?”

“Racks. Don't worry, nobody could hide in there. Too cold, anyway. Just above freezing. The key samples for the antidote work are in there.”

“Can I open it?” Naomi paused with her fingers over the handle.

“Yes. The sample material isn't particularly toxic. They're cell cultures.”

Naomi slowly pulled the door open and looked inside. A light came on and illuminated racks of test tubes on several shelves.

“Does it look like how you left it last?”

“It does.” She watched as Dante's head poked up from behind a lab bench. He gave Naomi some kind of hand signal and then she seemed to relax. She addressed Jasmijn.

“Okay, everything's clear in here. You can get to work whenever you're ready. If you need to leave for any reason, including the bathroom, one of us will go with you and the other will stay here. Okay?”

Jasmijn agreed. As she set about preparing her equipment and samples, she saw Dante tap an earpiece and speak softly. Looking closely at Naomi's left ear, she saw one there, too. She supposed they could communicate with Stephen, probably roaming the campus somewhere. Taking a deep breath, Jasmijn consulted her lab notes and tried to block out the extraordinary circumstances surrounding her while she got back into work mode.

EIGHT

Bethesda, Maryland

Tanner Wilson hadn't been fooled by the president's address. He harbored little doubt that while the official talk was hard line, the White House was now pursuing every available option behind the scenes, including both negotiations and meeting the terrorists' demands. The media was now in full fear-monger mode, spreading panic like wildfire. Reports of suspicious activity at high profile venues were everywhere, and everyone seemed to have seen something worth calling in. Meanwhile, Tanner thought, kicking his feet up on the conference table he now sat at alone, the clock was ticking. A day-and-a-half to go.

And while some of the talking heads on the news shows were willing to call Hofstad's bluff, Tanner calculated the odds at 90% that not only did they intend to, but that they *would* execute another attack according to their stated timeline. He knew Hofstad going back a long way. While they had stayed under the radar compared to flashier groups such as Al Qaida and more recently, ISIS, he had long noticed that they never failed to accomplish what they set out to do. Although their strikes, up to now, had been smaller scale, not generally commanding international headlines, they had always put their money where their mouth was when it came to executing them.

No, Tanner thought, shaking his head at a pundit on screen who was sure that the terrorists had already retreated back to Europe by now since it was too easy to keep America in fear without even having to do anything at this point—they had found a way to up the intensity of their attacks, but their gameplan was the same as ever.

And the worse part of it was that he doubted the White House would be able to stop it in time. As one live streaming view showed, the U.S. embassy in The Hague wasn't going anywhere anytime soon. Tanner watched as a heavily secured gate rolled open in front of the compound, admitting a black SUV. U.S. policy would be the same as ever, Tanner lamented, running his fingers through his thick, wavy brown hair. They would act after more people got hurt and killed, and those acts would likely result in the loss of further liberties for American citizens, giving the terrorists yet another victory. A never-ending cycle. It frustrated him to no end, and that frustration was magnified further by knowing that he had once been in a position to actually do something about it.

He still was, though, just not in an official capacity. But he nevertheless had some people on his side who still occupied influential positions within FBI Counter-terror and other agencies as well. The same was true for all of his OUTCAST operators. There was a reason they garnered support—in the form of both information and funding—from government insiders and captains of industry alike. Even from a few foreign heads of state. The government had thrown out combined decades of experience when it had ousted the OUTCAST 6 for reasons that had nothing to do with their actual job duties, and meanwhile interagency cooperation—just when it was needed most—continued to be mired in convoluted tangles of bureaucratic red tape.

Tanner placated himself by considering what the optimal action against Hofstad should be. If he could do anything, what would he do? Dismantle the embassy? Although it would likely save lives in the short term, Tanner agreed with official U.S. policy that in the long term it was not a viable solution. Once that happened, once they gave in—terrorist organizations who wanted something done would demand it through violence and threats of follow-up. Tanner drummed his fingers on the smooth table surface. No, there had to be a real solution, one that involved actually solving the problem; that is, eliminating Hofstad's key players.

How could he get to them? Waiting for them to strike next would likely produce no better results than last night's fiasco. By now the halftime show production company breach had been reported, and shadowy photos taken by stadium surveillance cameras of the Hofstad terrorist posing as a production assistant broadcast all over the world. But he was gone. Security video showed him leaving the stadium tunnel in a golf cart, and even showed him getting into a car—a four-door sedan whose license plate was not readable in the video images. Tanner silently agreed with a guest speaker who speculated that the car had likely been ditched almost immediately following the incident. Even so, finding it would be a solid opportunity for clues, and that effort was ongoing.

Tanner knew that police procedural work was a slow-going endeavor, though, and with only about a day and a half to go before the next attack, they needed something more expedient. Tracking the terrorists like hunters after an animal would not save lives quickly enough. Tanner recalled the summer trips he spent as a boy with his grandfather, who was a game trapper. He killed animals not with guns but by tricking them to walking into his traps. He'd take Tanner out into the woods (he called it "camping" to downplay the violent aspect and thereby appease Tanner's mother, although she knew exactly what they were doing), and teach him the ins and outs of hiding his traps, of presenting them in the most natural way from the point of view of their target as possible. It was much easier than hunting, if one had something the target wanted and knew how to offer it in a way that seemed unthreatening.

And Tanner's work now was not all that much different. He clicked off the news reports as he thought about what he could put forward to Hofstad as bait. What did they want? The American embassy closed. Yet Tanner, for all his connections in high and not so high places, could not control that. If President Carmichael didn't authorize the closing of the embassy—and he doubted he would—then it would remain open.

But there was something else. He flashed on Jasmijn, now toiling away in her Netherlands lab to work on the STX antidote.

The antidote.

Hofstad wanted the antidote, ostensibly to leverage their control over weaponized STX even further. They already stated their intention to pay a return visit to Jasmijn to collect it. But what if, Tanner postulated, staring at the track lighting on the ceiling, someone other than Jasmijn were to offer them an antidote?

Moving slowly while deep in thought, Tanner picked up the phone. There were people who owed him favors. It was time to call them in.

NINE

Tarfaya, Morocco

Hofstad leader Mustapha Aziz Samir was much more at home in the western Sahara desert than he was in the cooler, temperate climes of the Netherlands. Even though to most people this arid, brown coastal village seemed like a lost corner of the Earth that was best to remain that way, to Samir it was home. In a mud-colored stucco abode festooned with satellite dishes and antenna towers, he sat in a darkened room on the second floor, satellite phone in one hand, a TEC-9 automatic rifle leaning against the wall within easy reach. A small table in front of him supported a laptop and a tea setting, and a smattering of simple hand drums lay nearby on the floor—his only concession to entertainment.

He spoke in Dutch to one of his Lieutenants in the Netherlands, Bram Witte. Fifteen years Amir's junior, he had been recruited to Hofstad while still a teen, his weekly visits to the Mosque initially a harmless venture born of innate curiosity, then transforming into in-depth brainwashing sessions under the guise of religious studies.

“The Hague embassy is still open,” Witte reported.

“Proceed as planned,” Samir commanded, ready to end the call.

“There is more,” his Lieutenant said.

“Tell me.”

“A call was received. An antidote to STX has been developed by a private U.S. lab. They are offering to give us both a batch of working antidote as well as the formula for $10,000 U.S. dollars.”

Samir asked why it was so cheap.

“They say they the amount covers development costs only. They want us to have it, to prevent more deaths. They have proposed a meeting place.”

“Where?”

“Charleston, South Carolina.”

Samir thought about this location. East coast, but not close to the seat of power, Washington, D.C. But not all that far, really, either.

Witte asked him if he wanted to act.

“Yes. But only in such a way as it does not impact the next strike team. And send no one higher than Tier 2.”

“Understood.” Witte signed off.

Samir smiled, tenting his hands. Could it be a trap? Yes. He was not still alive after leading his jihad-style group for almost three decades without equal doses of wariness, extra-caution and paranoia. But that is what expendable warriors eager for the endless virgins in the afterlife were for.

TEN

Bethesda, Maryland

Tanner disconnected the call and grinned like a Cheshire cat. Unbelievably, it had worked. He had plied his web of contacts—some of them frighteningly tenuous—but he had managed to get through to a mid-level operator within Hofstad and set up a rendezvous for the antidote. There was no doubt that they truly desired the STX antidote, though, to be willing to jump through such hoops for it, and that in itself concerned Tanner greatly. They were planning something big. The football attack was just the beginning.

Next, Tanner placed calls to Liam and Danielle. He and Danielle would pose as reps from the biotech company and actually meet face-to-face with the Hofstad contacts. Liam would be dropped in the vicinity of the drop ahead of time, ready to forcibly intervene should things head in a wrong direction.

The meeting was set for tonight at 8pm, in four hours time. The next day would see the expiration of the threat window, so Tanner knew that this was likely the only chance they would get at climbing sufficiently high on Hofstad's hierarchy ladder to be able to make a difference. He knew that they wouldn't be careless enough to send high ranking members. The possibility of a trap would not escape them. Militia-wise, they'd send lower level sleeper cell jihadists. Men who were trained to kill but who didn't know too much about how the organization was run, should they be captured and tortured.

But they would need a scientist, or at the very least a highly experienced lab technician. This person, Tanner had a hunch, would be no more than one or perhaps two intermediaries removed from Hofstad's brass. He could be physically tailed, electronically traced or both in an attempt to find his superiors. But the first thing they would have to do is to convince him that they did, in fact, have a functioning antidote for STX, else there was no reason for him to even contact Hofstad's inner circle. Tanner had no idea how to accomplish that, but he knew who did.

#

Jasmijn looked up from her microscope to see Dante engaged in conversation. He wasn't talking to Nay, who catted around the room on patrol, and he wasn't talking to Jasmijn. Nor did he hold an obvious device like a cell-phone or radio in his hand, either, so she assumed he must be listening with his earbud and talking through a tiny mic, perhaps a clip-on. She decided not to get too distracted by it, and got back to her work on the antidote.

It was slow going. Progress was excruciating. The work was a vexing combination of tedious complexity and visual acuity with a microscope that mentally ground her down at an unrelenting pace. But with untold lives at stake, Jasmijn knew that resting was not an option. She sipped from a Diet Coke as she worked. She had almost lost herself in the protocols once again when she heard Dante calling her name.

She looked up from the microscope. He was walking toward her, arm extended, holding a smartphone he must have produced from a pocket since the last time she'd looked at him.

“Tanner wants to talk to you.” He handed her the phone and she put it to her ear.

“How are you? Everything okay? Line is secure, no one listening but me. You can talk freely.”

She recapped their travel and told him everything was fine so far. “I'm working on the antidote right now. Slow going, but it's going.”

“I wanted to ask you about that. Do you think you can create a fake antidote that might pass inspection by a scientist for at least a few hours, even though it ultimately doesn't work?"

Jasmijn pursed her lips as she watched the pair of OUTCAST spooks case the room.

"That's easy. You could take a glass of Kool-Aid and say it's an antidote. Unless they're willing to test it on a live subject whose been infected with STX, it'd take several hours at least to confirm the chemical composition. But this is Hofstad we're talking about, so it wouldn't surprise me if they used it on an infected lab animal. Or person."

In Maryland, Tanner frowned. He hadn't considered this. Still, his goal was only to gain access to whoever it was that was calling the shots for the next attack. In his mind, all he had to do was get close to them and he would take it from there.

"I just want them to agree to a meeting where I'll be posing as a biotech rep with an STX antidote for sale. Can you email me some information about an antidote that would sound legitimate?"

"Well yes, I—I can do that, but..." Jasmijn stammered as she comprehended Tanner's meaning. "I thought you wanted the real thing, though? If you try to bluff them with a fake, what happens when—if— I have the real deal? They won't believe it."

"They'll be the ones contacting you for an antidote, remember? In this case, we're going to them. They won't connect the two different sources."

"I hope you're right."

"We don't have much choice, Jasmijn. Another attack is coming tomorrow. If we're going to stop it, I need to get to them. I don't see how else to get to them but to lure them to me."

"I'll send you some convincing-sounding info along with a simple recipe you can use to make something in the kitchen that looks authentic at first glance."

"Great. I'll let you get back to work."

"Tanner!"

"Yeah?"

"Please be careful."

Jasmijn handed the phone back to Dante, who resumed his patrol with Naomi. Jasmijn shook her head at the audacity of the OUTCAST leader's plan and set about concocting his bogus antidote.

ELEVEN

Charleston, South Carolina

Tanner Wilson adjusted his tie in front of a mirror in his room at the Hilton near the airport. He disliked wearing a suit, but in this case it was good tradecraft. He was a biotechnology executive with a product to sell. He heard a coded knock at the door (two-one-three), checked the peephole anyway, then opened it.

Danielle Sunderland. She'd booked into the adjoining room as though they were traveling business partners, which in a way they were. Both of them were checked in under assumed names and using a business credit card obtained under the shell name, Helix Biotechnologies, L.L.C. Tanner carried fancy business cards which included a small circuit and flexible screen containing a simple but playable video game. A great gimmick, lots of wow factor, the salesman had said. But also a practical one, in Tanner's case. Besides the game, the card also concealed a miniature GPS transponder. He was banking on the fact that they wouldn't scan it for invasive tech while still in his presence.

If they did, he was prepared to fight.

"Do I look happy to see you?" he asked after Danielle had entered and he closed the door.

Her eyes roved up and down the contours of his suit and despite the role play, he found himself blushing a little.. "I don't see a pistol in your pants, if that's what you're asking. In fact, I'd say you look good, Mr. Kohler!"

He checked the mirror on the door to be sure the outline of his Kahr PM9 didn't show through his suit. Satisfied it was all but undetectable even to scrutinizing glances, he appraised his fellow operator. Danielle looked the part in a pressed pantsuit, hair in a tight bun and carrying a slim leather briefcase.

"You don't look half bad yourself Ms. Halifax." And he meant it. Somehow she'd managed to hide the dressed down computer geek that she truly was in the makeup and hairstyle of a corporate saleswoman. He liked it, but hoped he wasn't too obvious about that fact.

"Ready for our big date?"

"You bet."

"And our chaperone?"

"Liam is set up in the bar already." It comforted him a great deal—and Danielle, too, he was sure—to know that ex-SEAL Liam Reilly had their back down there should things get too dicey.

Tanner picked up a larger metal attaché case on the floor, carefully hefting its weight to make sure he had a good grip on it. Per pre-arrangements with Hofstad's contact made entirely through mobile text messages, all negotiations would take place in the hotel lobby bar. No private rooms or off-premises locales.

He glanced at his watch, now a Cartier more befitting a business executive than the waterproof G-Shock he normally favored. Twenty minutes until the arranged meeting time. He wanted to be there early but not too early, lest they appear suspicious. He decided fifteen minutes, while ordering a drink and appetizer, would be in accordance with a businessman wishing to be well settled in and prepared for an important meeting.

When they got to the lobby Tanner could see that Hofstad's man was already there. Green shirt, tan slacks, black hat, as stated in the texts. His was a dark skinned, swarthy complexion. He sat alone, also as stated, at one of the lobby bar's outer cocktail tables. Tanner knew he wouldn't really be alone, though. He'd have backup. The lobby was crowded with the evening rush. Perhaps it was the group of three men loudly watching sports three tables away. Or maybe it was the African American woman reading a newspaper on a lobby couch, facing the bar. Could even be the bartender, busy as he was. There was no time to stand here and try to pick them out. One person he knew it wasn't , though, was the young man wearing a sombrero style beach hat, shorts, T-shirt, and sandy flip flops occupying a cocktail table in the middle of the bar, because that was Liam. A backpack with a pair of swim fins sticking out was slung over his chair, and he buried his nose in the current issue of *Surfer Magazine* while he nursed a large brew. A pair of white iPod earbuds, actually connected to a two-way radio, completed the ensemble.

Tanner and Danielle made sure not to even look at him as they made their way across the lobby in plain view from the Hofstad contact's vantage point. Tanner knew to greet the man as Amir. He knew nothing more about him than that, other than what he said he'd be wearing and that he was affiliated in some way with the Hofstad terror organization. He doubted he was very high up, but he would try and find out.

“Small table,” Danielle said just loud enough for Tanner to hear as they approached the edge of the bar.

Tanner had noticed it, too. They'd be sitting very close to one another, well subject to personal scrutiny. The Hofstad man made eye contact, first with Tanner and then Danielle as they passed into the bar. Tanner walked up to the high table with four barstools crammed around it, including the one Amir occupied, and nodded at the terror agent. Amir stood and extended a hand.

"Mr. Kohler?"

Tanner pumped his hand enthusiastically. "Yes, and you must be Amir. Pleased to meet you. This is my associate, Ms. Halifax." Danielle shook Amir's hand and said a pleasant greeting.

"Please sit," Amir said, waving a hand at the cocktail table, where a glass of water sat in front of him. "I apologize for the cramped space, but as you can see," he said, turning around to look at the slammed bar, "it's a popular place."

“Not a problem. My briefcase here might take up my drinking real estate, but that's okay. We'll celebrate later, right?”

Amir smiled as he watched Tanner lay the case on the table and unsnap its hinges. “I like a man who gets right to the point!”

Tanner shot Amir a serious look over the lid of the open case. “No reason to waste time when we've got an antidote that can save people's lives, right?”

Amir nodded. “Of course not. We are very excited about your proposition. May I see the samples?”

“Certainly.” Tanner swung the case toward him so that he could view the secured racks of test tubes it contained. Within the tubes, a turquoise liquid suggested a antidote.

“Each tube contains how many human doses?” Amir peered intently into the case.

Danielle answered. “Ten.”

“And there are one hundred tubes?”

“That's right. One thousand doses total.”

“And what is the shelf life of the antidote?” Amir looked at them both expectantly.

“As long as it's kept out of temperature extremes and away from direct sunlight, they should remain viable indefinitely.”

Amir looked pleased. “And this is a one-time use antidote, not a vaccine. In other words, it does not prevent you from being affected by STX again, correct?”

Danielle nodded. “That's right. It's an antidote, not a vaccine.”

“We're working on a vaccine as well,” Tanner said, playing the part of zealous biotech exec. “But this antidote is a very exciting milestone step.”

“Most definitely.” Amir tore his gaze from the blue vials to look Tanner in the eye. “You have the requested technical data on this antidote?”

Danielle handed him a folder emblazoned with the Helix Biotech logo. “Full specifications for your perusal.”

He took the folder, opened it briefly, then looked up again. “And may I have a small testing sample with which to verify the efficacy of the antidote? Just a simple test. Only a few hours will be required. You will be staying here in the hotel tonight?”

Tanner nodded. He removed a smaller tube, half the size of the others, from the case, and handed it to Amir. “You may use this for testing purposes. I'm sure you will be quite pleased. Are you staying in the hotel as well?”

The question had some risk, as he didn't want to be seen as pressing for information on Hofstad's whereabouts, but he thought it was reasonable given that he had just been asked the same thing. He was surprised, however, at how promising the answer seemed.

"Yes, my company put me up in the penthouse. They have a block of dates reserved each year, and happened to have a couple of days left, so...lucky for me!"

Tanner and Danielle expressed suitable "great for you" remarks.

Then Tanner pulled a business card out of his suit jacket pocket and offered it to Amir. He took it, nodding at first as he read the Helix Biotech information on the front, then narrowing his eyes a bit as he flipped the card over and saw the circuitry on back. He looked up at Tanner with a bemused expression that clearly said, *what's this?*

Tanner smiled and tried to act just a bit embarrassed. "It's a video game. Remember Pac Man? You can actually play it right on the card." To Tanner, the game was also an allegory. One character being chased around a board by four more, always needing to stay one step ahead or else be captured.

“Really? I must try it right now!” Tanner wondered if Amir's enthusiasm for the game was genuine, or if he was really only checking to see if the circuit was in fact just a game. He pressed a tiny button on the card and Tanner watched his face alight with amusement as the classic arcade game started up with its jingly music.

“Remarkable! The wonders of technology never cease to amaze me!” Amir turned the game off and pocketed the card.

Tanner nodded at the racks of aquamarine test tubes inside the case as he shut the lid. “I quite agree!”

The Hofstad man stood and glanced at his watch.

“I assume that if we agree to the deal later this evening, you would be able to pay in cash at that time?”

“Absolutely.” Amir gave an assertive nod. “I will text you.” Then he turned and disappeared into the sea of people in the bar area.

TWELVE

Charleston, South Carolina

Tanner opened his hotel door and led Danielle into the room. He wasted no time setting the case of "samples" down and then removing a backpack from the hotel safe while Danielle drew the room curtains.

"Let's see if we get a signal on the transponder." Tanner removed a piece of electronic equipment about the size of a smartphone from his backpack and set it up on the single table in the room. He powered the unit on and drummed his fingers on the table while it initialized. He could have had Liam tail Amir right from the bar, but opted not to since Amir was sure to have his own spotters who would notice. They'd let the tracking device do the work.

"Signals transmit through walls okay?" Danielle asked.

"Yes, high frequency, limited range. Walls aren't a problem, distance is. Let's see what we get." He squinted at the device's LCD readout.

“I recognize that devilish smile,” Danielle said. “You've got a hit, don't you?”

“Yep.” He tapped one of the gadget's buttons and watched the display for a few more seconds. “He's off site. Let's go, before he gets out of range.”

Tanner grabbed the tracker and headed for the door, Danielle close behind. They ran down the hallway to the elevator . They were on the tenth floor so Tanner hit the call button and waited. After an agonizingly long minute the elevator opened and a gaggle of Midwest tourists poured out into the hallway, not sure if they were on the right floor. Tanner and Danielle politely asked them if they wanted to get back in. They didn't need to be remembered by anyone for seeming rude or hurried.

They rode the elevator down to the parking garage and found their rental car, a white compact SUV. Tanner handed Danielle the tracker and got behind the wheel.

“Still got him, he's heading north on East Bay.”

Tanner pulled the SUV out of their space while Danielle monitored the tracker. He saw a Vespa scooter pull out of a spot in his rear view. It was Liam, now wearing a black hoodie in place of the sombrero and T-shirt. He was tempted to tailgate the car ahead of him through the gate arm rather than wait to pay the parking lot attendant, but he knew that such attention would be foolish. Tanner calmly pulled up to the window, paid the attendant the fee with cash, and slowly rolled out of the garage.

“Looks like he just turned west onto Queen.” To anyone observing, it would look as though Danielle was Tanner's wife, using a smartphone or GPS while he drove. Tanner stepped on the gas.

“Wish we knew what he was driving,” Danielle said, eyeing the tracker. “Still on Queen.”

They made their way through the small city, lights coming on for the evening. Tanner made the left onto Queen just as Danielle announced a course change.

“He made a right onto King.”

Tanner accelerated down Queen until he had to stop for a light.

“He's slowing down,” Danielle squinted at the tracking gadget.

Tanner hit the gas again until he made the right onto King.

“He's stopped up ahead. Looks like right side.” Danielle looked out the window in that direction. The street was a commercial district, with shops, restaurants and hotels lining both sides, many done in the distinctive Georgian architectural style. Pedestrians crowded the sidewalks. Tanner pulled to a stop in front of a busy crosswalk and Danielle said, “There he is.”

She didn't point or even look in his direction, but instructed Tanner verbally. “One O'clock. Couple hundred feet. Metallic blue sedan. Porter's grabbing his luggage from the trunk. Tanner watched as Amir handed his keys to the valet. Green shirt, tan slacks. He'd ditched the hat he wore earlier, but it was definitely him. He walked toward the lobby entrance.

“So much for staying at the Hilton,” he said. He took a left before he reached Amir's hotel. He didn't think he knew what they were driving, but were they to be recognized, their cover would be blown. Better safe than sorry. Tanner wondered if other Hofstad personnel were staying here as well.

“What's our next move?” Danielle wanted to know.

“We know where he's staying now. We’ll head back to our hotel. I'll contact Liam and have him maintain surveillance on the entrance so he can follow Amir in case the transmitter fails or if he catches on to it somehow.”

“He probably won't have need to visit his superiors unless he actually buys the antidote,” Danielle pointed out, still keeping an eye on the tracker where the dot representing Amir's location remained fixed.

“Right. I was thinking that unfortunately, even if they do fall for it and make the purchase, it's also possible that he could maintain custody of it himself and not lead us anywhere with it.”

“First things first. I just hope he buys it.”

Tanner picked up a handheld radio and transmitted to Liam that he should maintain watch on Amir's hotel entrance.

“Copy that. If he leaves, you'll know about it,” came Liam's confident reply.

Tanner drove them back to the Hilton and they walked back into the lobby. Tanner and Danielle scanned the bar to see if any of the same people were still there and seemed to be watching them, but neither detected anything suspicious.

Once inside their room, Danielle consulted the tracker again.

“He's still in the hotel.”

Tanner checked his mobile phone to make sure it was ready to receive texts. It was the only way Amir had to contact him. Satisfied it was operational, he set it on the table next to the tracker and sat in one of the chairs.

“If he doesn't contact me by ten O'clock tonight, I'd say there's a problem. Either he detected the surveillance or found out the samples are bogus.”

“Or both,” Danielle added cheerfully. “What time is it now?”

Tanner scowled at his Cartier. He still hadn't gotten used to an analog watch that had no numbers on the face. “I think it's seven.”

Just then Tanner's radio crackled with Liam's voice. “I've got a make on him. He's walked out of the lobby and he's heading toward a waiting taxi.”

“Copy that. Stay with him.”

“He's getting into the cab. Cab is moving...”

They could hear the sounds of traffic emanating from the radio speaker when Liam transmitted.

“Can you follow without being seen?”

“Affirmative. Will do. He's moving north up King now in the cab.”

Danielle glanced at the tracking device and made a face.

“What is it?” Tanner asked.

“The transponder hasn't moved from the hotel.”

“Maybe he's still too close for it to register. I'm not sure what the accuracy is supposed to be for that thing.”

He keyed the radio transmitter and spoke. “Liam you still with him?”

“Copy that. Cab is moving pretty quick, we're coming up on Calhoun.”

Danielle shook her head, still staring at the tracker. “That's almost half a mile from his hotel. He left it behind.”

“I saw him put it in his jacket pocket right after I gave it to him. Maybe he changed clothes before he went out.”

“You sure are a glass half full kinda guy, aren't you Tanner?”

Just then the radio squawked with Liam's voice. “Bad news.”

“Go ahead Liam.”

“He's getting on Highway 26. My scooter's not highway legal. 50cc's, I won't be able to keep up anyway if the traffic breaks up. Right now I could, though.”

“Go for it, Liam.”

Tanner pocketed the radio, picked up his keys and looked at Danielle. “Grab the tracker.”

“But he left it in the room.”

“I know. We may have lost him, unless Liam is Evil Knieval on that thing, but we haven't lost his room. We can see if he left anything interesting in there.”

Danielle shot him an appreciative look. “There's that half full glass again.”

THIRTEEN

The Hague, Netherlands

Stephen Shah had a wildcard to play. He'd cleared the longshot tactic with Tanner, who had told him he was greenlighting it only because it wouldn't take much time to fail. As soon as it did, he was to get back to the university campus to provide external lab support there.

Shah knelt behind his rental car in the parking garage of his hotel. Each of the three OUTCAST operators were checked into separate hotels under assumed identities to avoid associations. He looked and listened to be sure he wouldn't be witnessed for the next minute or so. He'd already cased out the positions of the security cameras and deliberately parked in a blind spot.

Shah slipped a license plate from his leather messenger bag and then pulled a multitool from his pocket and deployed its screwdriver. In about thirty seconds he had the

Netherlands rental plate off and in his bag. Thirty more saw a diplomat plate affixed to his gray Peugeot 207. He put the tool away and dusted off the knees of his charcoal gray pants. Then he adjusted his tie and jacket in the window reflection and got into the car.

As he drove out of the garage and toward the U.S. embassy in The Hague, Shah hoped that his past experiences here would be sufficient to see this through. As a middle-Eastern specialist, most of his time abroad in the CIA had been spent there, but on occasion he did have reason to visit the Hague embassy over the decades, and he still had some contacts there. Today, though, he hoped he wouldn't see any of them, with one exception. Even of those who were still there, he highly doubted they would remember him. It was simply his familiarity with operating protocols of U.S. embassies in foreign nations in general that he was banking on.

Shah pulled up to a light and waited, deep in thought. Were his plan to fail, he would surely be imprisoned on multiple charges and cross-jurisdictional violations. Tanner would likely find a way to get him out of it, but it would take a while.

But it wasn't himself he was worried about. He'd seen the replays of that halftime show in Miami, and knowing that if he were able to delay another event like that by even just a few hours—maybe long enough for other options to work—any penalty he might pay personally would be well worth it. He'd already put in his time, lived a full life. The U.S. no longer trusted him, but he wanted to help the nation that had taken his family in when he was a young boy from a war-torn Iran and given him a future. Given him an education, jobs, a career. Given him a life. Sure, things changed gradually over the decades. He'd noticed some ugliness creeping into the lexicon that hadn't been there when he'd first started (or was he just too young and starry-eyed to notice it, he'd asked himself on many a sleepless night) , and eventually things had ended badly when he'd filed suit against the CIA for not being promoted due to his race.

Still, even after all that, he'd been welcomed by Tanner Wilson and OUTCAST. The group lacked the security and prestige of his former position, but in a way it allowed him to actually do more to combat threats to the United States. So America was still good to him. And he would do his utmost to be good to it.

Shah approached a dull-looking, gray cinderblock facade of five stories and instinctively checked his rear-views. No one seemed to be tailing him. Taking in the building, he smiled and shook his head. It really didn't look much different from his last visit here about eight years ago, when he'd stopped by on the way home from the U.S. Embassy in Saudi Arabia to share information on a budding jihadist organization he had been tracking, called ISIS.

Shah cleared the memories from his mind and mentally steeled himself as he drove up to the manned entrance. He had his fake CIA Special Agent badge, papers and falsified vehicle documentation at the ready. When he reached the guardhouse he rolled his window down and reached his hand out with the documents to the guard without smiling. The young man took the credentials, also without a smile, and studied them carefully, an M-16 slung over one shoulder and a handheld radio on his belt.

"How long will you be staying at the embassy?" He looked up at Shah.

"Just for tonight." That was the truth.

"And how long in the Netherlands?"

Shah looked away from the guard, feigning boredom while he looked around at the embassy grounds. He was buying time to formulate a response. He hadn't expected this question. He didn't think he'd ever been asked it before. Were they onto him already?

"Also just for tonight." That was not so much the truth. But it went along with his here-on-important-business-that-won't-take-long story.

"One moment." The guard retreated into the small guardhouse structure and typed something into a computer. Shah knew he was entering notes about this encounter into an electronic log. Then he turned back around and handed him his papers, wordlessly nodding him through.

Shah parked in the employee lot and carried his briefcase to the building entrance, also guarded. He flashed his credentials to the guard here as well, this time also submitting his briefcase to a search, which turned up nothing suspicious. Again he was nodded through.

Shah took the elevator to the fourth floor where he knew the highest levels of government decision-makers to be housed. While in the elevator he made certain the contents of his briefcase were still in the proper order after being rifled through by the guard. Satisfied, he relaxed and took a deep breath just before the chime rang announcing floor 4.

Shah proceeded down the hall past closed doors on either side until he reached the room number he sought. He paused there, steadying his nerves. Satisfied he was as calm as he could make himself, he knocked on the door. A female voice told him to come in and he opened it.

Inside was a bustling open space divided into cubicles. A receptionist sat at a low desk off to the left. She asked him how she may direct his visit. Shah gave her a name and she asked if he had an appointment.

“No, I'm afraid this is a matter of urgency which arose too quickly to make pre-arrangements. I have orders from the President of the United States of America to close this embassy.”

Shah lifted a piece of paper from his briefcase bearing the presidential seal and dangled it in front of her face.

FOURTEEN

Charleston, South Carolina

Liam snapped his head over his shoulder before making a lane change. Amir's cab was in the fast lane and properly making use of that designation. He coaxed his little Vespa scooter with epithets muttered under his breath, but the little machine was close to giving all it had to give. As it was, were he to be sighted by a police officer he'd likely be pulled over for having the scooter on the highway.

He stabilized the bike in the lane next to the fast lane and held the pedal to the floor. The speedometer crept up to eighty kilometers per hour, but meanwhile, Amir's cab one lane over in the fast lane was easily doing one hundred. In a few more seconds the cab would be out of sight.

Then he caught a break when a WIDE LOAD procession of trucks carrying mobile homes took up the two right lanes, squeezing traffic to the two left-most lanes. Traffic slowed, but Liam was able to ride between the lanes. When he was ten cars back he switched into the fast lane, deciding it was risky to pass the cab and be seen by Amir.

His headset warbled in his ear, Tanner's voice asking for a sitrep, a situation report.

“Target in sight on 26. Not sure how long I'll be able to stay with him but I got him for now.” He gave the exit he just passed.

“Copy that, stay with him.”

Liam braked as he came up on the rear of the cab. Up ahead the wide load convoy was exiting, traffic already beginning to flow normally once again. Liam decided he needed all the momentum he could get. He moved over one lane to the right and sped between that and the slow lane, passing the cab so that he would have a lead once traffic began to flow again. By the time he was two exits ahead of the taxi, the traffic flow was full speed again. Motorists honked at him to get out of the way with his slow vehicle. He was drawing attention so he moved right one lane into the slow lane.

That's when he caught the splotch of yellow in his rear view, moving left to right. The cab had changed lanes, all the way over. Liam cursed as he reflexively slowed his scooter.

The taxi exited one offramp behind him. He banged a fist on the handlebar as he shook his head. He transmitted to Tanner.

“Just lost him!”

Tanner's reply was instant. “Scooter too slow?”

“Mobile home convoy slowed traffic and I was able to I pull ahead of him so I'd have a lead on him when the flow resumed, but then he exited while I was two exits up.” He named the exit.

“Take the next exit, I'll give you directions; maybe you can circle back and find him on surface streets.”

“Copy that, getting off.”

Liam raced off the highway, turning right onto a main boulevard where he was able to make good progress toward the street on which Amir's cab exited.

The closer he came to that exit, however, the more discouraged he became. The area was commercial and busy with many buildings on both sides, lots of places to duck into. He experienced a powerful jolt of adrenaline upon sighting a yellow cab, but when he got close he could see that the number painted on the door was different from that of the one Amir took. He looked into the back anyway, in case Amir may have switched cabs, but the rear was empty.

He sped on, soon reaching the avenue that Amir's cab had exited onto. Liam stopped at a light, looked both ways, and had to admit defeat. The cab was nowhere to be seen. Nevertheless, he forced himself to patrol the area, circling block by block, looking down driveways, stopping to examine places where cabs congregated. Even if he had sighted Amir's cab empty, it would have given him a clue that he had been let off in this area. But as it was he could still be speeding down the street toward the other side of town, headed who knows where.

Liam gave a sharp sigh and transmitted to Tanner that for now, at least, Amir had slipped away.

FIFTEEN

United States Embassy, The Hague

Stephen Shah read the nameplate on the woman's desk. Lena Gandara. Didn't ring any bells, not that he expected it to. She was a receptionist, not someone he would have worked with.

"I haven't heard anything about this. Your name again, Sir?"

Now she wanted to know, Shah thought.

"Jacob Rahimi." He'd chosen the name carefully, to mirror his own in that he had an Americanized first name but a Persian last name matching his ethnicity. He knew they would be used to many employees and contractors with similarly structured names.

Lena pressed a button on her phone and waited with the handset to her ear. "I'm sorry, Mr. Peterson," Shah heard her say. "But there's a man here by the name of Jacob

Rahimi who says he has orders from President Carmichael to close the embassy. He asked to see you by name."

Shah nodded his approval when she looked his way. As with everything under his control for this sortie, he'd chosen Peterson carefully. He was high enough in the government's organizational structure to get the embassy closed if he believed the presidential orders were genuine, but at the same time he hadn't been at this embassy long enough to have met Shah previously, so he had no reason to recognize him on sight as might be the case with one or two other employees.

A door at the rear of the office space opened and a tall man wearing a rumpled shirt and tie with no jacket emerged, his gaze fixed intently on Shah. He seemed to hold eye contact with him as he strode across the room. When he reached the reception area he glanced briefly at the document in Shah's hand, and then at his plastic ID badge clipped to his jacket pocket.

“Join me in my office, please.”

Shah followed him across the space, where a few heads were already peeking over cubicle walls to watch him walk back. He could feel the grapevine growing in his wake as the employees speculated on the meaning of his visit. He and Peterson reached the office and Peterson stood to one side with an outstretched hand inviting him in.

“Please take a seat, Mr. Rahimi.” Shah sat on a simple leather chair in front of Peterson's desk, a nice wood affair but nothing that would trigger excessive government spending complaints. Peterson walked around to his chair on the other side of the desk and sat.

“You have a document for me?”

Shah nodded and handed him the false order. Peterson quickly flipped it over to see if there was anything written on the back (there wasn't), before placing it flat on the desk in front of him. He pulled a pair of reading glasses from a drawer and put them on.

Shah studied Peterson's face while he examined the paperwork. One hand rubbed the side of his face as if massaging a cramp, while his eyes alternately squinted and relaxed as he read.

"...in keeping with this directive, all embassy facilities are to be properly discontinued and the premises safely evacuated until further notice," he finished aloud, looking up at Shah, who nodded authoritatively.

"So they're caving in to terrorist demands now?" Peterson shook his head in disgust.

"Trying to save lives. Don't want another event like Monday Night Football, right?"

The embassy man threw up his hands. "But if we start giving in to demands, what happens when they want something else a couple years down the line? What kind of example does this set for other terrorists watching and waiting in the wings?"

"Hey, I don't make the rules, either. You know how it is. They say 'take that hill', and we take that hill, right?"

Shah hoped a little civil service camaraderie might make the man feel more at ease. Instead he stood and pointed out the room's single window, at a busy street down below.

"What's going to happen here without any kind of sanctioned American presence? It's an open invitation to terrorists—c'mon over to The Hague! It's the Wild West out here!" He turned back from the window and put his hands on the desk on either side of the bogus presidential shutdown document.

"I guess U.S. travelers who lose their American Express will have to find some other way to get an emergency loan for return airfare," Shah joked.

Peterson actually seemed to brighten a little at that one. "Hey, that is a service we provide from time to time. Just one of the many things we do here. I can't help but wonder if they're using this terror thing as an excuse for downsizing. You know, budget cuts! For all I know, it's a false flag thing and they set that damn chemical bomb off themselves just so they'd have an excuse to close down a bunch of embassies!"

Shah felt his gut turn over at that. Here was a career government man, highly placed at an American embassy, with such a lack of trust in his own government. It reminded him of why he'd joined OUTCAST.

"Let's not get carried away. All it amounts to is a temporary cease-operations order. You see it says, 'until further notice'." Shah immediately regretted refocusing Peterson's attention back on the document. He'd already seemed to have bought it; *no need to get him to look at it some more, you idiot,* Shah chastised himself.

"Yeah," Peterson said, scanning the paper once again, "but we all know what that means." He raised his head from the paper, thankfully without having concentrated on it further. But now he was staring at Shah's badge.

"Say, who're you with, anyway—White House?"

"State Department."

"So don't I have to sign off on this? Or Ebeling?" Shah knew Alfred Ebeling was the Ambassador of the Embassy, the top dog.

"You just have to close the embassy down, Mr. Peterson. The best way is to get most of your personnel out of here now. Keep on a skeleton crew for the safeguarding of critical documents, the shutdown of computer systems, data backup to the cloud, that kind of thing. When that's done, the rest of you leave and lock the door behind you."

Peterson appeared flabbergasted. "Lock the door behind us..." he stammered. Then he perked up. "And then what? Will we still get paid? Or is this some kind of furloughing, or even worse—layoffs?"

It never ceased to amaze Shah how much these government employees were really looking out for number one, even though they put on such a professional facade of caring about their country.

"...still two years away from my twenty years when my pension kicks in, you know, a lot of us are! I wonder if that has anything to do with this decision!"

Shah continued to shake his head. He was getting the opposition he'd expected all right, but not for the reason he'd anticipated. This guy wasn't worried about keeping the embassy running so that it could continue to provide needed services, he was worried about his own paycheck and his retirement package. It disgusted Shah to no end. He realized that these were the type of self-serving bureaucrats who had slowly but surely driven him out of government service.

"I assure you that if it does, it would be news to me, Mr. Peterson. To the best of my knowledge the decision to close the embassy has only to do with wanting to at least appear to comply with the terrorists' demands in order to prevent further bloodshed of innocent American citizens."

Peterson's eyes brightened. "So you think it's just a temporary ploy to keep Hofstad happy and then they'll reinstate us as soon as Hofstad is under control?"

"That is my understanding, yes. So the sooner you can commence with the shutdown procedures, the sooner everything will get back to normal again."

Peterson stared into Shah's eyes for a moment and then picked up his desk phone.

SIXTEEN

Charleston, South Carolina

Tanner Wilson and Danielle Sunderland approached the main entrance of Amir's hotel. They'd parked a block away so as not to be associated with a vehicle. Danielle eyed her tracking device and gave Tanner a nod. *It's in here.*

Tanner keyed his radio and transmitted to Liam.

"If you're not busy come to the hotel and meet us in the lobby."

The message was pseudo-coded in case someone managed to break the encryption on the secure frequency. Difficult, but not impossible. Given that they'd been chatting during the scooter chase, however, Tanner decided to exercise the caution that was hard-coded into his DNA. Liam would know now to come to Amir's hotel, and that Tanner meant for him to patrol the perimeter for any sign of trouble while they were inside.

Tanner and Danielle walked up the circular drive and into the lobby, then took the elevator to the second floor of the ten-story hotel. Tanner looked ahead as they walked while Danielle consulted the tracker. About halfway down the empty hallway she stopped. She jerked a thumb at the nearest room door on their right.

“I think it's in here.”

“You think? We don't need to be busting into random rooms.” Tanner was known for being sharp with his people, but he was also known for getting results.

“I know that. The tracker does give altitude—which is lucky enough as it is—but it's plus or minus about ten feet, which means it could be this floor, or the one above.”

“What about the first floor?”

“Looks like it consists of all common areas.”

Tanner put his ear to the door while Danielle continued to consult the tracking device.

"I don't hear anything in there and it's too early for most people to be asleep, unless there's a jet-lagged traveler in there."

Danielle didn't respond, but only kept her nose buried in the device.

"Something else wrong?"

"Maybe. The other problem is that this place seems to be built on a small rise—you saw how the driveway is raised from the street and the first entrance is out onto that?"

"Yeah."

"I don't have the blueprints, but since the tracker's elevation is from ground level and reads 30 feet, and floor one starts ten feet high..."

"Third floor."

"Right. Plus or minus ten with the error factor, though, which means it could either be two, three or four."

Tanner exhaled heavily. Then they heard the elevator open, a group of people talking loudly getting off. Tanner grabbed Danielle's hand and they started to walk like a couple toward the elevator.

"Three represents the average reading, so let's try that first."

They passed the group of oblivious twenty-something revelers and took the stairs one flight up. Walking down an identical-looking hallway, Danielle stared at the tracker until it indicated she was next to the transmitter. A sliver of light shone from underneath the door.

Again, Tanner touched his ear to the door and listened.

"Don't hear anyone," he said, slipping a hand into his pocket.

"Lights on in the room." Danielle pointed under the door. Tanner shrugged. They both knew many people left their room lights on.

"Let's try it."

It was an electronic key card lock by the largest manufacturer. Tanner removed a palm-sized electronic device from his pocket.

"What is it?"

"Arduino microcontroller. Hooks up to the DC power socket, here..." Tanner plugged a wire from his device into the barrel socket. "This should read the 32-bit key from the lock's memory and bounce the key back to the lock." He pressed a button on his microcontroller. "Got it. Now I just..." They heard a BEEP and exchanged quick grins. He turned the handle and the door opened.

Then they heard the elevator chime.

Tanner pushed his way inside the room, hyper-alert as his eyes scanned the new surroundings. He checked the bed. Empty and neatly made. Bathroom: clear. He waved Danielle in and she softly closed the door and latched it.

Tanner pulled his PM9 and did a more thorough search of the room, checking the closets, the balcony, and under the bed.

The room was clear.

"No used towels in the bathroom," Danielle noted.

"Place looks barely used," Tanner agreed. "Let's find the transmitter."

Danielle looked at the tracker and set it down on the bed. "It's in here. It's not accurate enough to tell us exactly where." She went to the furniture and started opening drawers. Meanwhile, Tanner moved to the closet. A single garment hung from one of the hangers—a suit jacket.

"I think this is what Amir was wearing." He searched the jacket and felt smooth plastic in the breast pocket. He withdrew his hand and held up the business card he'd given the Hofstad operator.

"Jackpot," he said without the enthusiasm that usually accompanies the word.

“On the plus side,” Danielle said, moving to the nightstand drawers, “it does appear as though he just forgot it, not that he was onto it.”

“Right. And he hasn't checked out of the room yet which means, at least at the time he last left, that he was planning on meeting us later tonight.”

Danielle moved to the second nightstand and removed a bible from the drawer. She rifled through its pages and put it back. Tanner moved to the bathroom and checked the drawers there while Danielle parted the balcony curtain to look outside.

“Nothing in here,” Tanner called.

“Balcony's clean. He must be taking the samples to his contacts somewhere in the vicinity. We should probably just head back to our hotel and wait for—”

That's when they heard a BEEP as a key card activated the room door lock.

SEVENTEEN

Charleston, South Carolina

"Under a bed, quick!" Tanner hissed as he jogged out of the bathroom to the nearest of two twin beds. Danielle put the balcony curtain back in place and slid beneath the other twin. From his tight hiding place, Tanner worked his pistol out of his pants pocket so that he was holding it. He knew Danielle would be doing the same. Hopefully it would just be the hotel cleaning service, but they were prepared for anything.

But as the hotel door closed and brown leather shoed feet trod inches away from Tanner's face, it soon became apparent that this was no room service.

Amir was speaking to someone, on a phone apparently, since Tanner observed only one pair of legs walk past the bed. The conversation was in Dutch, however, and gave neither Tanner nor Danielle many clues as to its content. Amir's tone sounded matter-of-fact at first, but then seemed to grow sharper, more questioning. Then they heard him slam his fist into the dresser and utter a single syllable.

Tanner wondered if his lab tech had just informed him that the samples were no good. Probably. He shifted the gun in his hand. He hoped he wouldn't have to neutralize Amir, which would be akin to cutting off the tip of a tentacle of the beast. They needed Amir to lead them back to the head.

Tanner also wondered why Liam had not alerted him to Amir’s returning to the hotel. Surely he must have seen him, or did he take a side entrance? Whatever the case, the last thing he needed was for his radio to make any noise now, so he carefully switched it off.

Tanner saw Amir's' legs pacing back and forth while he muttered under his breath. Then the legs stopped moving and Amir stood silently in place.

Had he noticed something amiss in the room? Was he looking underneath the beds?

Suddenly Tanner felt a vibration in his pants. His phone was ringing on vibrate. He quickly reached a hand into his pocket and silenced it, but even that motion was more than he was comfortable with.

Had Amir heard anything?

But then the terrorist's voice was speaking, in English. Tanner realized he was leaving a voice message for him.

“Mr. Kohler, this is Amir. I am sorry to report that after analyzing the samples you provided us, they have failed to meet our strict quality control standards, and we will not be able to move ahead with the purchase. Thank you for meeting with me, but further contact will not be necessary. Good luck to you, Sir, and goodbye.”

Tanner heard Amir snap his phone shut. The response was professional, Tanner noted. But from the way he was breathing heavy and cursing under his breath, it was clear that he knew they had tried something.

He thought fast. Now that he knew Amir's intentions were to cease all contact with himself and Danielle, alternate courses of action sprung to mind. A spider crawled over his left wrist, causing it to jump, but he remained silent while he smeared the arachnid into the dusty carpet, his mind staying on track like a freight train. Could Amir be deceiving them—telling them the meeting for tonight was cancelled so that they would let their guard down, only to accost them in the wee hours when they least expected it?

Even if that was not the case, Tanner deliberated from the cramped confines of his place of concealment, perhaps it was best to take action now. If Amir escaped back into whatever network of hiding places he normally frequented, then this little mission had been for nothing. Worse than nothing, Tanner corrected himself—it even had a slightly negative outcome, since Amir and his colleagues would suspect someone had tried to trick them.

He could wait until Amir left the room and then call Liam and have him tail him, perhaps from a cab this time. But that might not work. Amir was here, now, they should do something now. Tanner flashed on the gasping victims in Miami, the confused looks on their doomed faces, the panic spreading through the stadium crowd like wildfire...knowing a scene just like it was set to be repeated *tomorrow...*and suddenly his mind was made up.

Tanner gripped his PM9 and raised himself onto his two elbows for a low crawl. He watched from under the bed as Amir's legs walked out of his field of vision to the left, toward the closet. Then he heard the swipe of a coat hanger off the rack.

The card!

He'd almost forgotten about it. He could just let him leave with the tracker in his jacket. But the battery in the transmitter had a life of "hours, not days," he recalled his techie saying.

Tanner made up his mind.

He heard Amir pull his jacket on.

He watched his ankles travel past the bed toward the door.

Tanner slithered toward the edge of the bed. Left elbow. Right. Left. Right...silently, until he could tilt his head to the right and see Amir entering the short hallway leading to the room door.

Tanner put his body into rapid motion, squirming the rest of the way out from under the bed and springing to his feet in one fluid motion.

“Freeze or I shoot!” Tanner leveled his gun at Amir's back just as his hand landed on the doorknob.

“Open the door and I shoot!”

Behind him Tanner heard Danielle emerging from the bed she was under.

While Amir was frozen, Tanner reached for his radio with his free hand and brought it to his mouth. “Alpha to Bravo, 416, now.”

“Copy that, Alpha.”

To Amir he said: “Back away slowly from the door. Right now! Don't turn around or I shoot!”

“Is that you, Mr. Kohler?”

“Shut up and do it!”

Amir took a careful step backwards.

“What is the meaning of this? Why are you in my room?”

Danielle walked up next to Tanner, her gun also pointed at Amir's back.

“Do as we ask and you won't get hurt,” she said.

“Both of you are in here? If you needed a place to stay, you need only have asked!” He roared with fake laughter.

Tanner pantomimed to Danielle where he wanted to move Amir.

“Step backwards, slowly, into the main room. There are two guns trained on you. Do not try to fight or we will kill you. Is that understood?”

“Yes.” He began walking backwards.

Tanner backed up into the space between the two beds, by the wall. Danielle retreated to the foot of the second bed that she'd been hiding under, giving Tanner a hard stare as she passed that said, *what the fuck are we doing?*

Tanner removed a folding knife from his rear jeans pocket and used it to cut the cord from one of the nightstand lamps. He took the cord over to Amir.

“Clasp your hands behind your back.”

Amir did so.

Tanner bound his wrists so fast that it surprised even Danielle, who moved over to the other bed in order to cover Amir from the front. He scowled at her while Tanner cinched the cord tight.

“What are you doing with me?” He was yelling now, starting to panic. “What do you want? You want the ten thousand dollars? I will get it for you.”

Tanner opened his mouth to say that this wasn't about money, it was about protecting innocent lives, but then a thought struck inside his brain that caused him to close his mouth before having spoken. Did Amir have ten thousand dollars in cash on him right now? He carried no briefcase or bag with him, and he was preparing to check out of the hotel so he wouldn't have left it in the room safe...An envelope containing hundred dollar bills would fit in a pocket, though.

Tanner started to frisk Amir, first his back pants pockets, then the front, then the suit jacket.

“You think I would carry that kind of cash on me to a meeting with people I've never met before?” Amir spat.

Tanner stepped back having found nothing. So far this was going exactly the way he hoped it would.

“If you don't have it, why should I believe that you can get it?”

If Amir thought he was just a high class thug out for money, so much the better, Tanner thought.

The Hofstad agent laughed. “I can get it. You should have told me sooner you needed the money that badly. I would have gladly paid it not to have gone through this ridiculous ordeal. Now release me and I will see about providing you with the funds.”

Tanner looked over at Danielle and grinned like a Cheshire cat.

It was time to follow the money.

EIGHTEEN

U.S. Embassy, The Hague, Netherlands

Mr. Peterson stared at Stephen Shah as the embassy administrator began talking to whomever had picked up the phone on the other end.

“David, listen to me. A State Department envoy just handed me embassy shutdown orders from the White House.”

Shah heard an unintelligible line of inquiry emanate from the phone.

“Yes, *shutdown* orders. Right, they're complying with the demands. At least for now.”

Peterson listened for a few more seconds and then cupped the phone, looking at Shah.

“Where are we supposed to go? Do we stay in country or report for duty in D.C.?”

Shah hadn't considered this and had to think fast. As much as he enjoyed the vision of a couple of hundred foreign embassy workers suddenly showing up for non-existent duty in Washington, it was more consistent with his temporary closure story that they remain nearby.

"Stay in country and be prepared to resume operations when notified. You have a disaster plan in place, correct? Like if there's an earthquake or a flood or something?"

Peterson nodded.

"Treat this like that. Those type of plans generally tell employees how to contact each other once off the premises. Put your disaster plan into effect now."

Peterson spoke into his phone. "We need to evacuate everyone and then follow our disaster plan for coordination of activities while off-site."

For the first time since he'd entered the embassy, Shah allowed himself the faintest of hopes that his ploy might actually work. Emboldened, he pressed on, half-expecting that at any second a team of security men would burst into the office to escort him away.

“You also need to remember to announce the closure publicly just before or after leaving, to let the terrorists know that their demands have been met.”

“Hold on a minute, okay?” Peterson said into the phone. Then he said to Shah, “Shouldn't President Carmichael do that?”

He was right, of course. But Shah was hoping that since The Hague was Hofstad's base of operations that a local announcement would reach their ears soon, and they would put a hold on whatever they had in store for the citizenry of the United States for at least the next few hours. Who knows, maybe the White House would follow with its own announcement if they assume the embassy acted on its own best intel. Maybe they know something the president doesn't. But these thoughts took a backseat in Shah's mind to the situation right here, right now. He still had some convincing to do, and even if Peterson and whomever he was talking to were fooled, he was well aware that this little charade could have the rug pulled out from under it anytime in the next few hours.

"The president will do it, but sometimes local sources are taken as more authentic by local people, so we would like the announcement to come from the embassy itself as well."

That would have to do. Shah hoped it would be enough as Peterson conveyed the instructions to his colleague on the phone. Shah's inner voice told him he should get while the getting was good. The ruse would either work or it wouldn't. There wasn't anything more he could do here. The questioning would grow more pointed, more confirmations would be requested, so it was better if he left now and hoped the plan would be carried out. Based on his knowledge of federal administration of overseas assets, Shah gave it about a forty percent chance of success.

At least Peterson and his contact were now discussing the details of implementing the shutdown.

"Excuse me, Mr. Peterson?" Shah interrupted. Peterson raised his eyebrows at Shah expectantly.

"I've got to be on my way. I trust you can handle things from here?"

"Yes sir, Mr. Rahimi. You can count on us."

"Excellent. I'll be sure to let the president know what a first rate operation you run here. Just don't forget that announcement."

Peterson beamed. Thank you, Mr. Rahimi. Yes, Sir!"

Shah turned and left the office, closing the door behind him.

NINETEEN

Charleston, South Carolina

Tanner punched Amir in the face, a forceful, closed-fisted shot. He didn't enjoy violent behavior but time was short and he needed to get it across to this terrorist that he meant business. Blood erupted from the Hofstad agent's nose, staining the bedding as he keeled over. Danielle kept her pistol trained on him.

“What did you do that for?” He spat blood out onto the covers. “I said I would get you the money.”

“That's just to keep you from getting too comfortable. Just a little preview of what's to come if I don't have that ten grand in the next hour.”

“The next hour?” Amir struggled until he was able to right himself, sitting once more on the now bloody bed.

Tanner raised his fist as if he was about to strike a hammer blow. “Do I need to repeat myself?”

Amir seemed to shrink into the bed. "One hour, okay. I can do it."

Tanner wondered if Amir personally had ten thousand he could access from an account of his own, which would mean there would be nothing to trace to Hofstad. He hoped not. But regardless, it was worth a try.

"Where is it?"

"It is in one of my accounts. I can wire it to your account or I can withdraw it in the morning from any major bank."

"I said one hour."

"Then provide me with an account number and I will transfer it immediately from my phone."

In his line of work, Tanner had learned long ago to be prepared for this eventuality. He had an account setup for use by OUTCAST—an account that was well-funded and easily accessible online, yet that was also setup under the alias he was currently using.

Tanner glared at Amir, channeling some of the genuine hatred he felt for this terrorist who, if not directly responsible for killing those people in Miami, at least supported the organization that did. Tomorrow would most likely bring more devastation if OUTCAST was unable to do anything.

"I can give you an account number. But we use my computer." Tanner reached under the bed and retrieved his briefcase from where he'd been hiding.

"You could be recording my keystrokes," Amir stated.

Tanner backhanded him across the mouth, bloodying his lip. "I could be killing you, too. Would you prefer that?"

Amir said nothing.

"If I wanted more than ten thousand don't you think I would have asked for more? We use my machine and you transfer the ten thousand or else I will kill you right here in this room."

“Fine. Let’s get this over with.”

Tanner handed the notebook computer to Danielle, who was familiar with the OUTCAST account. She took it to the room desk to boot it up while Tanner aimed his firearm at Amir's head.

“To expedite things, I'm going to untie you so that you can use the computer. You will have two weapons trained on you the entire time and everything you are doing online will be closely watched. Do not try anything funny. Is that clear?'

“Yes.”

“It's ready,” Danielle said, pointing to the open computer, a web browser sitting at the ready.

Tanner made a show of opening his folding knife in front of Amir's face. Then he walked slowly around the bed until he was behind the prisoner.

“I'm going to cut your arms free now. Do not move until I say and you will not be hurt.”

"Okay."

Danielle moved over to the bed, standing in front of Amir with her pistol aimed at his chest while Tanner sliced through the lamp cord and stepped back.

"Stand up slowly."

Danielle backed up to the wall to give him plenty of room as he put his hands on the bed and pushed himself up to a standing position.

"Now walk slowly to the desk and sit down in the chair."

Amir did so, eyes fixed on the computer as he walked.

"I must warn you about something," Amir said, taking a seat in front of the computer.

In response Tanner cocked his PM9.

"I am not positive—this is the truth—but transferring this much money from my account, which is company linked—my own personal accounts cannot be accessed in this manner—may trigger an investigation."

Tanner smirked. “We'll be long gone by then. Let us worry about that.”

Amir turned his head away from the screen to look at Tanner. “No, you don't understand. I'm just trying to avoid surprises here since I don't want to get shot. But the company I work for has its own security measures, some of which are rather extraordinary, and *they*—not the bank—may come after us to see if the transaction is legitimate.”

Inside, Tanner was grinning hard. But outside, he kept up his impassive stare. Amir mistook his silence for anger.

“There is nothing I can do about that. It may work without incident. It may not. Usually when I transfer this much money my superiors know about it in advance. That's all I'm saying. If we can wait until morning I can go into a bank in person and withdraw the entire sum from one of my personal accounts. Not that I relish the thought of spending the night like this,” he said, looking over at

Danielle's pistol pointed at his face, "but if it means life rather than death then of course I will do it."

Tanner moved close enough to read the screen. "Do the transfer."

Amir nodded and put his hands on the computer. He typed in a dot-com web address. Tanner didn't recognize it, and it didn't suggest any connection to Hofstad.

Tanner watched closely as Amir used familiar looking online banking controls to transfer ten thousand U.S. dollars to another account. Tanner noted that he had to set the currency into dollars from Euros, strongly suggesting a European-based system.

Amir looked over his shoulder at Tanner. "Your account number?"

Tanner removed a piece of paper from his briefcase while Danielle guarded Amir. He read off the numbers, which Amir entered into the online system. He clicked enter and the site gave a confirmation that the transfer was processing.

“It is done.” Amir turned around to look Tanner in the eye.

Tanner waved his weapon toward the bed. “Go have a seat while I confirm the transfer.” He didn't really care about the money. He was just buying time. He hoped that someone in Hofstad would notice that ten thousand dollars had been transferred from one of their accounts immediately after one of their lab techs had declared the antidote samples to be ineffective and probably outright junk, and come running. But checking to see that Amir had actually initiated a transfer and not some kind of coded alert would be worth doing also, he thought, as he faced the laptop's screen away from Amir's view.

Tanner logged into the OUTCAST financial account and checked the recent activity. Indeed, there it was: a pending deposit for $10,000.

“Lucky for you it worked, Amir.”

“Can I go now?”

Suddenly Tanner's radio squawked on his belt. Liam's voice. Tanner picked up the unit and lowered the volume, holding it up to his ear as he took it into the bathroom. No need for Amir to hear Liam. Especially when he sounded so frantic, as he did now.

“Activity at the front entrance. Four guys just got dropped out of an SUV that I was watching. They're headed into the lobby now.”

TWENTY

Charleston, South Carolina

In Amir's hotel room bathroom, Tanner adjusted his radio's squelch setting, attempting to get a cleaner signal.

"Say again, Bravo—did you say *four* guys?"

"That's affirmative! Coming in now. Should I follow them in?"

"Yes! We've got control of the tango up here." He gave Liam the room number.

"Copy that, in pursuit."

Tanner felt much better knowing he had the ex-SEAL on his side. Three on four—or three on five if one counted Amir—were much preferable odds to two on five. Tanner considered that they might be able to use Amir as a hostage, but in his experience terrorists cared little for their own. They would not shed a tear for their fallen comrade.

He walked out of the bathroom and back into the main room, where Amir was pleading with Danielle to let him go.

"Shut up, Amir," Tanner said, collecting his laptop and tossing it into his briefcase.

"They split up," Liam said over the radio, audible to everyone in the room, including Amir.

"Two going up the elevator, two went ground level out back, by the pool."

Tanner ran to the balcony and pulled the curtain aside just enough to get a look outside. The pool deck was underneath, mostly empty at this evening hour but with a small group in the hot tub. He didn't see a fire ladder or any way to readily access the balconies from below, although he knew that a prepared team could make easy work of it.

"You have support on the outside!" Amir accused. "Who are you? You are not simply a biotechnology company wanting to help people with your product, are you? You don't even have a product—the sample you gave us was pure trash. Who do you work for? CIA?"

Tanner knew Danielle was too disciplined to look away from her charge, but he could see her flinch at the closeness with which Amir's verbal dart came to hitting the bullseye.

"Sorry, Amir, old buddy," Tanner said as he crossed the room to the phone on the nightstand, "But there's no time to chat now."

"What are you doing?" Amir asked.

Tanner pressed a button on the phone and waited a second before saying, "Yes, I'd like a bottle of your best champagne brought up immediately, please. Yes, charge it to the room. Thank you."

Tanner let the phone receiver drop and turned to Amir. "Sorry to pile on the expenses, pal, but your boss will understand, I'm sure." He raised his gun and walked toward Amir until the barrel pressed into his temple. "Who's coming up here? Do they work for you or do you work for them?"

Amir breathed heavily, his substantial gut heaving in anxiety-riddled gasps. A tracer of blood sluiced down his temple to his cheek.

"Answer the question!"

Danielle interjected. "They're here."

They heard men calling through the door in Danish. Tanner heard what he was pretty sure was a name, but it wasn't Amir, not that he thought Amir was his real name.

"Answer it!" He jammed the gun barrel into Amir's head at the same time as a little warning bell went off in his mind.

His hands are still untied...

They heard the door being kicked in at the same time as Amir rammed his head into the belly of Tanner, who had been looking at the entrance.

“Tanner!” Danielle fired two shots at the intruders, who wore black ski masks with their eyes blacked out and brandished sound-suppressed handguns. Tanner fired a shot of his own at the doorway and at that moment Amir made his move. Not bothering to get up from the chair, he lashed out with a vicious judo chop to Tanner's arms, both of which were holding his gun. Tanner's second shot went low, hitting the carpet. His gun went flying a couple of feet away onto the floor.

Tanner dove for his gun but Amir toppled over in his chair onto him, grabbing his legs. The OUTCAST leader wormed his way on the floor toward his weapon while Amir struggled to pull him away from it.

Danielle fired two more rounds at the advancing intruders. One of them grunted in pain as he took a bullet and spun into the wall, but the other kept shooting. Danielle used the end of the dresser as cover, crouching behind it just as a bullet chipped away a corner, missing her but spraying a splinter into her left eye and blurring her vision in that orb. She fired again, this time at the Hofstad man she hadn't hit, who was now advancing on Tanner's fallen pistol. She hit him in the gut but he kept coming and she knew he was wearing body armor beneath his clothes.

In another second, four things happened at once.

They heard a knock on the hotel door followed by a woman calling, “Room service!”

Tanner was grappling with Amir and the gunman who had advanced into the room.

Danielle saw an opportunity and shot the same man she'd hit before in the head, splashing his cerebral matter onto the cerulean wallpaper.

The sliding glass door leading to the balcony exploded in a shower of glass and two more Hofstad men crashed through into the room. Danielle's heart sank for a moment. Then she saw that they were both already dead.

“Freeze, don't move!” The terrorist inside the room shouted. He had his shoe on Tanner's gun and his own firearm pointed at Tanner's head.

Danielle swiveled the barrel of her gun from Amir to the balcony. When she started to swing it back to Amir, the terrorist yelled at her: “Put it down or I blow your friend away!”

Amir outstretched his meaty palm. “Give it to me.”

And then she watched as the head of the man pointing the gun at Tanner seemed to explode into a misshapen mass of extruded meat, his eyes suddenly traveling down the sides of his face. His gun flew up into the air as his cranial contents dripped to the floor. With a surprising degree of alacrity for a man of his bulk, Amir reached up and caught the weapon in mid-air.

Tanner gut shot him as soon as he did. Amir made a coughing sound and dropped to his knees, both hands, including the one still holding the gun clutching at his ruined mid-section.

Then they heard Liam's voice. “Balcony, clear!”

“Main room, clear,” Tanner responded. His voice did not sound nearly as energetic as Liam's.

The ex-SEAL stormed into the room, counting the bodies as he looked about.

“Got what we need?”

Tanner nodded.

“Time to go, boys and girls, unless you want to stick around to explain five dead bodies.”

Tanner got to his feet and looked around at the carnage, disparaged. Every single Hofstad man was dead. Quickly, the three of them searched each body for anything that might lead them higher up the terror organization's hierarchical structure.

But they found nothing.

Then came shouting coming from the hall, the trammel of fast-moving footsteps, and the room phone ringing.

"This way, please." Liam patiently waved an arm at the balcony. "Rope slide. Let's go."

He led them to the balcony, drawing the curtain and door shut as they heard loud knocking at the door, hotel employees calling into the room.

Liam jumped off the balcony, seeming to barely touch the rope on the way to the ground. Tanner and Danielle went next, their egress slower than Liam's almost supernatural glide but still serviceable.

With a flick of the wrist Liam pulled the rope down from the balcony as they ran down a maintenance path. The trio of operatives made it to Tanner's vehicle and they left the area, abandoning Liam's scooter.

Behind the wheel, Tanner felt the sting of failure along with the rush of wind through his hair. They'd dispatched five Hofstad agents, none of them key members. They were no closer than before to following the beast's tentacles back to its head.

The mission was a failure.

He could only hope that his agents were having more luck at Jasmijn's lab. Or that Shah—even though his objective had the lowest probability of success of all of them—was courting Lady Luck in the embassy.

TWENTY-ONE

United States Embassy, The Hague

Stephen Shah exited the elevator onto the first floor and passed through the cubicle farm. He caught some odd looks on the way. *Yeah, I'm the guy who just shut your asses down. Deal with it.* At least he hoped that's what the looks were about. But as he neared the end of the cube farm just before it opened into the expansive lobby area, he saw a man bolt upright, his head shooting above his workstation wall like a hyperactive prairie dog emerging from its hole in the ground.

Shah did his best to ignore him but saw the man point dramatically at him. Heard him say into the phone, "He's here! Yes, right now, he's about to walk out of here into the lobby."

Shah picked up his pace as much as he could without seeming like he was acting suspicious, but then came the shouted commands.

"Mr. Rahim! Stop, please, we need to talk to you! Mr. Rahim..."

Then a duo of suited security personnel emerged from a row of cubicles and headed right for Shah. One of them held up a badge. Shah didn't take the time to figure out what it represented. His ruse hadn't worked.

A few of the workers began to catcall at him.

"Close us down?"

"You with Hofstad?"

Shah took solace in the fact that they didn't yet know who he was.

One of the security men silenced these rabble-rousers with a wave. One of them touched an earpiece as if straining to hear better, and then he pointed assertively in Shah's direction. He and his associate ran toward the OUTCAST operator, blocking the thoroughfare to the main exit.

Shah sidestepped down a row of cubicles, eliciting screams from surprised female workers who feared what this imposter among their ranks might do now that he'd been outed. He was dangerous in the same way a wild animal was unpredictable when cornered.

Halfway down the row of cubes Shah jumped up on a desk surface and leapt over the cubicle wall. He landed on the desk of the cubicle on the other side. Fortunately it was unoccupied but he slipped on some papers before he regained his balance enough to jump to the floor.

“We just want to talk!” one of the guards implored.

“Don't make this worse than it needs to be,” chimed in the second.

Shah's voiceless opposition made it clear to the security detail that they would have to forcibly take this man down. No surrender here.

Shah, who had long practiced Krav Maga, saw potential weapons everywhere as he began to make his course more erratic. A pencil jar holding a pair of scissors here. A pewter paperweight there. A computer cable. Even a thin notebook computer could be flung into a windpipe with devastating force. But for now he concentrated on evasive action.

He reached the end of a row and knocked over a five-gallon water cooler as he rushed past, flooding the floor. A pair of hands stretched out to grasp him and he deftly snapped one of the wrists, little yelps of pain receding behind him as he crashed into double glass doors that led out into the lobby.

And then came the command he'd known was coming.

"Stop or I'll shoot!"

Shah grabbed a passing man with a briefcase, whirled him around and flung him through the still open doors into the work area. He took off at a dead sprint through the lobby. He got to the main entrance too late—four more armed officers poured into the lobby area from outside.

He ran past the main exit, mentally recalling the building design as he fled. The lobby was actually a rectangular hallway, sort of like a moat that circled the inner work areas of the building. He traced its way around looking for a way out. A few people stepped aside to let the fleeing man pass. One man, a forty-ish civil servant who looked like he maintained a strict fitness regimen, tried to stop Shah. He put both hands out, sidestepping to block the intruder's path.

Shah feinted right, then ducked left, sweeping his right foot across the back of his foe's ankles. He went down hard, swiping at Shah's legs with a hand as he passed but his fingers clutching only air.

"Over here!" the would-be hero yelled to the unseen security force in pursuit.

Shah guessed he was about halfway around the loop now. No way he'd be able to make it through the heavy security at the main entrance. He had to find a way out.

Behind him the heavy footfalls and squawking two-radios were catching up to him.

He spotted a door up ahead on the right marked ROOM A. He slowed his pace as he reached it, willing himself to slow his breathing. He pulled the door handle and was relieved to feel it swing open. Quickly he ducked inside, where a conference was underway. A white-bearded man was speaking at a podium to an audience of perhaps fifty people. No one turned to look at him as he entered. Shah casually walked down the rows of folding chairs until he found one with an empty seat on the edge. He took it and waited.

The speaker was droning on about Dutch-American trade deficits. A man two rows up asked a question and a heated exchange followed. Shah looked around until he was certain no one was watching him. Then he scanned the room for exits behind the speaker. Saw a green lit EXIT sign on the left wall behind the small stage. He had no idea where it led, but sitting here would only buy him a few minutes at most.

Just before he got up, Shah caught himself smiling, a huge shit-eating grin on his face. He was living, wasn't he? Goddamn if he wasn't. For a while there, after he was terminated from The Company, he'd thought his life was destined to be a parade of drudgery; that he was ordained to live out his days doing mundane things until he was shoehorned into some nursing home where the highlight of his day was to be wheeled out into the hallway to sit for a couple of hours. He was exaggerating his fate, perhaps, a form of mental self-flagellation, yet that reality was on the spectrum of his possible fates. But here he was, every nerve ending pulsing with electricity.

And he was at least trying to do some good in the world, to help people. Thanks to OUTCAST, his life had purpose once again. If all he cared about was getting a cheap thrill he could go throw himself off a bridge tied to a bungee cord, or take up sky-diving or race car driving some other self-serving adrenaline junkie habit. But he wanted, as he always had during his twenty-year career at CIA, to help his country, to help people lead better lives.

He glanced at his watch, a gold Rolex with Roman numerals, and reminded himself that more Americans were likely to die in the next few hours if he and the rest of the team were not successful. He had personally failed his long-shot mission, that much was clear. So the hope now lay with Tanner in South Carolina, and with Dante, Naomi and Jasmijn in the lab.

Speaking of which, Shah thought, rising as the audience erupted in applause, it was time for him to get back there. As the talk concluded, those not hanging around to try and engage the speaker in a little post-talk one-on-one Q & A were streaming out of the room from two exits. Most left the same way Shah had come in-through the main double-doors out into the perimeter hallway. But a smaller crowd vacated by way of the single door at the rear left. Shah mingled in with this group and followed them through the exit.

It led to a short hallway with two elevators at one end and a stairwell at the other. He followed the group to the elevators and got in when the doors opened. A man pressed the B button and Shah rejoiced at his good luck. He remembered from his visits long ago that there was a basement parking garage. His car was parked above ground, but he would be able to reach the outside from the garage.

The elevator doors opened just as Shah realized that a man was asking him what he had thought of the talk.

He looked at him and nodded agreeably. "Most liberating."

Shah saw the sliver of gray daylight and strode briskly toward it.

TWENTY-TWO

Waikiki Beach, Hawaii

Ali de Groot shouldered his daypack as he stepped into the bright yellow touring helicopter. As planned, he moved up front to the co-pilot's seat, which in this case was merely another passenger seat. He nodded amiably at the pilot, a middle-aged man of mixed Asian descent, who returned his good-natured smile as his fare settled in.

Behind him, two of his customer's associates, one Dutch and one Moroccan man in their early thirties, clamored aboard. They occupied the two rear passenger seats, maxing out the fare capacity for this flight, a quick jaunt from Honolulu International Airport over Waikiki Beach, Diamond Head, and out over the ocean to return. All told, maybe a twenty minute sightseeing trip.

Each of the other two men also bore backpacks. None of the three had been subjected to any kind of a search, as this was a private, tourist-friendly flight.

The pilot knew that his three paying passengers had been briefed by the touring company as to what the tour would encompass and what to expect. He checked to make sure that each of their seatbelts were fastened, that their headphones were working, and then engaged in some chatter with Air Traffic Control before lifting into the air.

The Pacific Ocean was instantly visible as the pilot banked their small craft toward world famous Waikiki Beach, already crammed with sunbathers on this eighty-five degree sunny afternoon. The pilot communicated with his passengers through the use of the headphones, which made his running tour much easier to hear.

"On your left is world-renowned Waikiki Beach. The pink hotel in the middle is the Royal Hawaiian, over 100 years old. Best *luau* in town!" The aircraft reached the end of the beach and made a turn to follow its length out in the surf zone.

"Good waves today!" the pilot added. He looked down through the windshield at the crowd of surfers jockeying for position in the Ala Moana swells.

Ali established brief eye contact with his associate in the left rear seat, which went unnoticed by their pilot.

"You see that barrel! He was deep in the tube! Great wave! Okay, now ahead, you see Diamond Head volcano. But it's no longer active, at least we hope so, right? I hear that—"

The pilot's words choked off as he noticed the M1911 pistol in the hand of his front seat passenger, aimed square at his chest.

"What do you want?" His voice was calm and low, transmitted through his headset mic to all three Hofstad passengers' earphones.

“Descend to an altitude of 100 feet and fly directly over the entire length of Waikiki Beach. Do you understand?”

“We can't do that. We have to maintain a minimum altitude above the beach!”

“I'm not asking about the regulations. I'm asking if you understand the command. Let me add, sir, that I myself am a licensed helicopter pilot. If you are unwilling or unable to comply, then we will simply dispose of you.”

The pilot brought the craft lower to the water but hesitated when the end of the beach came into view off to their left. They passed directly over a sailing catamaran, which looked terrifyingly close with its mast protruding skyward.

“Fly over the beach!”

The pilot white-knuckled the controls as if transferring rage he wanted to vent on the gunman to an inanimate object.

“What for! Are you going to hurt people?”

Ali looked back once at his associates. Then he fired a round into the right knee of the pilot, who wailed in agony. He clutched his knee with is right hand, temporarily losing control of the helicopter, which veered sharply to the right.

Ali raised his voice. “Regain control or the next shot is through your worthless neck!” His carotid artery appeared as though it was about to burst, his face red with fury as he aimed the 1911 at the pilot's Adam's apple. “I said regain control or die!”

“Okay, okay!” The pilot heaved as if hyperventilating, but managed to bring the aircraft to a stable attitude.

Ali looked out his window, could swear he saw spray from a breaking wave reach one of the landing skids. They had lost altitude but he smiled, deciding that was so much the better to accomplish their objective.

“Keep this altitude and fly over the sand. Now!” Ali waved the gun.

The pilot titled the helicopter's collective to the left and Ali watched streaks of foam-laced whitewater rush beneath them, in seconds transitioning to golden sand.

"Turn right!"

The pilot banked the craft right with his left hand while still clutching his massacred knee with his right. Below them heads tipped skyward as the helicopter's rotor wash sent umbrellas, towels and rafts tumbling across the sand.

Ali turned around to look at his colleagues. Both men had already donned biohazard suits and removed silver canisters from the backpacks they'd brought onboard. In front, Ali quickly removed his gear from the pack and put it on.

"What's going on?" the pilot squeaked. Ali silenced him by pointing the 1911 at his good knee.

Then he opened the door and the occupants of the helicopter were buffeted with a blast of warm, salty air. They could hear shouts from the beachgoers below, some simply excited at the low-flying craft, unaware it wasn't normal or legal, while others yelled because they feared something was amiss.

“Now!” Ali shouted.

“What about me? Do I need breathing protection?” The pilot shrieked into his headset but his question went unanswered.

The operative seated directly behind Ali gripped two handles on his canister and leaned partway out the door. He tipped the canister in the opposite direction of the wind flow and felt the can begin to grow lighter as an invisible mist dispensed from it, raining down onto the throngs below.

“Stay on course and you'll live!” Ali barked at the pilot. But as menacing as he tried to sound, it was hard for him to suppress a grin as the helicopter traced the gentle curve of the beach, dropping its aerosolized death particles in its wake. It was working!

Ali grinned as he saw the WARNING: Jellyfish signs posted on the beach. It meant that even more people packed the sand, unable to enter the water for fear of the tentacled sea creatures. Ironically, the STX neurotoxin being dumped on them was a million times more toxic than the jellyfish venom they sought to avoid by staying on the beach.

Pride welled up in Ali as he looked back and saw knots of panicked tourists beginning to form on the beach behind them. He heard indecipherable screams, perhaps an "Oh God!" as they raced over the strip of beachfront. He could no longer contain his elation.

"They pray to the wrong God! They should be appealing to Poseidon, the source of this poison!"

Behind him, his man shook his canister before letting it drop to the ground.

Empty.

He turned to his colleague and grabbed the second one.

"Hurry, hurry! We must get them all!" Ali bellowed.

His associate deftly unscrewed the canister's safety lid and held it out the open window. He steeled himself for Round 2, knowing his muscles would need to be strong to hold the can in place against the wind. But for Hofstad's victory, he would do it.

His canister began to dump toxic rain just as they passed in front of the iconic pink hotel, literally thousands of people from around the world jamming its beach. Asians, Americans, Hawaiians, Pacific Islanders, Europeans, Canadians... All of them succumbed to the hyper-potent neurotoxin as the death ‘copter flew above like an aerial demon.

The pilot continued to shout as he navigated along the beach. “What are you doing? What is going on?” And his three passengers continued to ignore him except for Ali who kept him in line with the gun when needed.

“Almost empty,” the man with the can reported, holding it nearly upside-down out the window.

Ahead of them the volcano of Diamond Head filled the windscreen. A particularly packed area of beach in front of a cluster of hotels lay before them.

“Get this! Then we're done,” Ali said.

The bomber in the backseat shook the canister as they flew over the end of Waikiki Beach. Then he gave Ali a thumbs up signal and let the container drop to the beachfront restaurant below.

Ali turned to the pilot, the pistol pointed at his face. “Go left, higher, fly to the base of the mountains.”

Despite not knowing what was in store for him, the pilot was happy to avert the looming volcano of Diamond Head and gain some altitude.

“Radio your base and inform them that you are having mechanical problems and will be setting down inside Diamond Head.”

“Inside Diamond Head? That's a weird place to land.”

"I don't care. Tell them you have no other choice. Do it."

The pilot keyed his transmitter and relayed the instruction. The person radioing from the base of operations continued to ask questions. Ali told the pilot to ignore him.

"To the Manoa hills."

Wordlessly the pilot set his course. Five minutes later, a series of rainforested mountains came into view, the air thick with mist. A rainbow arched across the sky. The natural beauty meant nothing to any of the men aboard the craft.

"Where do you want me to land?"

Ali pointed. There's a parking lot at the end of that road down there. Put us down there in one piece and this will all be over."

The pilot glanced down at the small square of dirt, a couple of cars left there by hikers who trekked up into the rain forest.

In the backseat, Ali's men had removed their hazmat suits and now tossed them out the still open door. Ali instructed one of them to cover the pilot with the pistol while he removed his own suit and tossed it out.

By the time that was done the pilot was hovering above the parking lot, easing the helicopter down. His radio still boomed with chatter that went ignored. They were searching for the aircraft now in Diamond Head crater.

The skids kissed the dirt with a gentle thump and the pilot sat there with his hands on the collective, looking over at Ali.

The two men in back hefted their backpacks and stepped from the aircraft, now wearing shorts, boots, heads wrapped in bandanas. They looked for all the world like day hikers out to explore the rain forest.

“Let's go!” They called to Ali.

Ali turned to the pilot and double-tapped his 1911, putting two bullets through his forehead. He watched him slump forward at the controls. Satisfied he was dead, he stepped from the chopper and fell into single file line with his men as they hit the trail that wound up into the rainforest.

TWENTY-THREE

Virginia

Tanner was behind the wheel of a rented SUV with Liam and Daniele on the way back to Maryland. They had just gotten over the sting of their failed sortie—the knowledge that not only were they unable to follow Amir to a Hofstad higher-up, but that now Hofstad was aware the antidote ploy was a ruse—when they got the news.

Tanner had kept the radio tuned to an AM news station, knowing that Hofstad's deadline to the government for shutting down the embassy would pass while on the drive home. Thirty-seven minutes after that deadline came and went, the stunning reports came.

Hundreds dead on Waikiki Beach in Hawaii after a touring helicopter flew low over the beach. Dozens more still seriously ill. Doctors report that victims inhaled some type of neurotoxin thought to be released by a man wearing a mask from a yellow tourist helicopter. The search for that helicopter continues.

Tanner pounded the wheel in frustration as he accelerated past a slow-moving camper vehicle. Liam shook his head in silence while Daniele reached up from the backseat to grip Tanner's shoulder.

“We tried our best.”

“Our best wasn't good enough.”

“Sometimes it's not.” This from Liam.

“Hold up—listen!” Daniele turned up the radio volume, where the reporter was saying something about transferring to a live feed. Then the same voice that Tanner recognized as having delivered the statement following the football stadium attack boomed over the airwaves.

“Americans: Hofstad claims responsibility for the Waikiki Beach attack that has killed hundreds, perhaps thousands, of your citizens. We executed these people because our demands have still not been met. The United

States embassy at The Hague remains open for business. And so do we. I reiterate our simple demand to the U.S. administration: close The Hague embassy. You have a two hour grace period after which you may expect further attacks at any time, without warning."

Tanner wasn't sure if a video accompanied the broadcast, but a radio announcer came on to signify that that was the end of the message.

The SUV was silent, all three OUTCAST operators lost in thought. Tanner knew by the fact that a second attack was carried out that Stephen's gambit had failed to pay dividends. That left the lab effort. He wouldn't be able to communicate securely with them until he reached the OUTCAST facility.

As they crossed the Maryland state line, Tanner could only hope that Jasmijn was making progress.

TWENTY-FOUR

Royal Netherlands Institute for Sea Research, Den Hoorn, Netherlands

Dante Alvarez exchanged shocked glances with Naomi Washington across the lab. Between them, Jasmijn Rotmensen sat at a lab bench, her head buried in a stereomicroscope. Dante held eye contact with Nay and pushed a hand toward the floor.

Easy. Keep quiet. Don't let her know.

Dante and Naomi each wore two earpieces. In anticipation of the Hofstad deadline, one was tuned to a news radio station, while the other was reserved for their secure wireless communication channel. They were both hearing at the same time the news of the Hawaii attack. For right now, at least, there was no need to distract their best hope of coming up with an STX antidote by exposing her to the horrible news. Let her work.

So the pair of OUTCAST operatives did their best to stay focused while they listened to the details of the new terror incident. At least a thousand confirmed dead, now. Some kind of airborne neuro-agent, released from a helicopter at low altitude. Hofstad claimed responsibility. The helicopter was located near the mountains, its pilot dead of gunshot wounds inside the craft.

Dante and Naomi continued to circle the lab like sharks on autopilot, guarding their scientist. Pistols drawn, they maintained a state of constant vigilance.

And that vigilance was about to pay off.

Naomi noticed a shadow block a portion of the sliver of light beneath the door, then pass by. Since Jasmijn's lab was the only door set into the end of a hallway, there was no reason for anyone to come this way unless it was to access the lab.

Must be a university security patrol, Naomi thought. Nevertheless, she waved to Dante to gain his attention. The university guards had maintained a regular presence since they'd been here, and they didn't usually walk that close to the door. She glanced at her watch. It had been almost an hour since she'd had a look outside for a perimeter check. She walked toward the door. Dante covered her with his firearm. She was lifting her hand to open the door when Jasmijn's voice nearly made her jump.

"I knew it!"

Neither operator turned to look at her. She looked up from her microscope and furrowed her brow as she caught them in mid-action—Dante's gun drawn, Naomi's hand on the door handle.

"Something wrong?"

"Probably not," Dante walked slowly toward the door as he spoke. "Please continue working. We'll let you know if you need to be aware of anything."

“Actually, I need you to be aware of something.” Jasmijn pointed to the slide under her microscope. Dante watched out of his peripheral vision only.

“I've made some progress but require further raw materials to continue.”

Naomi glanced down at the line of light beneath the door and held a finger up behind her. Dante crouched and steadied himself into a two-handed shooter's stance.

“One moment, please,” he said to Jasmijn.

Suddenly a knock came at the door. “Security. Checking in. Everything okay?”

The voice belonged to a younger Danish male, fitting the profile for the university sponsored patrols.

Dante relaxed his stance. He put his gun down, but did not holster it. He nodded to Nay, who did the same before indicating to Jasmijn that she should respond and come to the door.

"Yes, I'm fine. One second." She got down from the stool and walked to the door. She opened it.

A blonde head she didn't recognize poked into the gap left by the open door. "Afternoon, Doctor. Is everything okay?"

"Yes, yes. Quite alright, thank you." Jasmijn started to close the door but the man put his hand on its edge.

"Excuse me, Doctor. I don't know if you've heard, but there's been news I need to tell you about. May I come in?"

Dante could see Jasmijn check herself as she started to turn her head to look at him and Naomi. They were supposed to be scientists—colleagues of Jasmijn's, not a gun-toting mercenary detail—so she didn't want them to be seen if she could help it. But she needed their approval here. Did they know something she didn't?

Dante nodded and waved his hand backwards. *Come on in.* To deny them entry was suspicious and would only delay Jasmijn's work while the university sent more people to investigate. Better to put them at ease now and send them on their way if at all possible.

"Sure. I can spare a minute or two." She pulled the door opened and stepped back.

The blonde man walked into the lab. He was followed closely by another man, also wearing the yellow and blue university security officer's jacket, who entered the room with him.

Naomi and Dante quickly plucked white lab coats from hooks behind the door and put them on. They pulled clear plastic safety goggles from the pockets and wore those as well. They pocketed their pistols and each sat on lab stools as though they were taking a break.

The pair of security men walked inside, the second one closing the door behind them. They had a thorough look around, their gazes lingering over Jasmijn's two "associates," before addressing the scientist.

“How is your work going—the progress on the antidote?”

Jasmijn's eyes narrowed. It wasn't normal for university security personnel to be informed about the details of laboratory work. But then again, hers was a high profile situation, the very reason for the enhanced security in the first place. But a glance askew at Dante and Naomi told her that they weren't buying it , either. The two OUTCASTs were on the edge of their stools, trying almost too hard to appear casual.

“Going well. Need to get back to it, though. You said there was news to tell me?”

The first of the two into the room nodded. “There has been a second terrorist attack. In Hawaii. Thousands dead from an airborne STX neurotoxin. We need that antidote.”

The hairs on Jasmijn's arms bristled. “We?”

The second of the two security men took a couple of steps back, watching Dante and Nay closely before his associate continued.

“Yes, *we*. I believe you met with a colleague of ours, earlier, no? A colleague who informed you that the STX antidote was needed very soon. We are checking up on the progress of that antidote on behalf of that associate.”

“You—” Jasmijn stammered, suddenly very unsure of herself. “You don't—”

But she never finished her sentence.

Dante pulled his Sig Sauer so fast that neither of the two Hofstad terrorists knew what was happening. That speed came at a price, though. One shot found its mark in the midsection of the man talking to Jasmijn, but the other ricocheted harmlessly off the tile floor. The stricken man reached for something on his belt as he fell to the floor. Dante assumed it was a weapon and blasted his face off with the Sig.

Then a small electronic device clattered onto the floor and he saw it was a two-way radio. This reminded him of the fact that he and Nay both wore small headset radios that were highly advanced and would give away the fact that they were not simply scientists.

Jasmijn backpedaled away from the fallen intruder. “You're from Hofstad, aren't you? How did you get these uniforms?” Oh God...”

But no one else in the room was listening to her. The Hofstad man on the floor was dying, wordlessly hunched over the floor clutching his lacerated gut, chunky ropes of pink spittle swinging from his slackjawed mouth. The remaining Hofstad agent charged into Dante like a bull, smashing his back into the lab counter while Naomi aimed her handgun at the fast-moving combatants.

From there the fight grew furious, a blur of fists, knees and elbows until Naomi had no way to be sure who she'd be shooting. The two grappling men grunted and gasped, heads turning to avoid blows, the fisticuffs clearly taking a toll on both operators.

Jasmijn kept screaming but Naomi blocked it out, focusing her attention on Dante and the man he opposed. The two opponents moved so fast it was like trying to read the numbers on a roulette wheel while it spun. Still, she kept her eyes on them, waiting and hoping for a break that would give her an opportunity for a clean shot.

At that moment the fallen man's radio burst forth with Danish chatter. Only the two women in the room were able to listen to it, and of them only Jasmijn could understand it.

“They just told someone the room number of the lab! Someone's coming!”

Whether that someone was Hofstad reinforcements, university security or local police, she had no way of knowing, but it seemed to spur Dante into action. He grappled even more furiously, gripping the Hofstad man's head with both hands and whipping him into the bench counter. Then he took a well-placed knee to the groin, letting out a choking cough. It looked as though the terrorist was about to plant both feet on Dante's chest and push, but then he realized that his lack of separation from his target was the only thing keeping him alive. Instead of pushing him away, the Hofstad activist flung himself forward in a fluid rolling motion on top of Dante, so that both men now wrestled on the hard floor. Each tried to slam the other's face into the tiles.

Finally, with Dante straining his arm muscles to hold his foe's head up, Naomi saw her chance for a shot. She held her breath. Pulled the trigger back.

That was when the lab door burst open.

TWENTY-FIVE

Royal Netherlands Institute for Sea Research, Den Hoorn, Netherlands

Naomi counted four men, guns drawn, pouring into the lab. She ducked behind a lab bench. Dante still grappled on the floor with the Hofstad man. He was finally gaining the upper hand, rolling onto his side while pinning his opponent's arms unnaturally beneath him. Naomi heard the snap of bone followed by an agonizing wail.

Dante kicked the man away from him and was about to pull his weapon when two of the newcomers appeared to their left, and two to their right.

Four snub-nosed automatic weapons were aimed at Dante, Naomi, and Jasmijn. Dante could see that the extremists also carried backup weapons—pistols and knives worn on utility belts. Two of the men were typical looking light-skinned Dutchmen, early thirties, Dante guessed, while the other two had a more swarthy complexion that suggested North African descent. Regardless, all four them appeared deadly serious to the point of holding back anger.

One of them glanced down at their fallen comrade but did not bother to render aid.

"Search them for weapons," he said in Danish, understandable only to Jasmijn. She translated for Nay and Dante, who emerged slowly from the floor with his hands held high. His Hofstad opponent lay on the floor writhing in agony, favoring his broken arm.

"You three—line up!" One of the swarthy complected gunmen waved his auto-rifle at the lab bench behind them. Naomi and Jasmijn put their backs to it. Dante walked to the bench and did the same.

"Hands up!" Also in accented English. The trio of captured lab inhabitants complied.

The fallen Hofstad man looked up as his comrade approached. The Dutchman kept his automatic rifle leveled at the three prisoners while he looked down at his injured colleague. He directed angry words to him in Dutch. The wounded man responded, apparently trying to defend his actions, to explain why he had failed. Whatever he said, it wasn't enough.

The man standing over him grew red in the face, shouted something and then planted one of his black boots on the agent's broken arm. He continued to yell at him over his screams of misery until the man passed out in a messy fount of his own blood.

Dante watched the eyes of the other Hofstad men. They appeared to show no signs of apprehension or discomfort at what they were witnessing. Were these men higher up in the organization than the two they had just replaced?

“You!” A light-skinned Dutchmen pointed his weapon at Jasmijn as the other three gunmen converged on their three lined-up captives.

“We said we would be back and we are true to our word.” He leered at her two companions. “I see you have recruited help in the lab. Good. What is the status of the STX antidote?” He glanced at the microscope. “You have been working on the antidote, I trust?”

“Yes, I have.”

“Good. And if you've had a chance to check the news, you'll know that there are a good many people who could have benefited from it.”

“As if you would let them have it, anyway,” Jasmijn spat.

“We cannot give what does not exist. Or does it?” He looked again to her workstation by the microscope.

Jasmijn hung her head. “It does not.”

“Explain yourself.”

She looked up at her captor and took a deep breath before speaking. “I attempted a cloning technique I thought could be effective. It wasn't. Then I tried a variant cloning method utilizing an artificial instance of a key molecule that unfortunately does not seem to exist as a commercial preparation. That didn't work either.” She paused to catch her breath, staring at the unfriendly face aiming a gun at her that she knew could cut her to ribbons in seconds.

“If you have lost your usefulness to us,” the man with the machine gun said, then I suppose our work here is done.” He pointed the barrel of the snubnose at her neck.

“There is still hope! After the first unsuccessful trial, I stopped and I thought about it. I conducted a literature search, consulted some of my old notes, and then it finally came to me: the compound I need does exist, and I know where to find it.”

Naomi and Dante nodded, playing their roles as scientists affirming their boss's efforts.

“Where?” His eyes bored into hers.

“There is a species of sea anemone I have done nerve cell work with before that lives on the pilings of oil rigs in the North Sea. Not terribly deep—within scuba diving depths—that's how I used to collect them.”

“These...aneme-what?”

Jasmijn frowned at his lack of comprehension.

“Sea a-nem-O-knees,” she said, over-enunciating each syllable. “They're simple, primitive animals related to jellyfish that are fastened to a substrate of some kind—to rocks or some other hard surface, in this case the support pilings of oil rigs. They look superficially like flowers but are invertebrate animals that use their stinging cells to catch and eat prey like crabs, shrimp and even small fish.”

“They catch prey...” The man with the gun seemed to ponder this.

“Yes. The venom they produce is quite powerful. And I think I can use it as a key ingredient in my STX antidote.

But I need to get some of the anemones. About a dozen or so large, adult specimens should do."

The gunman turned to his associates and spoke rapidly for a few seconds in Dutch. One of them said something back to him and he turned to Dante and Naomi.

"Is what she says true? You require the anem—" He fumbled over the pronunciation and started over. "You require this sea creature to complete work on the STX antidote?"

Both of the undercover OUTCAST operatives nodded. The Hofstad man seemed to study them for a moment. Then he jerked his head at his colleague to his left.

"Search these two."

He indicated the closest man to his right. "Search her."

The man eagerly stepped up to Jasmijn and thoroughly patted her down, enjoying the look of revulsion on her face. After groping her longer than was necessary under the guise of a pat-down, he stepped back and turned to the team leader.

"She's clean."

The two men searching Naomi and Dante each came away with a pistol and two extra clips at about the same time.

The leader raised his eyebrows in their direction. "Scientific instruments, these are?"

Dante shrugged. "We were excited about being invited to work with our esteemed colleague, Dr. Rotmensen, but at the same time concerned about some of the attention around her lab lately."

"Which you can see was justified," Nay added sourly.

The man who found the weapons handed them over to the inquisitor. He turned them over in his hands appreciatively. "These are nice weapons. Sophisticated. Well cared for." He looked up at them as though he had asked a question.

“We both like to hit the shooting range in our spare time,” Dante said. A true statement. Though vastly out of context, it nevertheless gave him the confidence he needed to state it with conviction.

“If you were to obtain these...sea creatures,” the leader said, directing his attention back to Jasmijn, “how long would it take you from that point to complete the antidote?”

Jasmijn's reply was immediate. “About three days. A couple of hours to complete the integration, then forty-eight hours to incubate, then the rest of the time to check results and run test procedures.”

“Then we will see to it that you get these animals.”

“You are divers?”

He turned to his associates, all three of whom shook their heads. He conferred with them in a loose huddle for a minute, speaking Danish in hushed tones such that Jasmijn could not hear. After seeming to reach some kind of decision, three of the men fanned back out into formation, with the leader turning to address Jasmijn.

“We will arrange for a boat and escort you—all three of you— to dive on the site.”

“I need a dive partner. It's not safe to dive alone, and it makes the collecting work very difficult.”

“I'm certified, I'll dive with you,” Dante said.

“Really, I didn't know that!” Jasmijn was not lying, of course. She'd barely met Dante.

“I thought you work together, how could you not know such a thing?” the group leader demanded.

“Relax. We do lab work together, not field work. Usually when I need to collect specimens I go with a support team from the marine lab. They operate the boats, they have the equipment, experienced people to dive with me so that I can just stare at the bottom looking for my specimens.”

“Very well. You and he will dive to collect the sea creatures.”

TWENTY-SIX

Royal Netherlands Institute for Sea Research, Den Hoorn, Netherlands

Stephen Shah did not last as long as he had in a spy career—indeed, even live as long as he did—without being able to pick himself up off the floor and give things another try. His false embassy shutdown orders had fallen flat. But as he walked onto the campus through a side entrance, he was ready to rejoin the fight. Even though his personal side-mission had not succeeded, he could still assist with the lab effort.

To this end, Shah had donned a shabby suit and carried a beat-up leather messenger bag, assuming his new identity of visiting professor from a prominent Iranian university. Before visiting the campus he had checked in with Tanner, who had filled him in on the events stateside, including the Hawaii attack. Tanner had expressed mild concern that he hadn't been able to reach Naomi, Dante or Jasmijn, and was pleased to hear that Shah was heading over there.

As he approached the Sea Research Institute, Shah forced his mind to transition from thoughts of the overall OUTCAST mission to the kind of specialized tunnel vision he adopted when on an individual sortie. This kind of mental process had served him well over the years and he even found it sort of relaxing in a perverse kind of way. He was assuming another identity yet at the same time retaining the unusual abilities of his true self, the skills that allowed him to stay alive in the face of lurking danger presented by men and women a lot like him.

Shah smiled at a man and woman conversing softly, each holding a small stack of books, near the entrance to the research institute. They smiled at him politely and he nodded in return. He entered the building and was instantly on high alert.

He hadn't seen any security detail yet. Wasn't the university supposed to have beefed up its presence? He took the stairs to the second floor. As he moved down the hall at a casual pace, he saw a men's room and went inside even though he didn't have need of a bathroom. Decades of experience told him to check places like restrooms and supply closets whenever a situation was unfolding. He unlatched the safety catch on his holster and pushed his way into the restroom.

He took it in at a glance. Medium sized with three stalls on the left and two sinks next to those, three urinals on the right. No windows. Lights on, a couple of damp paper towels on the floor beneath an overflowing trash can. He walked to one of the sinks and turned it on, letting the water run while he backed up and bent low enough to peer beneath the stalls.

All appeared empty. He got up and turned the water off. Then he went to the door, saw the wedge used by the cleaning staff and crammed it underneath the door. He moved back to the sinks and climbed on top of the one nearest the stalls, allowing him to look down into the first one. It was unoccupied.

Like an oversized spider monkey belying its age, Shah crawled out onto the stall, hands on the front supports and legs on the side, until he could see into the second stall.

Clear.

He continued out along the middle stall in the same fashion until he could see down into the last one.

He suppressed a jolt of adrenaline at the sight of the dead body. Male, late twenties or early thirties, clad only in a pair of underwear. Quickly he dropped into the stall and felt for a pulse. None. A bullet hole on the right temple, no exit wound.

Shah rested the dead man's head against the toilet tank and exited the stall. He went to the trash can and lifted some of the paper towels out of the way.

There.

Dark material, cloth.

He pulled a pair of pants and a shirt from the waste receptacle. No doubt this was what the Hofstad actor had been wearing before taking out the security guard in order to appropriate his uniform. He carefully searched the pockets but they came up empty.

But he had seen all he needed to. Shah pulled the wedge from the door and walked out into the hall. He had no doubt that if he was to check other nearby restrooms or perhaps supply closets or little used areas such as rooms housing electrical / HVAC infrastructure, that he would find more stripped bodies.

On high alert now, Shah focused on maintaining a normal breathing rate as he passed down the hall, which was now empty although he could hear voices from behind some of the closed doors he passed. The lab was all the way at the end and there was little he could do to conceal himself as he approached. He mentally reviewed his cover story should he be confronted by anyone while he walked up to the lab.

I am Dr. Farid Soroush, professor of Ocean Sciences at the Tehran Institute for Marine Technology. I am here by invitation to work with Dr. Jasmijn Rotmensen...

But by the time he had reached the closed lab door, no one had approached him. He glanced down at the crack beneath the door and was careful to stand far enough back from it that he would not alter its light pattern. Old habits. Keeping his feet planted far back, he bent at the waist and placed an ear near the door where it met the jamb.

Voices.

He could only catch about every third or fourth word, but it was enough to tell him that they'd been compromised. He heard Jasmijn talking, something about scuba diving, and then who he assumed to be a Hofstad terrorist, speaking in Dutch. His hand reflexively dropped to his holstered weapon but he made no real move. From the sound of it there were at least three Hofstad operatives inside, perhaps more, and they had somehow gotten the upper hand over Dante and Naomi. Shah knew that in order to do that these foes must be substantially equipped, or else have had one hell of an element of surprise. Perhaps both.

Shah turned away from the door and padded softly down the hall. He knew the lab only had one entrance in or out, other than the windows. So they would have to leave by that door at some point. Better for him to surveil that exit than to walk into a possible firestorm, potentially putting his own operatives at risk.

He walked briskly down the hall away from the lab. He saw nowhere that offered a hiding place that would also allow him to see when the lab door opened, so he decided to hide in plain sight and hope that would suffice. If the lab team was in trouble, then he was most likely their only external hope of support.

About halfway down the hallway he saw an extensive bulletin board display featuring posterboard presentations of recent lab work. He stood facing one of them, something about predictability of El Niño oscillation cycles, and pretended to be absorbed by it.

He'd been staring at the exhibit for seven minutes when he heard the lab door open at the end of the hall.

He willed himself not to turn and look down the hall, but to keep staring at the information on the wall. As the footsteps grew louder and nearer, he registered people walking toward him in his peripheral vision. A large group, not one or two. He knew he would have but one chance to look their way such that it was disguised as a casual glance. More than that would arouse suspicions on the part of the captors, if in fact the lab team had been captured.

Shah told himself he was about to find out. He forced himself to wait a few more seconds until the approaching people were so close that it would almost seem strange not to turn and look at them. When he did, he saw Dante and Naomi walking side by side, with Jasmijn in front of them. The three of them were flanked on both sides by men wearing university security guard uniforms, as well as one in front and two in back, including the man with the broken arm.

Shah smiled curtly to the group as they passed, making ever-so-brief eye contact with Naomi, who opened her lips to silently mouth the word "Hofstad," and acted as though they had distracted him from his engrossing reading material. He turned back to the bulletin board display as they passed by him.

When they had reached the far end of the hall and he heard them open the stairwell doorway, Shah started down the hallway after them.

TWENTY-SEVEN

Royal Netherlands Institute for Sea Research, Den Hoorn, Netherlands

When tailing a target who has already seen you, it is imperative to alter their perception of you before continuing. To this end, Shah ditched his jacket and briefcase (removing his Spydeco folding knife first and transferring it to a pants pocket). He also donned a pair of dark sunglasses and a baseball cap that had been in the case.

Following Dante, Naomi, Jasmijn and their Hofstad escorts across the campus was child's play for Shah. Lots of foot traffic out here, plenty of criss-crossing foothpaths winding this way and that, trees and shrubbery, campus maps on kiosks. He easily kept them in sight while staying far behind until they reached a parking lot and made for a blue van. That was when Shah realized he could be about to lose control of the situation very quickly.

His own vehicle was parked on a different lot all the way across campus. He could try to run to it and then catch up with the van, which he now noted sported the university logo. Hofstad must have taken it from one of the guards they killed. Or, he could approach within earshot and try to overhear a clue as to where they were going.

Another split second decision to make in the field. He'd been confronted with lots of them over the course of his career, and he never second guessed them, even when they turned out to be dead wrong, literally in some cases. In this line of work, inaction was often worse than a wrong decision. If he were to do nothing for the next thirty seconds, that blue van would be out of sight, and along with it his colleagues' only hope for external support.

The neurons in his brain fired and he took off walking—not running, although he wanted to—toward the van. Just a guy walking across the parking lot. There were lots of vehicles here, not just the van, and there was no reason for anyone to suspect that something was wrong here. He only wanted to get to his car after a long day in the academic trenches, that's all. But to get to it he'd pass right between the van and the black pickup truck parked next to it.

As he approached, he turned his head toward the left as though he were looking in that direction, but beneath his glasses his eyes shifted right. He caught the outline of a pistol barrel pressed against the pocket of one of the "security" personnel's jackets. It was pointed first at Dante as he was ushered into one of the van's rear seats, and then Jasmijn.

As Naomi stepped up to the van, she tripped—or appeared to, reaching down to adjust her shoe. Now passing the van, Shah heard the guy with the concealed gun utter something to Nay that meant, *hurry it up, get in.*

As she stood, she glanced left and looked right at Shah, who continued to watch her only out of his peripheral vision to avoid being seen making eye contact. Then she turned away from him and stepped up to the van. As she climbed in, she said something loud enough for Shah to hear as he passed between the van and the pickup.

"Will our boat be waiting for us at the wharf?"

Attagirl, Shah thought. Excellent work. All he had to do now was continue to walk slowly through the lot until they left in the van, and then he could retrieve his own vehicle and go to the wharf. At least he had an idea of where they were heading. If he was lucky he'd even be able to tail them on the way over there.

But as he pretended to make a beeline for a car that wasn't his, Shah's inner voice nagged at him.

Why were they being taken to the wharf? He shook off mental images of his team being tied to cinderblocks and pushed into the water.

He stopped at the driver side door of a metallic brown sedan and pretended to fumble around for his keys while the van rolled past toward the exit. If they did cast any kind of suspicion on him, with any luck they'd now be watching for a tail to come in the form of a sparkly brown four-door sedan. Once the van had left the lot Shah waited for thirsty seconds to make sure it wasn't a ruse, that they would turn back in and spot him walking away from the brown car. But as he counted down...*two Mississippi...one Mississippi...*no van re-entered the lot.

Shah took off at a trot across the park-like environment toward his rental vehicle. Four minutes later he reached it, a subcompact SUV in white, the color chosen deliberately because it was the most common car color.

He drove slowly, within the posted limits until he had left campus property. There was no time to get pulled over now, and he could not afford to be chased when he needed to chase someone else. He took advantage of the slow speed to initialize his GPS and set up a route to the wharf. As soon as he reached a public surface street, however, he gunned the little vehicle until he was doing seven km/h over the speed limit.

Traffic was moderate, and Shah stuck to the fast lane when he had a choice. There was no highway to take to the wharf, so he followed the route the computer had plotted as being the most direct. It put the drive time at twenty-five minutes, and after about half that, the OUTCAST operator felt that familiar rush of sighting his target again after becoming separated.

Don't count your chickens—make sure, he told himself as he jockeyed for position around a pair of slow-moving work trucks. When he passed them he got a better look at the blue van. Same university logo.

Bingo!

He was back in visual contact.

Not too close.

Shah flashed back to his earlier days in the field when he was a true wheel artist, in command of vehicles designed for tactical use. These included headlights that could be individually controlled, blinking one out after a time to make it look as though a different car was there, brake lights that could be disabled with the flick of a switch, stall switches to simulate a vehicle breakdown in case he should reach a cheating command of the target and need to let them pass before starting up again as a "different" working car. Heavy-duty suspension, bumpers, batteries—various other modifications to increase the staying power during long follows.

But he had none of those advantages now, just a stock rental car by himself, no additional agents forming a box around the target. Still, he was highly trained to adapt to fluid situations and make do with what he had. Shah stayed four cars behind the van, one eye on the road and the other on his GPS. He was approaching what the map said was the exit for the wharf. Would the van take it?

He breathed a sigh of relief as he saw the right turn signal start blinking on the van.

Shah waited in his lane until the last possible moment to exit, allowing two cars between him and the van. He watched the van take the expected turn according to the GPS if they were headed to the wharf. Again Naomi's words haunted him.

Will our boat be waiting for us at the wharf?

He wasn't sure how he was going to deal with the boat. If it was a ferry with a lot of passengers he might be able to board it and mingle. But if it was a small boat...

He forced his mind to stay on task with his follow. If he lost them now it could all be a moot point. They wound through a semi-treed area with some open grassland on either side of the road until the ocean was visible in the distance, a spate of buildings partially blocking the views.

Some drivers had their headlights on for safety although it was daytime, and Shah flipped his on, knowing it would change the appearance of his vehicle in rear view mirrors. He hung back three cars, doing the posted speed limit. He kept watch on the van's windows for any signs of struggle coming from within—what if Nay and Dante were desperate and tried to fight their way out?—but he saw none.

The female British accent of his GPS unit announced that he should make a right turn ahead.

The van made the turn. Shah hung back, well aware that turning after a target vehicle brought high risk of detection. He checked the GPS map and saw that another road up ahead intersected with the one the van turned onto in about a mile. He decided it was worth the risk and passed the turn, then sped to the next right. He took it and cruised a little over the speed limit until he reached the road leading to the wharf. He stopped at an intersection, farm properties on both sides of the road. He waited to make sure he hadn't somehow come out ahead of the van, and then turned left onto the road.

Another mile ahead he caught up with the van. Beyond it he saw shimmering water, fishing boats in their slips.

Where were they going? He couldn't follow the van too much longer without being an obvious tail. After one more block Shah turned off onto a side street and parked. He observed the van from inside his vehicle until he was sure it was parking in the wharf lot. Then he exited and started to toward the wharf on foot.

He approached from a block over, walking at a normal pace. Small clapboard houses lined the street. At the waterfront there was a mild cluster of activity—fishermen unloading the day's catch, a row of shops and pubs, some industrial activity—loading and unloading of large containers. The tang of salt air filled his nostrils while the call of gulls assailed his ears. Shah turned to his left and saw that one of the two pubs had an outdoor seating area with a few old salts out there smoking pipes and playing cards at a small table. He ambled up to the place and swung open the wooden gate that led to the patio. He took a seat at a small table by himself, behind the men playing cards so that they shielded him somewhat from the van's view.

He observed two Hofstad men exit the van. One walked out along one of the wooden docks while the other proceeded to a storefront along the wharf, maybe six down from the pub where Shah sat. Everyone else remained inside the van.

Shah watched as the man on the dock reached a power boat he judged to be about twenty-five feet in length, with twin 250 horsepower outboard motors. The man ducked into the boat's cabin for a few seconds, then emerged and started the engines. Meanwhile, the other terrorist had entered a scuba diving shop.

A waitress emerged and asked Shah if she could get him anything. He ordered a pint of La Trappe beer without taking his eyes off the van. The server left and then the door to the van slid open. He watched as Naomi, Jasmijn and Dante piled out, surrounded closely by the other three Hofstad men. Shah noticed that they no longer wore the security guard outfits, but had donned commercial fishing gear—rubber aprons with hip boots and knitted caps.

Shah chugged half his beer in one gulp and left a bill to cover it on the table. No sooner had he set down his glass than the Hofstad agent emerged from the dive shop wheeling a cart full of scuba gear, headed for the boat at the dock.

Shah eyed the vessel again. The operative there was untying lines, preparing for departure. The boat was much too small for him to have any hopes of boarding undetected. He wished he knew the purpose of this trip.

What were they scuba diving for? He looked around the wharf. He could wait here until they returned.

But what if only the Hofstad members came back?

Then he saw an old man of the sea type step off a fishing boat that was smaller than the one Hofstad was using. Shah a glanced over to the dock, where Jasmijn, Dante and Naomi were now walking the plank, it appeared to Shah, out along the dock out to the boat, with Hofstad men in front of and behind them. He got up and left the pub through the front gate.

He forced himself to walk at a normal pace to the old man with the boat, his wallet in hand.

TWENTY-EIGHT

Netherlands, The North Sea

The ride out to the oil rig didn't take long, but it was unnerving having guns pointed at you in a bouncing boat. The boat driver slowed the craft as they neared the rig, and the leader addressed Jasmijn on the boat's aft deck.

"Set up your equipment while we are en route to the dive site." The Dutch terrorist indicated a rack of scuba tanks and a bag of gear, then looked to Jasmijn to see if she would object.

"He's going with me." She looked at Dante, who nodded.

The terrorist shook his head. "You will go alone."

Jasmijn raised her voice. It seemed to come from a place of genuine anger, not merely an act. "I have never before dove alone. I would not be able to collect the required specimens without a dive partner because I'd be too distracted out of concern for my safety."

“If safety is your concern, you are arguing with the wrong man.” The terror monger dropped his hand down to his holstered pistol.

Jasmijn gave a laugh that she hoped would sound defiant but it just came out sounding anxious. “I suppose you have a point there. Being shot and dumped overboard isn't very safe, either, I get it. But the fact remains that if you want me to collect the specimens I require to complete my work on the antidote, then I need to dive with someone who has scientific scuba experience, and that's Dante.”

She thrust an elbow in his direction. Although Dante was a certified diver and in peak physical condition, his experience was not in the line of duty as a former Secret Service agent, but rather recreational only, in tropical places where the drinks on the beach come in coconuts with little umbrellas on them, where the water is warm and the dives are shallow, the only objective to look at the pretty fish swimming over the rainbow coral reefs. He had absolutely no idea what was meant by *scientific* diving, and he had never done a dive as demanding as an oil rig in the bone-chilling cold of the North Sea.

He nodded confidently and said, “Let's do this.”

The Hofstad group leader summoned over another of his three henchmen and conferred with him in soft tones for a few moments. Dante saw the man who had come over turn to glance at him once while the other man was talking.

Then the leader said to Jasmijn, “Very well. You and he will dive. We will be following your air bubbles to see where you come up.”

She nodded. “Good. We don't want a long swim back to the boat in this freezing water. Speaking of which,” she went on, pointing at an exposure suit on deck, “these are dry suits, correct? A wetsuit isn't going to cut it down there at a hundred feet.”

The leader looked to one of his other men, a young Dutchman in his mid-twenties, for an answer. That man nodded.

“Yes. Put them on. Get going.”

“And you have the transport tank for the specimens like I asked?”

The same man who had assisted with the drysuit question lifted a hinged lid on a compartment and pointed to the bubbling water within. “Oxygenated livewell.”

Jasmijn nodded. They were normally used for fishing to keep bait alive. “That's good for the trip back to the dock, but then we'll still need something to keep them alive on the drive back to the lab. At least a cooler full of seawater, preferably with an aerator.”

“I'll see what I can do.” The man backed away. For a moment it was almost as if there was a regular working atmosphere aboard the boat, but that was quickly shattered.

“Enough delays! Collect the specimens!” The Hofstad leader aimed his pistol at Jasmijn. He stood there and leered at her while she stripped her pants off, leaving her jacket on to cover up while she stepped into the drysuit.

Dante put his suit on as well and then they were attaching buoyancy compensators and regulators to tanks, hefting them on, adding weight belts. After adjusting the straps on the gear and doing a check of each other's equipment, Jasmijn clipped a mesh collecting bag to her belt and announced they were ready.

They stepped over to the rear of the boat onto a platform where they put on their fins. Two of the Hofstad men stood immediately behind them on the boat deck, monitoring their movements. The leader stood back at the wheel, watching from a distance.

Jasmijn pointed to the nearby oil rig. “So we'll swim to that pillar there and drop down. The anemones we need should be attached to the structure about fifty feet down.”

Dante squinted at the oil rig just before he pulled his mask on. "Do we need to watch out for moving parts down there, like getting sucked into a pipe or something like that?"

Behind him one of the guards laughed softly.

Jasmijn shook her head. "I've dived on this rig before. This one has been slated for decommissioning and so there's no active drilling anymore. I'm not even sure if there are any people on it," she said, giving his foot a subtle stamp with her own as she looked over at the rig. "Active ones have a lot of boat traffic and as you can see, there's none of that."

"Enough talk!" The leader shouted from the wheel. "Get on with it!"

Jasmijn turned to Dante. She could see in his eyes that he was a little nervous. "We'll swim on the surface closer to the pillar to conserve air, then we drop down next to it. Ready?"

Dante nodded as he gazed out over the surface of the ocean. At least it was calm, by North Sea standards. Three-to-four foot swells.

Jasmijn nodded in return and the two of them splashed into the water.

TWENTY-NINE

Netherlands, The North Sea

Dante and Jasmijn dropped down into the ocean next to the oil rig's concrete column. They could see some thirty to forty feet in any direction, the water being clouded by floating microscopic plants and animals called plankton. Dante gripped Jasmijn's arm to halt their descent.

She opened her eyes wide. *What*?

He took the underwater slate clipped to the dive vest and wrote on it with the attached pencil.

DO U REALLY NEED ANEMS TO MAKE ANTIDOTE? He'd been wondering this since she brought it up in the lab, but this was the first opportunity he'd had to communicate with her alone.

Jasmijn gave an exaggerated nod that would not be hidden by the gear she wore.

Dante scribbled on the slate again.

SAW LADDER UP TO RIG DURING SWIM OVER. SIDE FACING AWAY FROM BOAT. WE COULD TRY TO HIDE ON RIG, LET THEM THINK WE HAD DIVE ACCIDENT.

They hung suspended in the water while Jasmijn comprehended what he proposed. Then she nodded again. What did they have to lose? There was no doubt that once Hofstad had the working antidote, she would no longer hold any value to them. She harbored no illusions that they would kill her. She took her own slate and wrote on it: OK BUT GET ANEMS FIRST. NOT FAR BELOW.

Dante gave her the diver's OKAY signal, thumb and forefinger in a circle, and then the pair descended further along the oil rig's support structures. When they reached a brace system at a depth of sixty feet where multiple struts branched off in various directions, Jasmijn tapped Dante on the shoulder and pointed to one of the flat metal surfaces.

It was covered with white sea anemones, outwardly resembling a bed of flowers. Thick schools of silvery fish swarmed in broad circles around the oil rig pillars.

Jasmijn approached the anemones and deftly pulled one off and dropped it into her bag. She repeated the process a few more times, the uprooted animals dropping to the bottom of her bag in a tangle of silky tentacles.

She signaled to Dante that she was ready to ascend. Their air supply would last longer at shallower depths, although they also needed to avoid detection. The water was not so clear they had to worry about being seen from the boat while they were underwater, but she recalled the Hofstad leader's words with a chill: *We will be following your air bubbles to see where you come up.*

She halted Dante and wrote on her slate: OUR BUBBLES?

Dante glanced at it and nodded. He pointed to her air gauge. 2,200 psi. Glanced at his own. 1,800. *Figures she has better air consumption*, Dante thought, shrugging out of his tank. Women usually do, and she was a much more experienced diver. He wished they could have Liam here, but things were what they were and he would deal with it.

He carefully inflated his buoyancy compensator device (BCD) until it was neutrally buoyant. Then he took a small reel of safety line and used it to tie the vest in place around a steel girder. He loosened the regulator's purge valve until a steady stream of air bubbles trickled from it and rose toward the surface.

They had to act fast now. It might not take long for the men on the boat to realize that there were two bubble streams far apart, the real one not as constant. But they weren't experienced divers, so it just might work. Even if they did spot the two streams, they would probably assume they had split up and would hopefully pursue the wrong one first.

Dante breathed from Jasmijn's "octopus," or spare regulator mouthpiece, designed with a longer hose to be an emergency regulator in an out-of-air situation. Thus tethered to her side, they swam upward at an angle toward the ladder Dante had spotted on the far side of the rig. They kicked through a maze of steel support beams encrusted with marine growth, the water growing lighter around them and more turbulent as they rose. They were extra vigilant to avoid becoming entangled in the myriad snags of monofilament fishing line, since Hofstad had seen to it that they not be allowed to carry dive knives, normally be worn for that purpose.

After a few minutes they could see the large pillars marking the far edge of the oil platform. Dante checked their remaining air: 1,000 psi. Enough to get to the ladder, but there wouldn't be much in reserve should something go wrong. He also worried that the ladder might not extend all the way to the waterline. If it was designed for boarding by boats only, it might be too high above the water for them to reach.

But it was time to find out. They passed between two massive support pillars at a depth of about ten feet, and looked up. They could see the watery, distorted shape of the oil platform above, beckoning. If they could get up there, they might be able to hide, to summon help.

Swimming to the far side of one of the pillars so that it would hide them from the boat, Dante and Jasmijn surfaced at the oil rig.

THIRTY

Netherlands, The North Sea

Stephen Shah eased up on the throttle of the small fishing boat he had paid an exorbitant fee to borrow. He was sure that the handful of gold Krugerrands he'd given to the old man at the dock were worth more than the boat if he didn't bring it back. But it seemed seaworthy and it had gotten him this far. The pair of binoculars tucked under the steering console were also a huge bonus.

He lifted the optics to his eyes and peered at the Hofstad boat from perhaps a quarter-mile away. One of the terrorists sat at the boat's wheel while a second was reloading what Shah recognized as a sub-machine gun. That man stood over Naomi, who sat on the stern deck, back to the rail. Her arms were by her sides but he couldn't tell whether they had been bound. The other three of the terrorists stood on the boat's rail, watching the water intently.

Shah felt a surge of blind panic. Had Dante and Jasmijn been killed and tossed over the side? Or had they been thrown overboard while tied together? But then he scoped the scuba tanks on deck and forced himself to stay calm. They must be diving. Why, he hadn't the foggiest notion. To retrieve something for Hofstad? They were close to the oil rig.

Perhaps Hofstad was forcing them to sabotage the rig somehow—plant explosives on it?

He scanned the water in the direction the men were looking but couldn't see anything. He supposed they might be looking for or watching their air bubbles. He searched the surrounding water through the binoculars but still saw nothing. He didn't 'like the situation. Jasmijn seemed to be the safest of the three of them, since she had the specialized knowledge to create the antidote. But Nay and Dante, although they were posing as scientific colleagues, were basically assistants— temp help—and Shah wondered if, after whatever objective they had for this dive was achieved, Hofstad wouldn't kill them off out here.

Almost subconsciously his hand dropped down to the Browning 9mm tucked into his waistband beneath his now untucked shirt. If he could only get close enough to the Hofstad boat, he might be able to neutralize them. But first he would have to find a way to bring his boat to them. If he were to speed over to them they would most likely gun him down.

He looked around the old boat, at the pile of nets and buoys on the deck, at the VHF marine radio on the console, at the battered old outboard motor mounted on the transom.

His eyes lingered there, then flicked back to the radio, then to the Hofstad boat. He found the switch to raise the motor and lifted its lower half out of the water. He then removed the cowling to expose its innards, as though he was working on it. He wiped some grease from the motor on his hands and smudged his forehead. Then he found the sparkplugs and removed one of them, pocketing it.

Shah walked back over to the console and picked up the radio. He verified it was set to the distress channel, then spoke in English while he keyed the transmitter.

"Attention, attention! Fishing boat requires assistance. Calling white boat near oil rig: can you help me? Motor won't start. Think I just need a jump start. Please help, over."

A couple of minutes passed during which Shah refrained from using the binoculars in case he himself was now being watched. Then the radio crackled to life in Dutch-accented English.

"Fishing boat, we acknowledge your transmission but we have divers in the water and cannot leave the area now, over."

Shah gripped the transmitter and spoke into it. "Please, I am begging you. I am taking on water with no battery power to run my pump. If I just had a jump start I could help myself."

About thirty seconds went by and Shah was beginning to think that they were ignoring him. But then the reply came.

"Fishing boat: all right. We can send a man over in our tender vessel to see if he can give you an assisted start. Stand by."

Shah thanked them and dropped the transmitter. He heard the buzzing of a low horsepower motor start up, and then he saw a small boat speeding in his direction from Hofstad's larger vessel.

THIRTY-ONE

Netherlands, The North Sea

Dante hauled himself over the top of the ladder onto the oil platform's lowest level. He shed his gear and then reached out to pull Jasmijn up. They crouched next to a large spool of electrical cable on a concrete deck and surveyed their new surroundings: a maze of pipes and catwalks. They could neither see nor hear any signs of people. The place looked deserted. Dante heard the sound of water dripping and located the source: Jasmijn's mesh dive bag containing the sea anemones.

"I thought you said you needed those to be alive, in water, in order to be useful for the antidote?"

She frowned at the bag of invertebrates. "Ideally, yes, but to be honest I've tried it with them before, delivered live, and it didn't work."

"So you lied to them?"

“Well, I guess so. But I don't know what else to try. I know these anemones are the key, somehow...”

“Good job. You got us out of the lab and at least now we have a chance. Maybe you should just ditch the bag now since they're going to die, lighten your load?”

She eyed the bag again. “I think I should hold onto them. For one thing, if Hofstad does recapture us, they might still be alive and I'll tell them they're still good. For another, maybe they'll work anyway, who knows. We went through a lot of trouble to collect them, after all. Not to mention I don’t want to take their lives for nothing.”

“Okay, then let's move.” Dante motioned along the edge of the structure, below which the waves slapped against the support pilings, echoing throughout the rig.

“What are we looking for?”

“Let's see if we can find a radio or a satellite phone in here somewhere.”

Jasmijn agreed. “We can work our way up, most of the rooms are on the upper level.”

They walked across the first level, which was mostly outdoors, with the second, more substantial level blocking most of the sunlight. Dante knew that they had only a few minutes before Hofstad discovered something was up. SCUBA air tanks lasted for somewhere between forty minutes to an hour, depending on depth, and, although he had no watch, he knew it had to be coming up on that now.

Dante pointed out some metal bolts laid out on the floor in front of them. “Step over them. We don't want to make any loud noises they can hear from the boat.” Jasmijn avoided the obstacles and they continued around the edge of the rig, which was roughly square shaped. They reached the end of the first side and laid out flat in what Dante thought of as a prone sniper position in order to get a look at the Hofstad boat below.

It was still floating there, the four men and Naomi visible as indistinct forms from this distance. Dante could see no signs that they were frantically searching for them yet. But then he saw something that gave him an adrenaline surge.

Another boat.

Smaller, a little further away than Hofstad's vessel.

Shah?

He'd been there at the dock. He wasn't sure if he'd be able to figure out where they were going, but Nay had gotten off the comment as a clue.

Even if it wasn't Shah, as long as it was someone besides Hofstad, it was great news.

"Who do you think is in the other boat?" Jasmijn asked.

"I think it's my OUTCAST colleague who followed us from the docks. I saw him there."

"No way we can swim to him or Hofstad will see."

“Right. We have to communicate with him somehow. A radio would be best, even though Hofstad might hear that. Or we could try to visually signal him somehow, like with a mirror or a flare if we can find one.”

But as soon as he said it, they heard the sound of a smaller outboard motor start up. They turned and saw an inflatable Zodiac boat making a fast beeline from the Hofstad boat to the newcomer's vessel. It would be there in a couple of minutes.

“Should we watch what happens here?” Jasmijn queried. Dante got to his feet and started moving toward the rig's main enclosed structure.

“We should see if we can get to a radio while they're a little distracted.”

THIRTY-TWO

Netherlands, The North Sea

Shah stood by his boat's motor as he watched the Hofstad Zodiac idle up to his craft.

"Speak English?" he tested.

"Need help with your engine?" one of them, the one not driving the boat, called out in the requested language. His tone was not friendly.

"Yes, please! Thank you for coming to help. It was working fine this morning." Shah pointed to the motor with a gesture of irritation.

"Perhaps mechanic is not your calling," the other man said. He killed the Zodiac's engine and tossed Shah a line. Shah tied it to a cleat on his boat, tethering the two vessels together. He was hoping that one of the men might remain in the Zodiac but both of them boarded the larger boat. The three of them huddled around the engine, its cover off.

“Let's have a look. Go ahead and start it,” the taller of the two men said. Both of them wore jeans and long sleeved shirts. One appeared to be of North African descent while the taller of the two was European.

Shah walked back to the console and turned the key while looking backwards, ostensibly to watch the motor, but really two keep an eye on the two terrorists.

“It's not turning over at all,” the shorter man observed.

“Like I said, I think my battery is dead,” Shah said. He worried that they were about to poke around in the engine and discover the pulled spark plug—that would be highly unusual since he'd managed to get out here—but then one of them leapt back onto the Zodiac.

“We'll try to jump it,” the one still on Shah's boat said, adding, “You should be more prepared before coming out here. You are a fisherman?” He cast his eyes about the deck, examining the piles of netting, buoys and traps.

Shah nodded. “I know it.”

The operator in the Zodiac tossed one end of a pair of jumper cables to his associate in Shah's boat. He clipped them to the battery.

“Try it now.”

Shah tensed. This was it. He knew the motor wouldn't start with the missing spark plug in his pocket. When it didn't, they would double-check the connections, and then once they saw they were good or noticed the missing plug, they would become suspicious.

“Okay, turning the key now.” He looked back at the motor, both of the Hofstad men also staring at it.

Shah turned the key.

“Did you try it?” the one in his boat asked, looking at him.

“Yes. Let me try again.” Shah turned it again, shaking his head when nothing happened as though he couldn't believe it.

“Check the cables on your end,” the man in Shah's boat called to his colleague in the Zodiac, who had connected the cable to his outboard motor. That man bent to the task while the one a few feet away from Shah did the same on Shah's battery.

Shah didn't hesitate. He snatched his Browning Hi Power 9mm pistol from his waistband and took aim at the man in his boat, who was on his knees, peering into the battery compartment. Shah took aim at the back of his neck.

He pulled the trigger, wishing it was sound suppressed but ready to act out a chain of events he'd already gone over in his mind. His target was lifeless before the sound of the report reached Hofstad's boat. The terror-fighter on the Zodiac recoiled sharply at the sound of the shot, arm reaching beneath his sweatshirt.

Shah aimed for his chest but a wave caused the boat to move at the instant he fired and the round hit the man in the shoulder. He was pitched backward by the impact of the slug until he tripped over a coil of rope and fell hard onto the deck. Shah saw the man's firearm fly from his hand and splash into the water. He might have a back-up weapon, though. Shah wasn't going to give him the chance to get at it if he did have one. He jumped across to the other boat, landing crazily on the man. He slammed his head once into the deck, hard, to stun him into submission, then pulled his arms behind his back.

Picking up the rope the man had tripped over, Shah used it to bound the terrorist's arms tightly behind his back. He patted him down but found no additional weapons. He did find a wallet, though, with an ID—a Dutch driver license. He took the license without letting the Hofstad man see he that took it and then returned the wallet to his pocket.

He considered whether to take the Zodiac but then looked at the little fuel can and wasn't sure it would be able to make it all the way back to shore. So he dragged the bound man back into his boat and set him down on the deck next to the steering console where he'd be able to keep an eye on him.

"Just lay there and don't cause any trouble, and I won't have to kill you." Shah pulled the spark plug from his pocket and showed it to his captor, who scowled upon seeing it.

"Maybe mechanic isn't your calling," Shah taunted, and then moved back to the motor and popped the plug back in. He didn't bother putting the motor cover back on, just left it open and jumped back to the console.

He started the motor and picked up the radio.

THIRTY-THREE

Netherlands, The North Sea

Dante Alvarez topped over the metal ladder onto the oil rig's upper deck. He examined the superstructure before him while he waited for Jasmijn to clamor over. Already two stories above the first level, this edifice rose two more. He moved to a steel door set into the bottom of the structure in front of them. Tried the knob.

Locked.

He felt in his pants pocket and removed a lock pick tool that had not been uncovered in the frisking Hofstad had given him. He applied it to the lock, which was of higher quality than most. Still, he heard it click into place after about a minute. He opened the door.

Inside, it was shadowy, lights off. He felt along the wall for a switch and found it, thinking they had probably left the power off and it wouldn't work, but a bank of overhead fluorescents flickered on. A battered metal desk occupied one wall, a corkboard above that covered in occupational safety warnings and tattered shift schedules. A computer occupied the desk but its screen was dark, no LEDs on anywhere. Dante tried turning it on but nothing happened. There was no phone that he could see. Jasmijn rifled through drawers and filing cabinets, finding nothing useful.

There was another door at the rear of the office and they took it into a narrow hallway lit by a single caged bulb into a larger work area. This space was enclosed but filled with machinery of some kind—pipework, metal ducts, various gauges and dials. A workbench occupied the left wall of the roughly rectangular room, backed by a pegboard containing a full assortment of tools. Dante grabbed a small hammer off its peg and handed it to Jasmijn along with a screwdriver.

"Here, carry one, put the other in your pocket."

She cast a doubtful stare at the implements. “I don't know if I...”

“Just do it. If nothing else I might be able to use them. I'll be carrying these.” He hefted a pipe wrench from the wall and slapped it into a palm. Then he selected a Phillips head screwdriver as a serviceable shank and put that in his back pocket. He scanned around the rest of the area but saw no communications equipment.

“Let’s keep going. There's got to be an electronics room somewhere.”

They moved on through the work room until they reached a door on its far end. It opened into a stairwell leading up only. They took it up two flights, traversing back and forth in a tight space to make the short vertical distance. At the top of the stairs they emerged on an open-air metal landing platform.

Dante pointed skyward. “Look at all those antennas. There's got to be a radio room somewhere.”

Jasmijn walked across the landing and looked down. "Ladder goes down here."

"Let's go." Dante looked out over the water while he waited for Jasmijn to start climbing down. The Hofstad boat was still there, as was the boat Shah was in, although now a Zodiac was pulled up next to it.

When Jasmijn was down a few rungs, Dante followed down the ladder. It ended in a metal enclosure with a five-foot drop to a metal deck. Jasmijn hung from the bottom of the ladder until she could step off. Dante let himself drop from a few feet.

They were situated on a square metal balcony of sorts with no other ladders leading down, and only one door set into the wall. He tried the door handle. To his surprise, it opened into a small, dimly lit room. There was no one inside. Racks of radio equipment lined workbenches on either side of the room. Much of the equipment was unfamiliar to Dante, although some he recognized as HAM radio gear—shortwave radio sets capable of transmitting over long distances. But right now they just needed to talk to the boat. His eyes scanned the shelves with the aid of his dive light until he found what he was looking for: a VHF marine radio.

He walked up to the unit and turned it on, breathing a sigh of relief when its backlit display lit up orange.

"Whatcha got?" Jasmijn watched Dante start to press buttons and turn knobs.

"Should be able to monitor the boat communications with this. See if we can reach Stephen..."

A burst of static emanated from the speaker and he adjusted the squelch. Still nothing intelligible. He wasn't sure which one was designated as the emergency channel in this part of the world, so he set the radio to auto-scan through the stations until a strong signal came though. After a few seconds, he was rewarded with a clear voice on one of the channels.

It belonged to Stephen Shah, with a background of engine noise. And one who didn't know him well wouldn't be able to tell, but Dante could detect the stress in his words.

"*...could make an exchange. Our woman for your man. Then we go our separate ways.*"

Dante held up a hand, knowing Jasmijn had questions, but he needed to hear what came next. He could already tell that a serious situation had developed. *Our woman* must be Naomi, and *your man* must mean that Shah had somehow taken one of the Hofstad men hostage.

A Dutch-accented voice, different background sounds. "*We sent two men to help you, not one.*"

There was a pause before Shah's voice came back. "*One has been eliminated. The other will be, too, if anything happens to the woman. But we can end the killing here. Your man for our woman. It's up to you.*"

"What about your other two people—the two scuba divers—you don't want them?"

Dante and Jasmijn exchanged a glance.

"Where are they?"

Dante eyed the radio transmitter. Should he break in on the channel to let Shah know they were on the oil rig? But that would be letting Hofstad know, too.

"*I don't know where they are. They were with you, what happened?*"

"*Forget it. Let us do this exchange.*"

Shah's voice barked over the radio channel. "*I'm on my way to your boat.*"

THIRTY-FOUR

Netherlands, The North Sea

Dante thought fast. He needed to communicate to Shah that they were on the oil rig, but if he announced it over the open channel, Hofstad would hear, too. He thought back to one of their OUTCAST strategizing sessions on communication, where Tanner had asked who knew Morse code. There had been a couple of snickers and words like "dated" and "primitive" thrown around, but in the end Tanner had insisted that all of them maintain proficiency at it. And right now, as Dante clutched the radio transmitter, he was glad he did.

He keyed the transmitter several times in a row without saying anything, alternating the time he depressed the button. Short-long-short, short-short, long-long-short, repeatedly for about ten seconds:

R...I...G...

He figured Shah would be monitoring the channel and that the duration would be long enough for him to interpret it to mean that he and Jasmijn were on the oil rig. Hopefully Hofstad would just think it was interference of some kind, or not be able to decode it if they did suspect a message.

The Hofstad man's voice punched through the channel. “What is that noise? What are you doing?”

“I don't know, but I'm on my way to you. Probably just engine interference, over.”

Shah got it! Why else would he pass it off as interference rather than simply saying , *I didn’t hear anything?*

But for Shah to go to Hofstad's boat alone was nearly suicidal. Even armed with his own weapon and those of the two men he'd taken down, he would still be facing four heavily armed terrorists. Hopefully he stopped by the rig before he visited Hofstad's boat. Dante turned to Jasmijn.

"Step outside and tell me if you can see where Stephen is heading in his boat. I need to monitor the radio, but if he passes near the rig maybe we can catch his attention without the guys on the other boat knowing."

She nodded, dropped her wet bag of sea anemones and stepped outside onto the square, metal landing area while Dante listened in on the marine channel. He heard no further conversation and so assumed that Shah was en route to the other boat.

"The Zodiac is coming toward the rig," Jasmijn called. A couple of seconds went by and then she added, "Around back—he'll pass behind us."

Dante listened to radio silence for a minute longer and then decided it was time to act. He left the radio on and joined Jasmijn on the landing platform outside. Suspended below the tower of infrastructure, it offered a 360 degree view of the sea around them, but one that was obstructed in places by various pipes and pieces of equipment. He followed Jasmijn's pointing finger to see the tiny Zodiac skirting around the rig, leaving a small wake as it traveled near the limit of its speed capabilities, about to make the turn around to the side they were on.

“Where do you think is the best place on this rig to get low enough to the water where Stephen will see us from the boat and we can jump down?”

“There's an access ladder down to the water from this side, too.” Jasmijn pointed between a latticework of metal supports down and to their right.

Dante nodded. “I see it. Let's go.”

The two of them went back through the radio room, where they heard no chatter coming from the systems, and proceeded to wind their way down through the rig. The whine of Shah's boat motor grew steadily louder as they neared the access point.

“This way!” Dante led them down a spiral staircase that opened up onto a deck platform made of a rectangular steel grate. Below that was the access ladder. Shah came into view, cruising around this side of the rig, slowing his speed as he neared.

Dante and Jasmijn leaned out as far as they dared over the edge of the platform while they waved their arms above their heads as Shah approached in the boat. Suddenly the boat's motor cut out and the inflatable fell back in the water.

Shah had seen them.

He idled the small craft up to the boarding ladder. Dante and Jasmijn climbed down to the water and stepped into the boat, carefully stepping around the bound and gagged Hofstad operator, who lie motionless on the deck. His eyes were open, watching.

Shah quickly addressed them. “I'm hoping to trade him for Nay. Weapons?” Dante told them about the pistols they each carried, then continued.

“I doubt it'll be an even matchup, but we have to go get her. What kind of firepower do they have?” He looked to Dante for the details.

“You took two out, so there'll be three left on the big boat, all armed with full-auto rifles and handgun backups.”

Shah shook his head as they bobbed in the motorized raft. “We can't just present ourselves to them like lambs to the slaughter. How about this: Dante, you go back up into the rig with our best long-distance pistol.”

Immediately Dante and Jasmijn raised their eyebrows. They'd only just gotten down from the rig.

“And take the southeast corner, there...” Shah pointed to the end of the rig facing Hofstad's boat before continuing. “That'll put you in range to take at least one, hopefully two operators out, and give us the element of surprise so that I can drop whoever's still standing.”

Dante nodded and showed him his weapon. Shah handed him a long-barreled pistol, trading for the one

Dante had and tucking it into his waistband. “Here, take this—a little better range. Fully loaded. Extra magazine, too.” He handed the spare bullets over to Dante, who pocketed them.

“Take these, too,” Shah added, handing Dante the pair of binoculars that had been in the boat.

Then Shah turned to Jasmijn. “What about you, can you shoot?”

“If I have to, I guess. I never have before.” She showed him her pistol.

Shah looked at Dante and pointed up at the rig. “Okay, let's go. They'll be getting suspicious.”

“What's the signal going to be?” Dante climbed up on to the ladder but waited to hear from Shah before ascending to the rig. He had to know when he was supposed to shoot.

“It'll have to be a hand signal. I don't have a handheld radio.”

“More like an arm signal. It's pretty far away.”

Shah nodded in agreement. “If I hold my arms out to my sides, like an *oh c'mon, be reasonable* gesture—that means take your best shot. Okay?”

“Okay.” Dante climbed the ladder. Shah put the boat back into gear and motored away from the rig.

At the top of the ladder, Dante oriented himself with respect to his target position and took off running. He would need time to get himself comfortably situated in a good sniper nest. A few minutes later he reached the end of the rig and turned right along the edge, crouching low behind a metal railing to avoid being seen by the men on the boat, which he could now see off to his left.

Shah's Zodiac was in his field of view as well, cutting a beeline to the larger vessel. Dante crawled on behind the railing until he reached a large diameter pipe situated like an inverted “U.” On the other side of it was a cluster of smaller pipes that he thought would make a good hiding place.

He dashed past the large pipe, temporarily exposing himself to the view of the boat, and then tucked himself into the maze of pipes. Eyeing the Hofstad boat, Dante was pleased that he was mostly concealed by the pipes. He blended in with the oil rig. No longer worried about being spotted, he turned his attention to the offensive. He rested the barrel of his pistol on one of the pipes and took rough aim at the ship. He laid his spare magazine out in front of him so that it was easily accessible. Then he peered through the binoculars.

As soon as he focused the glasses he could see the Hofstad leader gesticulating to his two other men on board. And there! Sitting on deck, wrists tied in front of her and ankles bounds as well—was Nay. He let out a sigh as he spied on the boat. Her position was far less than optimal. It was a very close-quarters environment and were he to miss, the shot could easily ricochet inside the boat and hit Naomi.

The sound of Shah's Zodiac motor decelerating reached his ears as it neared the boat and Dante turned his attention back to the gun. He played with the balance some more, getting the long barrel to rest on the pipe in front of him just right. He practiced looking through the binoculars held in his left and then quickly changing to the sight of the gun held in his right.

He watched as the Zodiac pulled up to within a few feet of the big boat. He tensed. This was it. Should there be a firefight without time for Shah to give the signal, he would need to be ready to cover them just the same. He peered through the binoculars, which unfortunately were cheap 7x25's, not nearly powerful enough to afford him the chance to read lips. But he could see the Hofstad leader pointing directly at Jasmijn clearly enough, no doubt asking what in the Hell she was doing aboard Shah's boat. *Shah must be explaining how he found her in the water but not me...*

As he continued to watch, the body language of all parties grew increasingly agitated. He saw one of the Hofstad men not doing the negotiating with Shah raise his automatic weapon to a semi-ready position...

And then Shah spread his arms wide in a gesture of exasperation.

THIRTY-FIVE

Netherlands, The North Sea

Dante reacted swiftly to the signal, moving his eyes off the binoculars and onto the gun sight as he had practiced. He saw the Hofstad man in the boat who had partially raised his automatic weapon swing it to a state of full readiness. Dante held his breath, aiming the pistol. He switched back to the binoculars one more time, then quickly back to the pistol.

Now!

He let loose two rounds aimed at the chest of the shooter. Through his naked eye he saw the man twitch violently and fall backwards, discharging his weapon into the air as he landed hard on his back on the deck, not far from where Naomi sat in her trussed position.

Dante heard other shots now—Shah returning fire from the Zodiac as he ducked behind the steering console. Dante consulted the bino's one more time as he took aim on the henchman who was swinging his machine gun toward the Zodiac in response. Back to the gun sight. Held his breath. Put pressure on the trigger, slowly...

He squeezed off two more rounds, watching in grim satisfaction as the second gunman contorted in shock and dropped to the deck.

Only one enemy remained standing.

But the leader was already on the move, backpedaling to reach the cover of the boat's console, instead tripping over Nay. Dante could hear Shah firing at the remaining opponent, but through his binoculars he could see that he missed his mark as a fiberglass door to the cabin shattered. And the Hofstad leader was pushing himself up off the deck...

...and turning his attention to Naomi.

Dante popped the fresh clip into his weapon and took careful aim, well aware that Naomi was in very close proximity to the intended target. He squeezed off four rounds, two of them missing but two snapping the terrorist's head back in a whiplash motion.

Dante heard the whiny acceleration of the Zodiac's outboard as Shah threw the boat into gear. He ate up the remaining distance to the Hofstad boat in seconds and jumped onto the larger vessel while Jasmijn remained in the Zodiac. Dante observed through the binoculars as Shah ran to the terrorist and kicked his auto-rifle away from him. He saw him reach out and place his fingers on the man's neck, feeling for a pulse. Then Shah looked back toward the rig and drew his hand across his neck in a slashing motion.

Dead.

That was five Hofstad men eliminated. It should mean that there were no more terrorists on the boat, but when your life depended on being right you didn't make assumptions. Shah cautiously circled around the boat's deck, carefully checking all areas, even lifting open storage compartments with his pistol at the ready. When that was cleared, he moved to the cabin. He yanked the door open and aimed his gun down inside. Then he descended slowly into the interior space. Dante watched and listened for signs of gunfire.

A couple of minutes later he emerged from the cabin, nodding his head and holding up his hand in the “okay” sign.

The boat was clear, the entire Hofstad squad dead.

Shah pointed in Dante's general direction, off to his left.

Go to the ladder.

Dante made his way back through the rig's catwalks and spiral ladders until he reached the steel platform at the top of the ladder. He heard the Zodiac approaching and when it was within sight he climbed down the ladder until he hung just above the water. Shah pulled up to him and he dropped into the raft, giving Nay and Jasmijn a hug. Then Shah took them back to the Hofstad boat where they boarded, leaving the Zodiac tied up alongside. After a few rounds of congratulatory talk and expressing thanks over being alive, Shah got down to business.

"We should sink this boat and the Zodiac and take the old fishing boat I came out here on back to port. But before we do we need to search it top to bottom—and the bodies—for anything that might lead us to the people pulling the strings."

Jasmijn immediately volunteered to search the cabin, knowing there were no bodies there, and headed below.

"I'll search the bodies," Shah volunteered. "Dante, you search the rest of the boat topside. Nay—why don't you go down below and help Jasmijn." The two OUTCAST operatives nodded and went about their tasks. It was a good call, sending Naomi below. Jasmijn was a scientist, not a spook, and likely wouldn't know what to look for unless it was blatantly obvious.

Shah searched the bodies of the two subordinates first and found nothing on their persons. He was a little surprised since one of the men he'd neutralized in the Zodiac had been carrying a wallet. So there were inconsistencies in the group, Shah mused. They were not a perfectly programmed machine.

He moved on to the body of the fallen, bearded unit leader who lay in a messy smear of blood near where Naomi had been held. The man was older, for this business especially—about fifty years of age. Shah had to admire that. He was about there himself. The jihadist's eyes were open but rolled all the way back, showing only whites, so Shah closed them while softly intoning a quick Muslim prayer . Then he proceeded to rifle through the pockets of his casual outfit—slacks and a long-sleeved shirt with a wool pullover. He found a 9mm pistol with an extra magazine secured on a side holster—his backup weapon. Shah took the entire holster, removed his own jacket, put on the holster and then donned his jacket again. Later he would see if he might be able to trace the weapon, although he doubted that particular route of inquiry would come to anything.

He searched the man's pants pockets and came up with a single item: a business card for a London yacht dealership. Shrugging to himself, Shah pocketed the card, adding it to the ID he'd found on the fighter he'd dispatched.

Dante returned from his inspection of the bow area and reported finding nothing of interest. Naomi and Jasmijn emerged from the cabin, also reporting no significant discoveries.

"Time to send this old scow to Davey Jones' Locker," Shah said in his best pirate imitation. His attempt at humor in the face of the grim situation was not enough to elicit a laugh from the group, so he simply set to work.

"Dante, take the Zodiac to the fishing boat..." He pointed off their starboard rail to where the old rental vessel lie adrift. "...and bring back the fishing boat and the Zodiac. Meanwhile I'll get this thing ready."

Dante nodded and jumped into the inflatable boat, started the outboard and motored away.

Shah then addressed Naomi and Jasmijn. "Go around the boat and gather up anything that might float—for example the life rings—and put them down in the cabin below. Before we sink her we'll close that door so that there won't be so many loose objects floating around to attract attention."

It was best to be as discreet as possible. Leaving a floating ghost ship was a surefire way to trigger an investigation. There would likely be one anyway when people familiar with this vessel notice it hasn't returned to its dock, but that delay was beneficial to OUTCAST's operation.

Shah looked up at the sound of the approaching motor to see Dante returning with the fishing boat that would take them back to land, the Zodiac in tow. He had Dante simply remove the inflatable's motor and drop it into the ocean. Then Dante used a knife to slash the boat's air chambers. But even in that deflated state, the material the raft was made from wouldn't sink, so he and Shah hauled it aboard the big boat and dumped it inside the cabin with the other buoyant items, and closed the door.

"That's it!" Shah had Dante, Naomi, and Jasmijn board the old fishing boat while he walked to the stern of the Hofstad vessel. Jasmijn found an old bucket on the fishing boat, rinsed it out, filled it with seawater and then placed the anemones in it for the trip back to shore. Given the trouble they'd gone through to get them, she wasn't about to let anything happen to them.

While Dante got behind the wheel of the fishing boat, Shah leaned over the transom and pulled the boat's drain plug. Seawater began to pour onto the deck. It would take a while, but the boat would sink. What's more, there would be no messy explosions or tell-tale holes bashed in the hull with some kind of implement to indicate foul play. If the vessel was discovered before—or even after it sank, as a wreck—the obvious assumption was that it was either deliberately scuttled for insurance purposes or else the plug had simply come out. It had been known to happen.

Shah took a last look around the boat to make sure they weren't leaving anything behind. Satisfied all was in order, he leapt into the fishing boat and Dante pointed the bow toward port.

THIRTY-SIX

OUTCAST Facility

The lowly fax machine, that red-headed stepchild of modern information technology; somehow it found a way to remain in use in this age of wireless Internet, scanners and email. For OUTCAST it offered a couple of distinct advantages, which was why one occupied a space in the nether regions of Danielle's workstation, presently spitting out a transmission.

For one thing, it was simply another way to communicate. When you had agents in the field the world over, options were desirable, regardless if they were little used. There were still a few places where there might not be computer access, but if not, a fax machine could often be found. For another, the mode of transmission itself was oftentimes more secure than a standard e-mail message or text. What made it not so secure for some people was that the printout could sit around in the machine until someone picked it up, but at the OUTCAST facility, Danielle would always be the first person to see it.

She snagged the paper from the machine and put it under a desk lamp, squinting in concentration as she discerned its meaning. After briefly examining the message header information as well as the content of the transmission, Danielle took the fax into the adjoining conference room where Tanner sat conversing quietly with Liam. Their mood had been somber since returning from their failed mission to Charleston, and Danielle hoped that this fax might contain a positive development for OUTCAST. Something they could use. She held up the printout as she entered and put it face down on the table in front of Tanner.

“This just came in by fax.”

“Fax?” Liam screwed his face into a puzzled expression. “What's that?” The youngest of the group, he was kidding but liked to poke fun at the technology of the older generations.

Danielle smiled and shook her head. “It's something created before you were born that actually works in a reasonably secure fashion.”

Tanner ignored their friendly bickering and picked up the sheet. “What am I looking at?”

“It's a fax sent from a print shop in a small port town in Netherlands. I verified the headers and cross-referenced the business online. It checks out.”

“So it's from either Shah, Dante or Nay.”

“Correct. As to the content, it contains only the two scanned documents: the Dutch driver's license and the business card. No other messages of any kind.”

Liam leaned in over Tanner's shoulder to get a better look at the man pictured in the driver's license. It showed a thirty-year-old Dutchman with a shaved head.

Tanner looked up at Danielle. “You run this license yet?”

“No, it's hot off the press, I wanted you to see it right away.”

“Go ahead and run it. And while you're at it,” he added as she turned to leave, “see what you can dig up on this yacht dealership, too.”

Danielle left the room and Tanner stared at the fax for a few seconds more before letting it slide onto the table. He looked Liam in the eye. “You know what these documents are, right?”

He gave a solemn nod. “From a guy or guys they killed.”

“Bingo. I wish they would have given us more info but they must have felt the fax wasn't secure enough for any more than this.”

“If they were there to guard Jasmijn in the lab, then something must have went down there for them to have come into contact with tangos.”

Tanner nodded. “And in another town, too. The lab must have been compromised in some way.”

“They had university police *and* our guys, though.” Liam looked puzzled. “Must have been some heavy action to get through that.”

“Seeing as how they've already killed masses of people in two different public crowd settings, I'd say that heavy action is something they're used to.”

#

About thirty minutes later Danielle returned to the conference room with a laptop. She set the computer down on the table across from Tanner and Liam and took a seat in front of it.

“Based on the two items contained in the facsimile, I picked up some intel on the Internet that I think may be worth looking into.”

Tanner urged her to continue.

“Using the name on the driver's license—Berg Minten—I was able to trace some interesting Web activity that indicates Minten is—or was, as the case may be—a Hofstad operator.” She held up a finger to indicate more was forthcoming. “Not only that, but following his name I came across specific details of an operation Hofstad apparently refers to as *The Poseidon Initiative*.”

“As in the Greek God?” Liam wanted to know.

“God of the Sea, that's correct,” Danielle returned.

“What's the objective of this initiative?” Tanner studied the driver license photo again.

Danielle tapped a key on her laptop and focused on the screen for a second before responding. “To...and I quote...'harness the power of the sea's unique biochemicals to exact vengeance on enemies of a pure State.'"She looked up at Tanner and Liam.

"This was posted publicly under the Hofstad name for all to see?" Liam looked incredulous.

Danielle shook her head. "News site message board postings under an alias I tied to Minten's real name. Minten is Hofstad, though, for sure, so on the chance that he was mouthing off about Hofstad's future plans thinking it was safe to do so as long as he didn't specifically mention Hofstad and used a message board moniker, I searched other known Hofstad members for web activity related to *Poseidon.* 'You can spell *poison* from the word *Poseidon'*, one of them noted on a known anarchist website forum."

"An anagram," Tanner clarified.

Liam gave him a stare. "What are you, an English major? You pack a poetry book in your go-bag?"

Tanner gave him a mock punch to the shoulder, which Liam deflected.

Danielle interjected. “I also found several references—all under assumed names tied to known Hofstad members—to ocean-related inquiries, including red tides and the micro-organisms that cause them.”

Tanner perked up, recalling one of his conversations with Jasmijn. “Anything about STX?”

Danielle raised an eyebrow. “Yes. Saxitoxin and its abbreviation, STX, were both mentioned in tactical and logistical discussions. Not actual Hofstad discussions, mind you, but informal strategizing or brainstorming online sessions with at least one Hofstad member participating anonymously.”

Tanner picked up the fax and dropped it back on the table again. “Okay. So this guy's definitely in Hofstad and was researching something called the Poseidon Initiative, which sounds like it may be related to the STX terror attacks. We don't yet know for certain. But what about the business card? Any leads on that?”

Danielle glanced briefly at the fax as she answered. “That yacht dealership—Royal Yachts, Ltd., is a well-established London business. So well-established, in fact, that I don't think we need to worry about this company being a front for anything. It's the real deal. But there is something that raised a flag.”

“What's that?” Tanner eyed the simple business card.

“They sold President Carmichael his current yacht.”

THIRTY-SEVEN

OUTCAST Facility

“The Presidential yacht?” Tanner asked.

Danielle shook her head. “There is no official Presidential yacht right now, that is, a yacht paid for and maintained by the government for the exclusive use of the president. There hasn't been since the *USS Sequoia* in the late 1970s.”

“So we're talking about a private yacht, here?” Liam asked.

Danielle nodded. “That's right, President Carmichael's private yacht, which he named *Lincoln*, after his hero and distant predecessor in office.”

“Does he ever use his yacht, or does it just sit around like a lot of them, or get rented out?”

“Good point, Tanner,” Danielle said. “I was able to confirm that he does not rent it out—I'm sure Dante could tell us how the Secret Service would object strenuously to that. However, he does in fact use it from time to time. More importantly, he'll be using it tomorrow, on a publicized vacation to Boothbay Harbor, Maine. The *Lincoln* will already be there with full crew when he arrives by Air Force One. A cocktail party for unspecified VIPs of the president's choosing is also scheduled."

"I've been to Boothbay," Tanner said. "It's a Summer hotspot, crowded with tourists. Beautiful place."

"And it's Labor Day Weekend," Liam added. "End of Summer blowout."

"So he's going to be there tomorr—" Tanner cut himself off as he realized the implication of what he was about to say.

Liam perked up. "Tomorrow's when Hofstad's forty-eight hour deadline is up."

Tanner rubbed his temples while he looked down at the tabletop in thought. Slowly, he raised his head and looked at Danielle. “Coincidence? This yacht dealership is a major business, known all over the world. Just because a Hofstad operative had one of their cards doesn't necessarily mean they plan to attack the President on his boat tomorrow.”

Danielle frowned in his direction. “Unfortunately, it also doesn't mean that they don't. Combined with my other Internet data mining results, my modeling program puts the odds of a Hofstad attack on the president tomorrow at seventy-seven percent.”

Tanner quietly issued a curse under his breath. Danielle's program-driven estimates were usually spot on.

“Hold on,” Liam interjected. “Tell me exactly how having the card of the dealership means that Hofstad intends to target the *Lincoln* tomorrow, the timing of it aside. It's a big leap.”

Danielle's fingers erupted in a flurry of activity across her laptop keyboard for a few seconds and then she turned to face the two men. “It goes back to the Poseidon theme.

The ocean. To eliminate the POTUS on a yacht would represent the ultimate expression of Hofstad's power via the sea. I'm picking up a steady stream of insurgent chatter that leads me to believe it's something they're considering."

"Even without the president there," Tanner said, "Boothbay Harbor will be full of waterfront tourists. They just hit a beach, so it's not like they don't see any value in the location alone. If they did strike Boothbay, it would be symbolic—*we can strike your shores anywhere from Hawaii to the eastern seaboard.*"

"The president is just the icing on the cake, is that it?" Liam asked.

Tanner replied at length, his expression thoughtful. "Anytime you go for a president, there are no guarantees of success. The odds are long, especially when it comes to the POTUS. Being on a boat may lower expectations of security, but even so, it wouldn't surprise me if they had a backup target should the POTUS hit prove too problematic."

Liam nodded. And that backup target is the Boothbay waterfront?"

"I think so." Tanner addressed Danielle. "Start gathering intel online for Boothbay. Maybe something will turn up."

She nodded and left the room.

"Liam, you ever been there?"

The former SEAL shook his head. "I do like cold water, though," he said with a grin.

"Good. Let's get packed. While the Netherlands team guards Jasmijn so she can hopefully develop that vaccine, you and I are taking a little vacation to Maine."

THIRTY-EIGHT

Royal Netherlands Institute for Sea Research, Den Hoorn, Netherlands

Naomi and Jasmijn walked side by side up to the lab door, Stephen and Dante trailing behind. The scientist carried the bag of sea anemones, the mesh dive bag now hidden within a an ordinary looking shopping bag. They saw no security presence. It seemed the bodies of the murdered security guards had not been discovered.

Thankfully, no surprises awaited them in the lab. It was as they left it. Even so, Stephen and Dante performed a crouching sweep of the space, making certain that no person or booby-trap lurked behind one of the lab benches.

"Clear." Stephen stood from behind a counter by the back wall.

"Clear." Dante popped his head up from another.

Jasmijn immediately set to work preparing the anemones. She ran tests on the water quality of one of the aquaria. Once the conditions were optimal, she carefully released the anemones into the tank, where they drifted down to the bottom. Then she moved to a rack of chemicals and began preparing a mixture.

While Jasmijn worked, the OUTCASTs circled the lab slowly like hyper-aware sharks sniffing out blood in the currents. They occasionally peered from a window, put an ear to the door, or monitored radio frequencies in their ear buds. While the male operators roved the lab, Naomi was planted beside Jasmijn at all times like a personal bodyguard, her pistol always drawn.

An hour went by, Jasmijn lost in her complex procedures, and then Stephen received a communication via his earbud from Danielle. She filled him in on the Poseidon Initiative intel, and how Tanner and Liam were en route to Maine. She cautioned them not to let their guard down in the Netherlands, since it was anyone's guess what Hofstad was up to. They may even be planning to flex their budding international terror muscles by maintaining operations on two fronts. Stephen gave a brief sitrep on the lab and signed off.

The OUTCAST team kept a coffee pot brewing and passed the time by having one of them leave the lab for an external check every hour or so. They avoided exact, to-the-minute scheduled watches lest they create suspicion should the lab be under some type of surveillance. This type of VIP guard duty could be boring, but the specter of Hofstad's looming deadline kept them on edge.

After a while Jasmijn moved from the chemistry equipment to a computer workstation. She placed a well slide into a machine connected to the PC and it began analyzing the compound in a program, displayed as a colorful graph on screen that meant nothing to the OUTCAST operators. Suddenly she thrust a fist in the air in a triumphant gesture.

“Yes!”

The outburst caused Dante to whirl around with his gun at the ready. He immediately lowered it with a roll of the eyes upon seeing Jasmijn staring at the computer monitor. She got up and bounced over to the anemone tank, clearly excited.

"Stage 1 is complete." She grabbed a long-handled dip net. "I'm ready for the combinatorial phase."

The three agents looked at one another and shrugged while she scooped two of the invertebrates from the aquarium, their tentacles waving as they were dragged up through the water. "First I need to extract the active compound from our friends here," she said, talking to herself, or perhaps the sea anemones, as much as to her escorts, who understood none of the lab procedure and knew only that she needed to try to make an antidote to the STX in order to save lives should there be another attack.

Jasmijn took the anemones over to a wet station where she proceeded to snip tentacles from the creatures and place them in a beaker of the solution she'd prepared earlier and verified with the computer program.

“Hey, if you guys want a thrill while you wait, touch your tongue to one of these anemones,” Jasmijn said, smiling. “You know how if you touch your finger to one, they feel sticky? That's the stinging cells—nematocysts—firing. They can't really pierce the skin on your finger, though—it's too thick. But on your tongue the epidermal layer is very thin. It'll give you a nice shock, but isn't really dangerous. If you need a wake-up shot...”

“Pass,” Stephen said without hesitation, glancing out one of the windows.

“Ditto,” Nay said, wrinkling her nose while looking at the anemones.

“I’ve licked some strange things before, but...maybe later.” Dante eyed the sliver of light underneath the lab door, then resumed his patrol.

“Suit yourself.” Jasmijn placed one of the isolated tentacles under a stereomicroscope and adjusted the device's focus for a close look. “But you must agree. It's amazing that this simple animal developed such a sophisticated chemical weapons system through evolution, isn't it?”

Stephen nodded. Hopefully they'd be able to put it to use. He knew that as the hours wore on, they would find out one way or the other.

THIRTY-NINE

Boothbay Harbor, Maine

It was a town defined by seafood like no other—and shellfish in particular. Lobster, blue crabs, shrimp, clams, oysters, mussels, scallops... A thriving harbor fishery brought them to shore each day, and the social scene revolved around it. There were seafood restaurants galore and right now a huge summer seafood festival was in full swing at a grassy park. Tanner and Liam threaded their way among the open air booths that were crowded with long lines of tourists waiting to sample the offerings. Although the seafood looked delectable and smelled great, neither of them had the stomach to sample it, knowing that it was the ultimate source of such a deadly poison that might currently be the focus of Hofstad's sinister initiative. They opted instead for hamburgers and corn on the cob.

The hair on Tanner's neck raised when he saw a young boy start to throw up into a trash can. He and Liam rushed to his side, wondering how Jasmijn was progressing with the STX antidote back in the Netherlands, but after hearing the boy's mother elicit from the child that he'd eaten three plates of lobster, they quietly walked away, leaving the mother to scold her child for overeating.

They wended their way through the park until they reached a fence on a bluff overlooking the town's namesake harbor. There were several wooden piers with harbor tour boats , a multitude of moored fishing trawlers and shrimp boats, and numerous small pleasure craft flitting about the picturesque harbor. In the bay beyond, large sailboats plied the waters with several small islands in the background.

One boat in particular stood out—a yacht. Blue in color and easily one hundred feet long, the sailing vessel lie at anchor near the edge of the harbor, as if overlooking the entire town. Looking carefully, they could see the U.S. flag proudly displayed from one of the masts. A smaller tender vessel hung from a crane on the ship's stern.

President Carmichael's yacht, the *Lincoln*.

Tanner and Liam both knew that in addition to the Secret Service Agents on board the vessel, there would be others in some of the neighboring boats, attempting to blend in; they couldn't tell which by looking. Liam produced a pair of binoculars and scanned the harbor, looking for suspicious vessels. He saw nothing to indicate anything out of the ordinary.

"Time to deadline?" he asked Tanner from behind the glasses.

Tanner glanced casually at his watch and replied, "Six hours." That put the zero hour at 4:00 P.M., when the bay, harbor and town would be in full swing. The sound of gulls wheeling above mingled with the festival crowd as Tanner wondered how a scene like this could go bad. But he knew all too well that it could.

Presently his earpiece crackled with Danielle's voice. "News update: major media outlets running a piece on The

Hague embassy, how it's still open for business. White House says it will remain open, over."

"Copy that. It's a beautiful day and we're having fun. Out."

Tanner frowned as he watched the sailboats take their tourists around the islands. Not that he expected the President to kowtow to the terrorists' demands, but it would have been nice had the embassy shut down for any reason ahead of the deadline. If Hofstad had plans in place to do something about it, no doubt they would be putting them into effect now. His reply to Danielle had been simple coded language. "It's a beautiful day" meant that they were on site, and "we're having fun" signified that they were actively monitoring the situation but had encountered no action yet. The transmission itself was nearly as secure as possible, but you never knew who was listening physically, possibly even with long-range directional microphones.

Tanner searched the sky while Liam continued to scope out the water. Aircraft of all types were a serious threat, too. Small fixed wing planes, helicopters, drones...Hofstad had proven their versatility when it came to methods of attack. Of concern to Tanner right now were the numerous sky-ad planes that pulled banners over the bay, visible all across town. Presently, one reading LABOR DAY SEAFOOD FEST IN THE PARK was being towed through the air. In Hawaii, Hofstad had used a tourist helicopter to camouflage their assault. One of these banner planes could achieve the same purpose—it could be used to dump STX over the President's yacht, the whole Seafood Fest, or both.

They could issue an alert to the White House, giving them the same intel that OUTCAST had. But would tipping their hand really achieve anything? Either the President would dismiss the information and decide not to act on it, or if he did, what could he do? Evacuate Boothbay Harbor and cause a panic? Hofstad would simply move the strike somewhere else. It would cause a delay, but wouldn't solve the problem. They needed to catch Hofstad in the act and stop them.

And there was already a palpable defensive presence here, Tanner noted, switching his attention back to the water. It was not as if threats in general had been ignored. A sizable Coast Guard cutter was stationed about a quarter mile out from the president's yacht, while Boothbay Harbor Police and Harbor Patrol boats crisscrossed the harbor at regular intervals. Should a suspicious aircraft be sighted, fighter jets could be called to the space within minutes. Up here in the park, police patrolled on foot as well as on horseback. Volunteer Community Ambassadors, wearing bright yellow shirts and carrying radios circulated throughout the event, assisting visitors, looking for anything out of the ordinary and notifying police when necessary.

Tanner finished off the last of his food, savoring the rich flavors. He eyed the stately *Lincoln*, floating serenely out on the bay.

What could possibly go wrong?

FORTY

Royal Netherlands Institute for Sea Research, Den Hoorn, Netherlands

Stephen Shah glanced at his watch again, pacing the laboratory like a tiger. Less than six hours to go and Jasmijn was still working away. She'd moved on from the sea anemones under the microscope and now stood in front of a centrifuge, test tubes full of a special solution whirling around inside the machine at hundreds of times per second, separating the various compounds by weight.

They'd had only a single interruption so far, when a university police officer knocked on the door. Jasmijn waited until the three OUTCASTs had put away their weapons and made themselves look like they were doing some kind of lab work before opening the door. The officer had simply asked if everything was all right, giving the lab a cursory glance. Jasmijn said she was fine, thank you for checking, and the man had left, assuring her that they now had extra men on patrol around the lab.

The centrifuge wound down and Jasmijn opened it and removed one of the tubes. She stuck this tube into another machine and then stood up and yelled, “Yes! I think I've got it!”

Next the operators watched as she went to the freezer with the biohazard warnings plastered all over it and removed the vial of STX sample. She loaded the vial into a special mister that would produce an aerosolized plume. They noted her extreme economy of motion around the sample. She passed around respirator masks to everyone in the room and told them to put them on.

Once all of the masks were secure, she ran to a cage with lab rats and extracted one. She held the rat on its back in one latex gloved hand and sprayed it with the mister. Then she put the animal in an empty cage by itself.

“In a few minutes it will start to die.” Jasmijn eyed the clock on her computer. She moved back to the centrifuge and used a hypodermic needle to collect fluid from one of the test tubes. She held the tube up to the fluorescent lights.

“My next gen STX antidote!”

“Does it work?” Naomi wanted to know, as did they all.

“We'll find out in a minute,” Jasmijn replied, nodding at the lab rat, which stumbled once as it walked across its cage. When it reached the end of the cage and started to turn around, it fell over onto its side and didn't get up. It scrabbled its front paws a few times in the air and then lay still, stomach rising and falling with labored breathing.

“Down for the count,” Dante said.

“It's time.” Moving quickly, Jasmijn picked up the syringe containing the new STX antidote and pulled the dying rat from the cage. She held the animal on its back in one hand while she administered the prospective antidote through the syringe in her other hand. The rodent jerked its head once as the needle penetrated its skin and then lay still.

Stephen shook his head. "Looks pretty dead. How long should it—" He was interrupted by Jasmijn's yelp of surprise as the rat wiggled in her hand. She set it down in the cage.

"It's alive!" Dante grinned.

"Wow!" The surprise on Naomi's face was evident.

The rodent ran around in fast circles, its movements hyper-quick. "Slow down, turbo!" Dante said.

And then the lab rat did slow down. It slumped against the wall of its cage and closed its eyes. It lay perfectly still.

"Is he—" Naomi couldn't bear to finish the question.

Jasmijn reached into the cage and gently placed a fingertip against the rat's abdomen.

"He's dead." She grimaced. "Something's not quite right. This solution had more effect than the previous one—at least it temporarily revived the subject—but obviously the effect isn’t lasting. I think I know what it is, though...” She walked back over to the computer station as if in a trance, the three OUTCASTs watching her.

She turned to them as she sat down in the workstation chair. “I'm sorry. Unfortunately it's sort of a trial and error process. I've got a long night ahead. I need to do a whole 'nother round of redevelopment before we can try the test again.”

Nay headed for the coffee pot. “I'll fire up the caffeine machine.”

Dante looked at Stephen. “Hopefully they have some good luck in Maine.”

FORTY-ONE

Boothbay Harbor, Maine

They sat on a park bench, Tanner pretending to read a local newspaper as he overlooked the bay, occasionally directing Liam to scope out particular things in more detail with the binoculars. He flipped a page of the paper and then registered motion out of his peripheral vision. Well outside the bay, a speedboat appeared to his right, visible only as a white streak that Tanner knew was the huge wake from the craft's powerful engines. He continued to watch the boat move from right to left.

He glanced around at the crowd in the Seafood Festival, seeing nothing that raised his internal alarm sense. But when he looked back out at the water, the white streak that represented the speedboat was oriented differently. Instead of lying horizontally, it now appeared as a vertical line, meaning that the vessel had changed direction. It was traveling toward the bay. There was nothing unusual about that, Tanner knew. Lots of fast boats plied the waters outside of the bay at high speeds. Inside the bay, though, traffic was heavier and the speeds were lower. He was sure this one was returning home after a day of boating and would slow down any minute as it approached the bay.

But as he continued to watch the incoming craft, its speed didn't waver. When it reached the mouth of the bay and proceeded to motor toward the harbor at high throttle, Tanner nudged Liam, who had the binoculars trained on the president's yacht.

“Take a look at the speedboat.”

Liam looked up from the glasses and immediately spotted the approaching watercraft. He lined up his spyglasses and focused the optics on the moving target. “Jet boat,” he observed, referencing a type of boat that used an unconventional engine to suck water in and expel it in order to provide high thrust, similar to a waverunner engine, but scaled up. “Only one man aboard. Don't see any weapons.”

“Okay. Stay with him.” Tanner had the bird's eye view of the boat's overall direction relative to the president's boat and the harbor, while Liam monitored activity onboard. They continued to observe in this manner for another minute, until it became clear to Tanner that something was wrong.

“I think we may have a problem, Liam. This boat's not slowing down.”

“Oh crap!”

“What is it?”

“The pilot just put a plastic tank up onto the bow.”

Tanner's heart sank. If it contained a liquid STX solution, it would likely shatter on impact if the boat hit anything. Yet as he watched, the swift boat veered sharply *away* from the *Lincoln.*

"Heading away from the target," Tanner stated for Liam, who was still glued to the binoculars.

"Where to?"

Tanner assessed the view below. After the president's yacht, he didn't see an obvious target for the speeding boat. Was it possible that the pilot of the fast vessel was simply a recreational boater who had lost control of his craft—mechanical problems—the tank containing only extra fuel or perhaps even just water?

But then his gaze tracked inwards, all the way to shore, extrapolating the vessel's current course. If it didn't deviate from the heading it was on now, the boat would run into the seawall in front of a busy waterfront walkway, lined with shops and restaurants.

Damn! Tanner felt helpless as he clutched his fists. They'd been so worried about the president that they hadn't considered the general populace, like a football team concentrating all of their defense on covering the star receiver, and meanwhile the ball is handed off to a no-name running back with a clear path to the end zone. He hadn't known what exactly they were expecting, but he didn't think the attack would be so open, so brazen. If that's in fact what this was.

"Ooooh!" Liam sucked in his breath. "He just ran down a paddle-boarder!"

"Accident?"

"Don't think so. Even if for some reason you couldn't shut down the boat's power, you could still steer it out of the way. What are the chances that he's lost both the ability to shut off the engine *and* the steering cable broke?"

"About the same as us being able to stop that boat from hitting whatever it's going to hit."

FORTY-TWO

Boothbay Harbor, Maine

They witnessed the speedboat convert itself into a fireball. Impacting at what must have been full throttle into a stone wall—about sixty miles-per-hour—the explosion was instant and terrifying to behold. Tanner wondered what was in that tank on the bow. Then, with a sickening realization, he understood why it had been perched atop the boat, unsecured.

When the vessel hit the wall, the tank of liquid would have shot forward with the sudden loss of forward momentum. This motion would send it over the seawall and onto the crowded oceanfront walk. There, it would shatter on impact, releasing a deadly splash of STX. Not as effective as an aerosol mist, but certainly deadly to those in close range.

Tanner pondered this. If it was an STX attack, why the shift in dispersal method? The football stadium attack had utilized a mister...Waikiki beach—same. The methods of disseminating the aerosol were different, but they were definitely mist. Here, the liquid in the tank would only be able to affect anyone who was splashed by it, who breathed in the fine droplets. Still, it was a formidable threat, but the deviation from past protocols troubled Tanner. In his experience working Counter-terrorism, once a group succeeded in creating a death toll, they pursued that method, perhaps refining it, but never abandoning it until they were neutralized.

So why would Hofstad want to go through all the risk and expense of carrying out a terror strike only to take out a handful of victims at best, when they've been striking en masse? Especially when the POTUS was here. Simply to cause mayhem in the presence of the president in his homeland? But surely they would try to get to him even with a high probability of failure, given the significant degree of resources devoted to protecting President Carmichael on his yacht. Those resources would make it doubly likely that this small boat attack would be contained...

Tanner felt a surge of adrenaline as the realization struck. He slapped Liam on the shoulder to get his attention away from the binoculars.

"Liam! We have to get down there!"

The ex-SEAL tore away the glasses from the view of the walkway on fire." What—why?"

"What if this—" He pointed down at the fiery fiasco below—" —is only a distraction for the main event?"

Slowly and with mounting awareness, Liam raised the binoculars to his face and aimed them in the direction of the *Lincoln*.

Tanner continued. "While emergency responders are focused on this..."

Liam nodded. “The *Lincoln* is more vulnerable. But I don't see any unusual activity on board yet. The party looks like it’s in full swing,” he added, letting the binoculars hang around his neck. “What's our best bet for helping once we're down there? We won't have this bird's eye view anymore.”

“Good point. But I think it's safe to say that we want to focus on the yacht. If we can rent a powerboat, we can get out on the bay and be able to respond in short order.”

Liam made one more scan of the yacht and the bay with his binoculars, then stood up.

They made their way through the park, walking against the flow of heavy foot traffic as people rushed to the bluffs to get a look at the explosion they heard.

“I feel like a salmon swimming upstream.” Liam said, shouldering past a mother towing twins who both gnawed on blue cotton candy.

They could hear people speculating that there had been an explosion or maybe a bomb. The president is here! We're under attack! A local news reporter-cameraman team ran toward the bluff.

Tanner and Liam walked purposefully, but did not run, out of the park. They didn't want to alarm anyone, nor did they wish to tip their hand that they had something to accomplish. Once they cleared the seafood festival the going became easier. They moved down the incline to the waterfront area, only to find that a barricade had already been put up, detouring people away from the section that had been set ablaze. It was from here that they got their first good look at the devastation.

They could heard screams of pain—agony. They heard a man wailing, “What's happening to her?” over and over again. A line of police officers kept repeating that they had no information at this time except to stay clear of the area.

They could hear sirens as fire trucks raced in to battle the blaze. The fuel-fed fire raged uncontested.

Tanner wanted to know if this had been a saxitoxin attack but they had no time to wait around and find out. They followed the detour directions, which fortunately led to a different part of the waterfront. Looking out across the harbor, he found he could no longer see Carmichael's yacht, which made him nervous. What's more, the entire waterfront would be locking down tight, soon.

"We need to rent a boat, quick." He pointed to a small shop that advertised fishing trips and boat rentals and ran to it. Just as they walked up to the counter the employee started to pull down the drop-down shutter to close up shop. "Sorry, forced closure by the Harbor Patrol. Emergency. No rentals until further notice." Tanner watched as a Harbor Patrol officer watched them to make sure a rental transaction would not occur, and then the officer moved on toward the next establishment down the line.

“Should we try that one?” Liam suggested, pointing to the rental shop the officer was heading to, maybe a couple of hundred feet away.

“No way we'd have time to do a rental before the officer gets there first. And he just saw us. But look.” He pointed at a shop three down from the one the officer was on the way to. “That one's far enough away that we might be able to run over there and rent before the Harbor Patrol guy gets there to tell them to shut it down.”

Liam eyed the establishment. “Waverunners?”

Tanner shrugged. “They're fast and maneuverable, and we don't have much gear.”

Liam nodded. Each of them carried only a pistol with extra clip, a folding knife, and the binoculars. “Right, then. Let's pretend we're fitness freaks.”

Liam removed his shirt, revealing his toned physique. Tanner did the same. They began to jog, moving fast under the guise of casual exercisers oblivious to the tragic event that had just occurred rather than two guys running pell-mell through the aftermath of a possible attack. When they got to the waverunner place, Tanner strode to the outdoor counter with his wallet open.

“Two waverunners, please, half-day,” he said. It was possible the proprietor had already been notified via phone to close up shop, but he was relieved to see a girl of perhaps eighteen years of age, long blonde hair dyed with green streaks and a lip ring, bopping her head to an iPod with earbuds in, looking at a social network page on her phone. Decent chance she hadn't heard yet.

She gave him a slightly annoyed look, she a year-round resident in a resort town that swelled with tourists each summer, he just another one of them. He noticed that she did give Liam a second glance, though, but still acted like she could care less about anything.

"Fill this out, sign here, credit card or cash deposit required, driver license required from both of you." She slid a clipboard across the wooden counter.

Yes! Tanner gave her the cards while he scribbled as quick as he could to complete the form. Liam monitored the Harbor Patrol officer, who had just completed his stop at the establishment two doors down and was on his way to the next. If he were to see them in the process of renting, there was no doubt that he'd come straight here. Tanner slid the clipboard with the form on it across the counter.

She eyeballed it more carefully than Tanner would have guessed, passing a finger over each box. The finger stopped on a blank one.

"Phone number required," she said, passing the clipboard back to Tanner and turning once again to her smart-phone.

Tanner took a deep breath to steady his nerves and entered the phone number for his pay-as-you-go trac-phone that he kept for this type of purpose. It matched the address on his bogus driver license. “Okay.” He eased the form back her way, not wanting to seem rude, which could lead to a delay they couldn't afford. She swiped the form back without looking at it and stood, grabbing a set of keys with a float on them. “Right down here.”

She exited the booth and trotted down to the floating dock where the waverunners sat. Thankfully she seemed to be in a hurry to get back to her phone. Tanner and Liam were right behind her. She pointed to a pair of red Yamaha waverunners, side by side. She began giving instructions on their use while the two men each straddled one of the machines, but Tanner interrupted her while starting his engine.

“That's okay, we've done it before.”

“We're good, thanks!” Liam echoed, his vehicle expelling a plume of exhaust as it roared to life.

“Yeah? Okay. Have fun!” She smiled at Liam and then bounced off back to the rental stand, where the Harbor Patrol man now approached. He had one hand raised in the air.

“Now, Liam!” Tanner put his craft into reverse in order to maneuver out of the tight dock space. Liam did the same. As they turned, they saw the officer had caught up with the shop girl, talking to her, while she pointed at her two most recent rental customers.

They watched as the officer raised an arm in their direction and started to run down to the dock.

Tanner and Liam got their waverunners turned around and ready to head out. With the patrolman pounding down the dock behind them, they gunned the throttles and sped out into the harbor.

FORTY-THREE

Royal Netherlands Institute for Sea Research, Den Hoorn, Netherlands

Boredom and familiarity bred complacency. It was something with which the members of OUTCAST were all too familiar. After hours of standing watch over the same confined space, of seeing the same things over and over again, repeating the same actions, one could easily let their guard down.

But as Stephen Shah looked out the window again, he never would have guessed that this truth applied to scientists as well.

Jasmijn checked the readout on a mass spectrometer and rubbed the sleep from her eyes. Almost time for the next phase in the experimental antidote development. More coffee would be good, though. She glanced over at the coffee machine where Dante was brewing another batch.

First prep the solution. She was nearly ready to try an intermediate stage on a test subject, another lab rat. This time, though, she would infect the rat by injection rather than aerosol cloud, to see if that made a difference. She glanced at the spectrometer again. A couple of more minutes.

She opened the STX sample vault, reminding herself that only two of the precious vials remained. After the terrorists stole her vat supply, these tiny vials were all she had left with which to experiment in order to create an STX antidote. She pulled one of the clear glass tubes from its secure holder and lay it on the lab bench. She did a syringe pull, emptying the contents of the deadly neurotoxin into the hypodermic. Then she moved to the rat cage and withdrew one of the lab specimens. It wiggled in her hand and she clamped down on it. She walked it over to the lab bench where the STX hypo waited.

Picking up the syringe, she clutched the rat tightly in her gloved right hand. It was a procedure she'd done literally hundreds of times before. The muscles in her hands knew what to do. She flipped the rat onto its belly and in slid the thumb of her other hand up the syringe. The rat kicked its hind legs once and she squeezed it gently, cooing at it to calm down, this will all be over in a second. When it stopped, she brought the needle close to the animal's skin.

The room was quiet, and she concentrated on the task before her while listening to the clock tick on the wall. It reminded her of the depressing deadline she faced. Only a few hours until more innocent people died, unless she could make this work...She depressed the plunger on the syringe.

"Coffee's ready!"

Whether from shock or coincidence, the rat squirmed at the sound of Dante's voice, struggling mightily in Jasmijn's hand. It flopped over to one side as Jasmijn glanced over for a split second at Dante. When she looked back down she was horrified to see the needle plowing through the thin latex of the glove into the palm of her hand.

She gave a little yelp of surprise on feeling the prick of the needle penetrating her skin and jumped, shaking her hand as if she could undo the needle stab. The rat went flying onto a lab bench and the coffee pot crashed to the floor as Dante drew his weapon, thinking that some kind of enemy tactic was playing out. Naomi and Stephen also raised their guns, heads on a swivel as they looked around for threats.

All three OUTCAST operators converged on Jasmijn, slowly circling her while she stared at her open palm. The syringe lay on the floor. Jasmijn's mouth was slightly open, her eyes wide as she gaped at a tiny speck of blood that bloomed in the center of her left hand. Meanwhile, the rat scrabbled away on the lab bench.

"Do we need to get the rat? Is it contaminated?" Naomi asked.

“N-no.” Jasmijn stuttered, now holding her hand upside down and squeezing it. “I'm contaminated. I—” She couldn't finish her sentence.

“You stuck yourself?” Stephen eyeballed the syringe on the floor. No fluid seemed to be leaking from it.

“Yes!”

“Are you sure?”

“Yes!”

“What can we do?” This from Dante.

No one said anything. At length, Stephen asked, “What's the status of the antidote?”

She shook her head. “Not ready! This injection for the rat was supposed to be an intermediate step to clarify something by using injection rather than aerosol as the delivery method.”

The trio of operators stared at her, stymied. There was not a single person on the planet who could help her now, except possibly herself. Worse, from past STX exposure cases they knew that without a successful antidote she only had about ten minutes to live.

Just then Stephen's earbud crackled with Danielle's voice. “Situation developing in Boothbay Harbor, Maine. Tanner and Liam on scene. Small-scale STX attack confirmed. President Carmichael's yacht as yet unharmed. Update only, no action required. Requesting Euro sitrep, over.”

Shah turned away from Jasmijn and spoke softly into his transmitter. He didn't want his reply distracting her at this crucial moment—which may be one of her last.” Copy that, home base. Internal situation developing here, do not require assistance as of yet. Will report back, over.” It felt strange for him to say they didn’t need any help when a key member of their team was dying, but the sad truth was that no assistance could be provided for Jasmijn.

Dante implored the scientist with his eyes." Dr. Rotmensen. You've got to try it anyway. There's no other way."

"You're right." She bent down to pick up the syringe but Naomi stopped her. "Doctor. Please. We can take care of that for you. Focus on administering yourself the antidote. Anything at all you can tell us to do—anything—just tell us and we'll do it."

"Okay." Jasmijn moved to the spectrometer and eyed the readout. She took a deep but shaky breath. "I can feel it," she said. "The STX taking effect."

"Is your dose of antidote as ready as it can be?" Stephen asked.

The scientist shook her head, a gesture of helplessness. "No. But it's already becoming harder to breathe. Legs feel wobbly..." She sat on a lab stool in front of her workstation. "I need to make it now and take it, while my symptoms are still manageable. Looks like injecting it rather than breathing it in didn’t slow the onset.”

“What can we do to help?” Naomi inquired.

She instructed the OUTCAST team on what equipment to gather in order to prepare the antidote shot. They moved efficiently and in three more minutes the dose was ready.

Dante handed Jasmijn the hypodermic and she took it, but her hand was shaking so badly that she couldn't hold it steady.

“Let me give you the shot,” Naomi offered, taking the syringe.

Jasmijn bared her shoulder to her.

Naomi plunged the needle into her skin.

FORTY-FOUR

Boothbay Harbor, Maine

"Circle the yacht—give it a wide berth!" Tanner called over to Liam. They rode their waverunners only a few feet apart as they raced out into the harbor. They could already see the president's ship just beyond the harbor in the bay. The cocktail party was in full swing on the main deck.

"Not too close, don't want them to think we're on offense!"

Tanner nodded his understanding and they jumped the wake of a passing motorboat. He was glad to see they weren't they only jet-skis out on the water. They continued to ride out toward the harbor mouth. The sun was out, but the water that sprayed them wasn't warm, and a light wind added to that chill factor. Still, the adrenaline pumping through Tanner's system kept him from noticing. They looked around in all directions as they jetted toward the president's yacht.

For all the pandemonium on land, out here there still seemed to be a lot of people having fun. They passed a pontoon boat filled with elderly people drinking wine and listening to Frank Sinatra doing it his way. Not far away a young woman wakeboarded behind a small boat, the occupants videotaping her and cheering her on. Beyond it all President Carmichael's vessel still floated serenely at anchor, and still Tanner and Liam detected no threats.

As they pushed further out into the harbor, Tanner began to wonder if maybe they were making a mistake by coming out here. There was an actual attack, after all, right behind them on the waterfront. They were in fact running away from it. But years as a counter-terror agent had imbued him with a sort of sixth sense that told him when things weren't quite right, and right now that sense bristled. The first attack was a distraction. It had to be. The logistics involved in transporting even a small amount of STX across state lines, the agents, the boat...it all seemed like way too much to do and far too much risk to assume not to try and hit Carmichael's boat. He was the very man, after all, who had refused to grant their demands. The U.S. embassy in The Hague was still operational. And he floated right over there...Even an unsuccessful attempt of some kind on the yacht would generate international headlines for Hofstad, something that the low-key terror organization apparently desired, seeking to up their visibility.

They heard the blast of a large boat horn—low in pitch—carry across the water and tensed, white-knuckling the waverunner handlebars. Looking to their left they saw a ferry carrying passengers toward the dock. Tanner slowed to get a good look; it was only the captain being cautious, warning the small craft in its path that it was coming through.

Tanner resumed cruising speed and the pair of OUTCASTs plowed across the harbor. Before long the *Lincoln* loomed, and Tanner knew that at least one of the dozen or so vessels anchored within one hundred yards of it had to be Secret Service, watching for any vessel to breach an invisible perimeter. Get too close to the *Lincoln*, and action would be taken. He motioned to Liam that they should take an outer perimeter approach. They knew better than to take a direct route.

They fell into a long oval pattern that took them around the yacht. During the first trip around Tanner scouted the presidential asset for signs of trouble and saw none—no evidence of terrorism, and no indication that he and Liam had aroused sufficient suspicion to warrant action against them. That didn't mean that they hadn't been noticed, of course. There could well be a pair of marine binoculars focused on them now, not to mention video surveillance, and possibly even firearms. Tanner put on his best tourist-having-the-time-of-his-life grin as he banked into a sharp turn out in front of the yacht's bow. The truth was that he disliked waverunners and jet-skis—the motorcycles of the sea, as he thought of them. They were loud and obnoxious, just large enough to sit on but not really relax. He'd much rather be on a boat, even a small one. But the skis were very fast and could fit into tight quarters if necessary.

After yet another circuit around the target, Tanner was about to suggest they break off—the same repetitive pattern for too long would also trigger increased scrutiny—when he caught a flash of something far out to sea. A glint of sunlight off glass, perhaps. He wasn't sure, but once the flash attracted his eye, he could pick out the outline of a slow-moving vessel of some kind. He couldn't yet discern its direction. It could be heading out to sea, or straight past the harbor. He couldn't be sure, but since it was possible it could be headed their way, he decided to keep an eye on it. It did come from a somewhat unusual angle of approach, he noted—threading between the outlines of two distant islands, which kept it somewhat hidden from direct line-of-sight to the harbor. He gripped his handlebars as he rounded the yacht's stern.

Liam waved to get his attention, wisely reminding him that they needed to break out of the pattern they'd been holding. Tanner looked out toward the bay and Liam aimed his craft in that direction. Time to leave the harbor for open water. They could check out the big, incoming vessel.

The mouth of the harbor was choppy where the bay water slacked out with the tide, and they had a bumpy ride through the chop out into the bay. They dodged a pair of racing sailboats before pointing their waverunners toward the slow craft Tanner had noticed.

Liam ramped off a sloppy swell made unpredictable by a passing boat wake and slammed head-on through another wave, his entire ski and body submerging for a few seconds as he passed through the swell. He shook his head like a dog shedding water after getting out of a pool and kept going, looking over at Tanner and giving him a thumbs up sign. A small crowd of people on a passing boat whooped and hollered, loving the show. *Now that's good tradecraft*, Tanner thought, maintaining course with the mystery ship.

As they neared their vessel of interest Tanner could see that it was some kind of barge. Not rusty and decrepit looking, but simply a Spartan workhorse, plowing through the waves as if it had all day to get wherever it was going but would definitely get there. It wasn't easy to tell for sure, bouncing around as he was on the ski, but he could see no persons aboard from this distance. He signaled to Liam to loop around the back of the ship, so that they could follow it from behind. Liam nodded and they raced out to sea.

Overhead, the sky buzzed with activity as Coast Guard choppers patrolled the skies, vying for airspace with media helicopters and police aircraft. Tanner knew that an SR-71 Blackbird fighter jet squadron was lurking in the clouds, ready to strike on a moment's notice should an aerial threat to Carmichael's yacht materialize. He and Liam could make a difference out here on the water, though, should danger rear its ugly head. At least he hoped so, as he led Liam into an arcing turn far behind the barge's broad stern.

The number of boats thinned out here, but there were still large sailboats visible plying the island waters in the distance. Tanner scanned the waters to make sure he wasn't ignoring some other suspicious vessel or even aircraft, but saw none. He wished the whine of the waverunner engines wasn't so deafening, but there was nothing he could do about that other than to stop, which could also arouse suspicion.

He and Liam began following the barge in toward the harbor. Although the workboat kept a straight-as-an-arrow path, they were sure to keep up a series of carving, swerving turns as they followed the boat, so that to anyone watching they would look like a couple of guys having fun on their toys.

Before long they entered the harbor, by now having gotten used to the skis, Liam in particular really putting on a show, ramping off boat wakes in spectacular aerial displays, while Tanner tried some trick-riding of his own, standing with one hand on the handlebars while circling, having a good time for the benefit of all who might be watching.

Still, he couldn't help but notice that the plodding barge inexorably continued its course toward the *Lincoln*, while the brunt of law enforcement was centered on the waterfront walkway, containing the fire, treating victims and bracing for possible further attacks. He waved an arm at Liam, indicating that they should close the distance to the barge. The two riders veered away from one another in a V pattern, into the harbor, closer to the barge. And the president's yacht.

As Tanner passed by the starboard side of the barge's stern, with the yacht in front of him and to his right, maybe an eighth of a mile, a blur of movement caught his left eye.

He eased back on the waverunner's throttle just a bit in order to get a better look.

There!

What was a black streak had temporarily steadied before setting into motion again off the barge's rail.

A tiny helicopter...but of course to Tanner, coming from a barge in close proximity to the President of the United States of America, this was no remote controlled kid's toy.

It was a drone. A quadracopter—a simple helicopter consisting of a basic circular frame containing four rotors, the entire craft no more than a foot in diameter. He knew they could either be pre-programmed to follow a particular route, or remote controlled by a human operator. He also knew that they could carry specialized payloads, such as cameras, bombs...*STX misters*?!

A micro-drone.

FORTY-FIVE

Royal Netherlands Institute for Sea Research, Den Hoorn, Netherlands

"It's been five minutes now and I'm still getting worse." Jasmijn sat on a stool in front of the lab bench, watching the clock on the wall tick away her final remaining minutes. Her legs suddenly felt rubbery. She would have fallen from the stool if not for Dante and Stephen who moved quickly to hold her up.

"It just needs a little more time to take effect," Naomi offered. She of course had no idea if this was true, but didn't want Jasmijn to give up hope.

"No." The scientist held her head in her hands. "Oh God, no. I remember now. It's not going to work."

The battle-hardened trio of operatives were taken aback to see Jasmijn so distraught.

"What is it?" Naomi put a hand on her shoulder.

"No," she said, lifting her head and wiping away a string of tears. "It *can't* work the way I did this last iteration. I realize now what I did wrong but I don't have time to explain it to you."

Stephen got down on one knee so that he could level his gaze right into her eyes." Then don't explain. Just do it. Make the next iteration."

Jasmijn took a very deep breath and looked at the ceiling for a second. "I can prepare it. I can set it up and leave instructions to you as to how to complete it..."

She started to cry. "...but there won't be enough time for me to use it. There are multiple stages—mix these two samples together, autoclave for twenty minutes, chill in the fridge for thirty minutes and so on. Over an hour prep time altogether. By then, I'll be..." She broke down again.

"Stay with us, Jasmijn," Nay said. "There's no time to feel sorry for yourself."

“Or to kick yourself for mistakes you might have made,” Dante added.

The scientist took another deep breath—or was it just a normal breath that was more labored than usual? “You're right. Let me get to work. I'll write out the instructions so that you will be able to cookbook it to completion. Then you just need to test it on a rat. Be extremely careful handling the STX—I'm spending my last remaining minutes trying to save people, not get more of them killed.”

“Don't worry, Jasmijn, we'll be careful. Please, document the procedure.”

“Help me over to the sample 'fridge.”

Dante and Stephen carried her over. “She shook her head and mumbled to herself as she worked, no doubt chastising herself for sticking herself with the STX needle, or for not getting the antidote right last time, which would have saved her. Or both. But she worked, pausing after a major step to think, to make certain she was getting it right this time.

Dante also noticed that her movements were becoming more labored, more difficult. “If you need us to do anything for you, don't hesitate.” She nodded in response, lost in thoughts that he couldn't even imagine. Meanwhile, Stephen was on the other side of the room softly reporting to Danielle over the comm system, and receiving an update from her on the Boothbay status. Naomi stood next to Jasmijn, physically supporting her on the stool so that she wouldn't fall off.

“I can't believe I didn't think of this before,” Jasmijn said, staring into a fluid-filled test-tube. Then she placed the tube into a rack and looked up at her three guardians. “I've gone as far as I can go. I feel extremely weak.”

Dante came and gently held the arm that Naomi didn't have. “I need you to put this tube in the autoclave for twenty minutes. After that...” She picked up a pen and began to write in a lab notebook, but frowned when she looked down at what she had written.

“Jesus. I'm sorry, this chicken-scratch won't be legible. My hand—it's shaking...” Her voice cracked with the realization that her body was rapidly breaking down.

“I'll write for you.” Stephen ran to the lab bench and picked up the notepad and pen.

Jasmijn proceeded to dictate the remaining procedures to him while Naomi steadied her on the stool. Dante would move to the different apparatus and specialized machines she talked about, clarifying the specifics of their use, including the computer programs. When she had finished, Jasmijn had Stephen read the notes back to her while she listened, now being propped up almost exclusively by Naomi.

“Good. You got it.” Her voice had lost much of its tone and sounded like a wheezy rasp. “I need to lay down,” she told Naomi, who eased her on to the floor.

"Jasmijn, do you want me to take you to the hospital? You'd be more comfortable..."

"No. There's nothing they can do for me. By the time I even explained what was wrong, I'd be...gone." She closed her eyes.

"Jasmijn!" Naomi pleaded with her to open her eyes. A few seconds later, she did.

Stephen gained Naomi's attention by waving a cell-phone in her direction and looking down at Jasmijn, his meaning clear. Nay gently shook the dying scientist.

"Jasmijn...listen to me. We'll carry out the lab procedure to create the antidote. But is there anyone you want us to call for you? Anyone you want to talk to..." She couldn't bring herself to say it—*before you die.*

Jasmijn's movements were very slow now, her breathing shallow. Even her eyes opened slowly as she looked at Naomi. The OUTCAST agent leaned in close to hear the words Jasmijn struggled to project.

"I'm at peace with everyone. Tell Tanner I'll miss him."

Naomi leaned in close. "I will. He'll miss you, too." Naomi had heard the rumors that Tanner and Jasmijn were romantically linked in the past.

"Jasmijn..." Naomi wasn't sure what she wanted to say to her. She supposed she just wanted to reach out to her to let her know that someone else was there. "Goodbye," was all that came out.

And then Dr. Rotmensen went into her death throes. As she herself had watched her lab assistant do, she began to convulse, her throat constricting, her lungs no longer powerful enough to perform their own expanding and contracting. The death wasn't a pretty one, and although all three of the OUTCASTs had witnessed many people die in various situations, later they would all agree that this was one of the very worst.

Jasmijn's lips turned blue with lack of oxygen. Her arms and legs twitched but couldn't really move. The neurotoxin had fully taken hold over her nervous system. She had lost all motor control including the ability to regulate her breathing. Dante and Stephen tried to hold her still so that she wouldn't bash her head into the tile floor. Naomi did her best to soothe the scientist. She might still be able to hear and process what was going on.

"Relax, Jasmijn. It's okay. Let go. Let go. You've done great work. The world will be a better place for it. They will know how important your work was. It's okay..."

She continued cooing to her for another minute and then the researcher's body lay still, a yellow foam issuing from her mouth.

Dante felt her wrist for a pulse. He looked up at his two colleagues and shook his head.

Dr. Jasmijn Rotmensen was dead.

FORTY-SIX

Boothbay Harbor, Maine

The micro-drone made a bee-line for the president's mega-yacht. Tanner watched it move off and realized that they would not be able to stop it. He could reach it by waverunner before it got to the yacht, but it was flying about twenty feet over the water. He wasn't sure where on the *Lincoln* the president was, but hopefully indoors. He was about to suggest they try and warn Carmichael somehow, when Liam pointed urgently into the sky in front of them.

Another micro-helicopter had just been launched from the barge.

Followed by another.

And another.

Tanner's heart sank as he watched the squadron of what he knew to be MUAVs, or Micro Unmanned Aerial Vehicles, flock toward the vessel that carried the POTUS.

Now, with four MUAVs airborne, there was definitely no way he and Liam would be able to defend the yacht. He studied the barge while he idled his ski. The drones were being controlled from it. They were much closer to it than to the yacht. He signaled to Liam.

The barge.

The ex-SEAL caught on to his meaning immediately and directed his waverunner toward the low, flat vessel pursuing the yacht. Tanner took the starboard side of the barge while Liam ran past the port. Unlike many barges, this one actually had a structure on it, rather than consisting of only a flat, open deck. Most of the deck space was open, but there was a single story structure occupying the forward-most quarter of the vessel. It must be from inside that that the terrorists were controlling the MUAVs.

Tanner eyeballed the side of the barge as he neared. They would have to find a way to board it somehow. At least all of the crew were inside, which would make boarding much easier without anyone on deck to repel them. This vessel was all offense. All they had planned to do was to get near enough the president's yacht to launch the micro-drones, make their strike and then...Tanner doubted they cared what happened after that. The people on board were no doubt simply doing the dirty work for those in command. Whether they believed they would be rewarded with endless virgins in Heaven for carrying out their holy jihad, or would actually be able to escape after striking the yacht of the POTUS, it made no difference. They would stop at nothing to achieve their objective.

Tanner saw no trailing lines or access ladders from which to board the barge, but there was a row of tires along the top rail, used as fenders. He brought his ski up alongside, throttling down to match the slow pace of the barge. Then, eyeing two tires a few feet ahead of him, he gunned the ski's throttle and leapt a couple of seconds later, arms outstretched, reaching for the open tires.

His right hand grabbed one, and, not wanting to let the momentum of his jump go to waste, he swung his legs up into the well of another tire. He scrambled up to the deck, threw a leg over the wet planks, and rolled onto the barge.

Tanner ran to the opposite side and held out a hand to Liam, who had guided his waverunner to the side of the vessel. Liam jumped and Tanner pulled him aboard. The two operatives crouched low on deck, scanning their new surroundings. The forward structure had no rear-facing windows. Tanner held two fingers together on his right hand and pointed to the structure. He and Liam ran to the rear wall, glad for the cover it gave them from nearby boats. They had no way of knowing if Hofstad had other craft in place in the harbor.

Tanner controlled the river of adrenaline surging through his body. Behind the wall he leaned on were terrorists controlling drones about to spray the POTUS with a deadly neuro-agent. At least he and Liam both carried small arms. He pulled his Kahr PM9 from the hip holster concealed beneath his *I HEART SEAFOOD* T-shirt and checked the action. Liam readied his Smith & Wesson 686 .357 revolver. Tanner made a box-like motion with one finger from each hand, indicating that they should split up and move around the structure, meeting in front by the only door they'd seen.

The two OUTCAST operatives converged on the front end of the structure, one on either side of a door with two high windows set into it. They each gave the other a hand signal to indicate things were clear on their respective sides of the enclosure. Looking across the expanse of water toward President Carmichael's yacht, Tanner saw the squadron of micro-drones perhaps halfway to it. They had to act before the pleasure boat was blanketed in deadly mist.

Liam put the hand not holding his gun on the rusty piece of metal bolted to the door. Tanner nodded, his own weapon at the ready.

Liam pulled the door open.

FORTY-SEVEN

Royal Netherlands Institute for Sea Research, Den Hoorn, Netherlands

The mood in Jasmijn's laboratory was beyond grim, but the three OUTCAST operators had a mission to carry out. An alarm sounded, indicating that the STX samples had spent enough time in the chiller machine and could now be removed.

"That's it," Stephen said, carefully opening the chiller and removing the rack of test tubes. It was unnerving, working with the body of Dr. Rotmensen lying nearby on the lab floor, even draped in white lab coats. But there was nothing that could be done for her now, and OUTCAST knew that if they were to report the death, the lab would be overrun by crime scene investigators and they wouldn't be able to complete the antidote preparation for which Jasmijn had given her life.

“What's the next step?” Dante asked. Naomi picked up the written procedure Jasmijn had dictated to Stephen just before she died.

“Testing! Prep the STX syringe—be careful! I'll get a rat.” Naomi went to the rat cage and withdrew one of the specimens while Dante—his movements slow and deliberate—filled a syringe with the last of the STX liquid samples.

“I'll hold it.” Stephen took the rat from Naomi and cupped it in his meaty hand. “Let’s wait a few seconds to make sure it's not moving.” The very last thing he wanted was a repeat of Jasmijn's accident. Dante walked up to him with the loaded hypodermic. After the rat was still for several more seconds, Stephen nodded. *Ready.*

Dante brought the tip of the needle to the rat's abdomen as he had seen Jasmijn do. He injected the animal. It squirmed but Stephen's grip remained firm while Dante withdrew the hypodermic without incident. Naomi called out the time, as the procedure indicated, while Dante disposed of the needle in the labeled biohazard container. Naomi took the injected rat and placed it in the solitary cage, where it was expected to die within the next few minutes unless the antidote worked.

Naomi read from the procedure. "Prep the antidote syringe."

Dante selected one of the freshly prepared tubes of antidote solution and carefully drew it into a hypodermic. He walked over to the rat cage and stood watching the animal scuttling around, pausing occasionally to sniff the floor. He was joined shortly by Naomi and Stephen. A couple of minutes later this rat, like the one before it, began to stumble and shake. They waited another minute to make sure that the neurotoxin had taken a firm hold. It was not easy to watch the rat struggling in the grips of the STX, knowing that Jasmijn had just endured the same fate. Nay wiped a tear from her cheek as she watched the rodent battle to remain upright.

"Inject him," she said, eyes on the written procedure. They repeated the injection process with Stephen holding the specimen and Dante administering the shot. This time the rat did not squirm. When the antidote had been administered, Naomi noted the time and Stephen put the rat back in the quarantine cage. A couple of minutes passed where the rat did not appear to improve; it barely moved at all, simply lying on its side on the floor.

"C'mon, little guy!" Naomi urged. If this antidote was not effective, then it meant that Jasmijn was wrong about what had kept the antidote from working, her last effort in life unsuccessful.

"She was under an unthinkable amount of stress," Stephen said, watching the rat quivering on the floor of its cage. No one had a response. They just stared at the specimen.

“Five minutes,” Naomi intoned, looking up at the lab clock.

And then the rat righted itself. Its muscles stopped spasming. The three operators held their collective breath as the specimen began to walk once more around its cage, its movements no longer tentative. Its gait was steady, deliberate. Normal.

“It's working!” Dante exclaimed, a smile appearing on his face for this first time since they'd entered the lab. They continued to monitor the rat for fifteen more minutes. After that time it was still acting normally.

Stephen addressed Naomi and Dante.” Pack the remaining samples for travel. I'll put a call in to Danielle and update her on the status. We’re taking this antidote to Maine.”

FORTY-EIGHT

Boothbay Harbor, Maine

The barge wheelhouse was unnervingly small. There were no labyrinthine passageways or stairwells leading up and down—nothing like that. Just a single wall partitioning the space into two distinct areas. The forward area, in which Tanner and Liam now found themselves, housed the barge's steering controls and navigation equipment. A simple wooden door, slightly ajar, divided the two spaces.

They weren't yet sure what the second area contained, because to get to it they would first have to defeat the man standing at the helm of the barge, eyes open in surprise at the sudden entrance of the two spooks.

Liam knew he had to take the opponent down before he could scream and alert his associates in the other room. The former SEAL was already crouched low, his eyes at knee level with the barge driver. Not wanting to use his gun, which was not sound suppressed to avoid raising suspicions during travel, he reached up and grabbed the hand of the terrorist, yanking him down, hard. At the same time he lashed out and jammed a foot down on the Hofstad man's shoe, preventing him from backing away while he was pulled to the deck.

The foe managed to get off a garbled yelp before Liam slammed his forehead into the deck, knocking him out instantly. The impact was so brutal he wondered if the sound of his head hitting the deck might be heard in the next room, and he and Tanner braced themselves for a shootout.

But no one came, and they could hear normal conversational voices carrying on from beyond the partition. Tanner searched the unconscious man and relieved him of his weapons—a Sig Sauer pistol and a folding knife. Liam took point and crouched at the inner door. Tanner positioned himself behind and to the right, weapon drawn.

He gave Liam the signal.

Go!

Liam opted for stealth mode, easing the door open slowly with his left hand rather than barging in gun blazing. What he saw stopped him in his tracks.

The interior of the space was decked out more like some futuristic command center than a rusty old barge. A bank of LCD monitors lined either side of the room, which was carpeted and overlain with plastic to allow the workstation chairs to roll about with ease. Red LED lighting illuminated the space. No less than four men occupied this area. Fortunately, all of them were intensely occupied operating the micro-drones—one to each of four tightly spaced control stations.

Although there were no windows in this dimly lit area, Tanner and Liam could see on the monitors the drone controllers stared at that the MUAVs were rapidly closing the gap to the *Lincoln*. The drone operators conversed in short, clipped bursts of both Dutch and an Arabic dialect. But their intent was clear enough. When these drones were over Carmichael's vessel, they would release their deadly payloads of aerosolized STX, killing all who breathed it in, including the POTUS.

Tanner was not about to let that happen.

He tapped his own chest and then held two fingers out toward the two operators on the right. Then he pointed at Liam and held two fingers at the two on the left. Liam nodded his understanding. They would each be responsible for eliminating the two men on their respective sides of the room.

They sprung at the same time. Tanner put a hand on each of the terrorists' heads and slammed their foreheads together, mashing both of their noses into a single, pulpy mass. They both slumped to the deck without a fight. One thing Tanner hadn't anticipated, however was that the two drones, which had been in forward motion, didn't drop into the sea but instead continued their forward course toward the yacht. He didn't know if the STX sprayers were programmed to automatically trigger when they reached the ship or if they had to be manually activated. Regardless, he would do his best to keep them away from the *Lincoln.*

He heard the sound-suppressed *pffft* of one of the terrorists' guns discharging and whirled around in time to see Liam grappling with one of them, the other already unconscious on the ground with blood running out of one ear. Aware that the four MUAVs were still airborne, Tanner moved to expediently dispatch their remaining active foe. Liam had the man from behind, a hand on each arm, including the one with the gun. He turned so that the abdomen of the terrorist faced Tanner, and the ex-Counter-terror operative slugged the opponent in the gut. The Hofstad gun went flying.

"Get it, Alpha 2, I got him!" OUTCAST usually made it a point to refer to themselves in the presence of enemies using code names, in order to protect their identities. On this op, Tanner was Alpha 1 and Liam Alpha 2.

Liam scrambled for the loose firearm while Tanner put the terror operative into a control hold. Liam picked up the gun and tucked it into his waistband, keeping his own weapon aimed at their adversary.

Tanner flipped the gun in his hand so that he held it by the barrel, about to deliver a knock-out pistol whip to the man's temple, when he checked himself. This was the last member of the terror organization aboard. Tanner looked around the cabin. He didn't see the big vat of STX that Jasmijn had described. The amount that even all four mini-drones could carry was miniscule compared to that. Not that it wasn't deadly, but it meant that most of the STX that was stolen was still unaccounted for. So where was it? He lowered his arm. He might need this man alive.

“Alpha 2, tie this guy up.” Liam removed his belt, which was actually a braided length of 550 paracord (“Don't leave home without it," was his motto). He unraveled a suitable length and used the folding knife Tanner had confiscated from his enemy to cut it. Then he quickly but effectively bound the prisoner's hands behind him and his legs at the ankles.

Tanner pointed to the screens that showed a drone's eye view of the president's mega-yacht across the water. "Handle these two drones! I'll take the two on the other side."

"I don't know how to—"

"Neither do I. Figure it out. Unless Mr. Jihad down there wants to help us out?" He eyed the trussed jihadist, who had no reaction. He could try to threaten him with torture into controlling the drones, but that could easily backfire. Knowing he was about to die, the terrorist could decide to crash them into the ship, or even the barge.

Tanner jumped up and went to the drone station on his side of the space, and Liam to his. Tanner eyeballed the two joysticks, one beneath each monitor. One man had been at each station, and now he would have to control two of the MUAVs simultaneously, as would Liam from the opposite side. Tanner looked up at the monitors. In each he could see a landing skid of the drone in the foreground, and then some water with the *Lincoln* looming larger by the second. It was coming up alarmingly fast. He estimated he had about ten seconds before the micro-drones reached the port side rail.

"A few seconds! Drop 'em in the water!" Tanner pulled the joystick down on the right-side drone, to see if it would work before doing the same thing with both. It did, and that MUAV nose-dived into the harbor with a tiny splash. But now the other was nearly to the target. He swiped at the joystick without taking his eyes off the monitor and felt his hand slip off into mid-air.

Missed!

He tried again, this time slamming the micro-copter into the hull of the *Lincoln*, down low by the waterline. He was terrified to see a plume of mist eject from the craft as it slid into the water. At least it was far from the boat's deck and below the concave hull shape, but it was a close call that chilled him to his core. He called out to Liam.

"How're you doing?"

"One down." Liam moved to the second of his twin drone stations. Tanner turned in time to see the video feed of the remaining drone. This one was running at higher altitude than its dispatched squadron-mates, perhaps twenty feet above the level of the yacht's main deck. Tanner saw that this presented a huge problem, since the cocktail party was presently underway there. He saw men dressed in tuxedos dancing with women in evening gowns as servers circulated with trays of champagne and hors d'oeuvres.

"Liam!" He forgot all about using the code name in the urgency of the moment. "Crash it. Crash it!"

On screen, the view of the deck grew more expansive. He watched as Liam jammed his thumb down on the joystick.

"It's not working!" He pulled the stick in different directions but still the drone headed toward the yacht.

Tanner looked up at the monitor. "Target coordinates must be locked into an onboard chip."

The quadracopter's video feed now showed that it was above the yacht's party deck. A couple of the guests apparently noticed it as their heads tipped skyward. Liam worked the station's controls to no avail. In frustration he stamped his foot on the deck.

The prisoner started to laugh. Liam drew his foot back to kick him but Tanner stopped him.

Then, to Liam: "Stay here, watch him and keep trying the controls."

He headed for the exit.

"What's your plan?"

"Damage control."

FORTY-NINE

Boothbay Harbor, Maine

Tanner emerged from the wheelhouse onto the barge's deck. He drew his PM9 and focused on the MUAV now hovering over the mega-yacht's deck full of VIP guests. It hadn't yet released its STX payload but he was all too aware that any second now that's exactly what could happen.

If Liam was unable to stop the drone via the controls, then he would have to take drastic action. He aimed his gun toward the quadracopter, which bobbed and weaved in and out of his sights. The Secret Service agents aboard the *Lincoln* were now on deck looking up at the potential threat, busily communicating into their radios. By the time they took action, it would almost certainly be too late.

Tanner squeezed off two rounds at the micro-drone, both missing. Knowing he would now draw the wrath of the

Secret Service on him, he fired again, a single shot, but a good one. He watched as one of the MUAV's rotors broke away from the body and flew off into the water.

"Take out the drone!" Tanner yelled to the Secret Service guys, but it was no good. They began firing on the barge as the MUAV, still airborne, struggled to maintain a hover with only three-quarters of unbalanced power.

Tanner ducked behind the structure and ran around to the opposite side, pounding on the wall as he went to let Liam know that the situation was critical. He came out on the other side and knelt on one knee, steadying his aim. He had maybe a couple of seconds before the agents became aware of his new position.

He squeezed off three more bullets, feeling relief more than satisfaction as two of them found their mark and pieces of the MUAV shattered into the air, the micro-copter plummeting toward the yacht's starboard rail. Tanner held his breath as he lowered his weapon and scoured the

MUAV for signs of a plume of STX ejecting from it, but he saw none as the contraption impacted with the rail. For one heart-stopping moment Tanner thought the micro-copter was going to fall back into the sea, where it would no longer pose a threat. But instead the broken machine tilted and fell onto the deck of the yacht. Those nearby stampeded away from the wreckage.

And then a Secret Service round splintered the wooden wall above Tanner's head, and the OUTCAST operative wheeled away. He got to his feet and dashed to the door of the structure. Throwing it open, he ran to the inner room where Liam stood guard over the Hofstad prisoner, watching the monitors.

“Good work! It landed on the yacht but I haven't seen any plume.”

Tanner nodded. “Secret Service is all over us, though. Patch a call through to Danielle and tell her we need comm. I'll try the manual method.”

Tanner moved to the VHF marine radio that was part of normal marine vessel equipment. Maybe he could explain himself to the yacht's captain and establish a line of communication with the president's team that way.

They heard the thudding of lead slugs against the structure's outer walls as they reached out to communicate. It was Liam who made contact first. Flashing on how much the communication system had cost to implement, Tanner was grateful for it now, and he made a mental note to look into having it upgraded upon their return. If they returned.

Liam quickly conveyed the situation to Danielle, who promised to contact the White House and brief the appropriate people on the breaking situation. She did not want to distract them with the horrible news about Jasmijn, but did say that the antidote had been developed successfully and that Dante, Stephen and Naomi were en route to Maine with doses of it now via supersonic air transport, should it be needed.

Tanner, meanwhile was having trouble raising anyone on the *Lincoln*. He was using channel 16, the one reserved for marine emergencies, and getting no response. He switched over to a vessel-to-vessel channel and hailed the president's yacht.

"Barge to *Lincoln*, barge to *Lincoln*," he began, wanting to make it crystal clear where he was transmitting from. A few seconds passed and then he received a reply from a stressed-sounding male voice.

"This is yacht, *Lincoln* to barge. You are ordered to surrender. I repeat, you are ordered by the United States Secret Service to surrender. Show yourselves on deck with your hands *up*!"

"Just tell President Carmichael that this is Tanner Wilson of OUTCAST. I'm on board the barge with Liam Reilly, my team member, and a suspected Hofstad terror operator we are holding until he can be placed in custody, over!"

The reply came quickly, suggesting that nothing was being done to authenticate Tanner's story. “You will need to surrender regardless of who you are!”

Tanner looked over at Liam, who stared with concern at the remaining drone display. “Special Forces team incoming,” he noted, watching an assemblage of black-clad men aboard a black Zodiac inflatable boat approaching the barge at high speed.

“We better comply.” Tanner waved an arm toward the exit.

“What about him?” Liam pointed to the terrorist bound on the floor, who had become more alert at the sound of the gunfire.

Tanner considered using him as a human shield but decided it increased the risk that he and Liam would be seen as the terrorists.

“Leave him. Let's go.”

Tanner and Liam tucked their guns into the front of their waistbands, where they would be visible, but kept their hands raised high as they exited the structure onto the deck of the barge.

FIFTY

Boothbay Harbor, Maine

"Do *not* move!" The icy male voice issued from a megaphone held by the driver of the inflatable boat that now deployed a special forces team onto the barge.

Tanner and Liam froze with their hands high in the air. They stood two feet from the barge's rail, on the side facing the president's yacht.

"We're on your side," Tanner stated as two of the team scouted the barge deck for more people.

"Former SEAL Team 6, here," added Liam.

"Shut up! Keep your hands up!"

They were scared. They trusted nothing. Tanner couldn't blame them.

"On your knees. Now!"

The pair of OUTCAST operators complied with the instruction.

Their hands were bound behind their backs with flex cuffs and they were taken aboard the small boat, which motored over to the mega-yacht. The entire inflatable was lifted aboard the yacht by crane, and then the two operators were dragged across the deck where the party had been happening, the guests having been cleared to other parts of the ship.

As soon as they were taken inside the door to the salon, President Carmichael was there to greet them, flanked by several of his cabinet and additional security personnel.

Tanner smiled as he looked at the president. The look on the face of the POTUS transformed with recognition. He addressed the Secret Service agents holding onto Tanner and Liam.

"Wait! I know this man! Tanner Wilson?"

Tanner grinned. "It's a pleasure to see you, Sir. Wish it could be under better circumstances."

Carmichael nodded before continuing to address his people. “He saved our asses during that god-awful reaper drone thing!” One of the men standing next to Carmichael said something softly to him that Tanner couldn't hear, but they heard the POTUS reply, “Yes! That's him!”

“Liam Reilly, here, was there, too, Sir.” Tanner cocked his head at Liam. Carmichael nodded solemnly before commanding his agents.

“Free these individuals at once. See to it that these two men are given five-star treatment. Have them debrief you and then show them to a suite. Now!”

“Yes, Mr. President.” While one of the agents cut the flex cuffs from his wrists, Tanner spoke.

“Mr. President, you should know that we detained one of the terrorists in the barge's wheelhouse. He's tied up in there now.”

One of the Secret Service men touched his earbud and nodded. “They just found him. They're bringing him out on the barge deck now.”

“Can we go out and get a look at him?” Carmichael asked. “Maybe one of us knows who he is?”

The Secret Service agents locked gazes with each other for a second, one of them shrugging before quietly intoning commands into his lip mic. Then the agents held the salon door open while the president and his entourage exited to the yacht's main deck. Tanner, Liam and the remaining Secret Service men followed.

The door to the barge's wheelhouse opened and the terrorist was brought outside, literally dragging his feet. An evil grin occupied his face when he looked up and saw the line of people gawking at him from the rail of the *Lincoln*, but he said nothing.

“I don't recognize him. Do we know who he is?” Carmichael asked no one in particular.

“Hofstad member,” Tanner said, preempting the Secret Service agent who shot him an irritated look.

“Speak English?” the president asked.

The terrorist said nothing. “Probably Dutch, but maybe English, too,” Tanner explained.

“Anyone speak Dutch here?” Carmichael looked around.

An elderly woman had just raised her hand when the terrorist called up to them.

“You will all die for failing to meet our demands!”

Two agents grabbed the terrorist and began dragging him to a waiting inflatable boat.

“Where will he be taken?” Carmichael asked.

“Your time is up!” The jihadist screamed.

Suddenly a powerful explosion rocked the barge.

FIFTY-ONE

Boothbay Harbor, Maine

"Down!" Tanner grabbed President Carmichael and flung him flat to the deck, several Secret Service agents dog-piling on top of them. Tanner looked to the side and saw Liam with his eyes open, crouched, watching the barge. He knew he had a lot of demolition experience, having been through BUDS training as a SEAL. If he felt comfortable to be in an upright position already, then he must be anticipating the force of the explosion to be non-lethal.

But with the exception of the Secret Service agents and the terrorist on the barge, the force of the explosion was the least of their problems. Tanner got to his feet and looked down on the terror vessel. A huge hole had been blasted in its middle, amidships. It was taking on water fast. Tanner felt fine droplets rain down on him. He assumed they were seawater from the explosion.

And then he saw with horror the pieces of white plastic floating away from the barge, and he knew.

The STX container!

Jasmijn had described the vat to him that Hofstad had stolen from her. Why else would Hofstad rig this barge to blow if not to trigger another neurotoxin blast? The previous attack—the warm-up act—had operated on essentially the same principle—exploding open a container of STX, but by sheer force of collision rather than incendiary. Tanner watched the slivers of white plastic drift away from the hole in the sinking vessel's side. The terrorists had gambled everything on the yacht of the president, even more than Tanner had suspected.

He had thought they would be holding on to their precious supply of neuro-agent to milk the fear factor for as long as possible, to let the world know that they were capable of inflicting a deadly strike anywhere, anytime. But instead, they'd put all of their eggs in one ultra-poisonous basket, and now that basket had been dumped on the POTUS and everyone else aboard his yacht. Including Tanner. Including Liam.

No sooner had Tanner gripped Liam's shoulder to break the news than he heard the first coughs of irritation start among those aboard the yacht.

“Liam. Liam!” The ex-SEAL looked up at his friend. Tanner continued.

“We have to assume that the explosion was an STX bomb using the rest of the stolen vat.”

“Shit.” Liam pulled his shirt collar up over his nose and mouth, but his eyes told Tanner that he knew it wouldn't matter.

“I'll see if I can get through to Danielle.” Liam stepped back from the crowd where people were still screaming and talking loudly. He tapped his earbud and waited. Meanwhile, he looked over the rail at the barge and counted the bodies floating away from it. He cringed when he spotted the stump of a leg bobbing by itself, then sighted the body of the man he'd tied up, minus a leg. *Got what you wanted, I guess.*

And what of his own fate? Liam thought back to the account Tanner had relayed from Jasmijn of how her lab assistant had died from the stuff, of the news-reel footage he'd seen of the victims in Hawaii and Florida clutching their throats...

"Okay! Yes!" He heard Tanner say with excitement into his bone conducting mic. "We are aboard the president's yacht, the *Lincoln*, anchored in Boothbay Harbor. Liam—" He turned toward his colleague.

"Yeah?"

"Find out from the Captain if the *Lincoln* is preparing to move. Tell him we have help on the way but they need to be able to find us right away."

Liam had questions of his own but he knew better than to stall things by asking them now. He moved to the president, who was kneeling between two Secret Service agents, each of whom had a hand on the back of the POTUS.

"Excuse me Mr. President—"

"Not now!" one of the agents growled.

Liam wasn't deterred. "I need to know for sure if the ship will be at anchor for the next few minutes. We have a possible solution en route."

The agent started to wave him down but Carmichael spoke. "You have help on the way? We'll stay right here. That's an order!" He turned to the agent who had told Liam to be quiet. "Tell the captain not to move us. Now!"

"Right away, Mr. President." He picked up a two-way radio and spoke softly into it, used to keeping operational instructions on the lowdown.

Tanner walked over to the group, finished with his conversation with Danielle. "They've got an antidote and they're in the air now to bring it to us." His expression and manner didn't seem to carry the same degree of optimism that uttering those words should.

“Is there a catch?” Liam wanted to know.

“Jasmijn's dead.”

“What? How—”

“Not now. We're not out of the woods yet ourselves.”

“What's happening?” President Carmichael demanded.

“Mr. President,” Tanner returned, “it's likely that the explosion on the barge was a deliberate attempt to expose you—and every one of us onboard this yacht—to the same STX neurotoxin that Hofstad has been using in their latest run of terror attacks.”

The president’s eyes were wide with fear. “Give me some details.”

Tanner laid it out for him, forgoing the use of formal titles for the sake of expediency. “The barge may have been on a timer to detonate so that a remaining tank of STX would blow, becoming aerosolized and disperse wherever it was."

"And it just so happened to be right next to my yacht." No one replied, so Carmichael continued. "You mean to say..." He struggled to formulate his words. "...that what happened to those people in Miami, in Honolulu..."

The president seemed to buckle under his own weight and had to be supported by two Secret Service agents, one of whom started into a coughing jag as he did so.

"Unfortunately that is the situation we seem to be facing," Tanner replied, "but there is hope."

The president looked up from the deck into Tanner's eyes. "What hope? Those victims died within minutes."

"My OUTCAST team has been working in conjunction with a scientist..." Liam looked over at Tanner as he heard his voice catch. The STX taking hold, or something else, something triggered by the mention of Jasmijn? The interruption was brief, however. "...and an antidote to this particular STX formula has been developed in the Netherlands."

"*Netherlands*?" Carmichael erupted. "What good does that do us? We've got maybe ten or fifteen minutes to live!" At this, a few of the passengers overheard the president's raised voice and began to panic, telling the others that the air was contaminated with some kind of poison.

Tanner took a step closer to the POTUS. "Stay calm, please. Our team was dispatched hours ago with the antidote. I've just been in contact with my base of operations and they are en route now from Portland International."

"How soon until they get here?" Carmichael demanded. He pulled at his shirt collar.

"Should be about five minutes, Mr. President."

"Five...minutes..." Carmichael muttered, lost in thought. Then suddenly he came back with, "How will they get out here? Do they know where to go?"

Tanner smiled. “They know where to go, and let's just say that they're trained to find a way.”

Around them they could hear labored breathing as the STX began to manifest itself. Tanner spun away from the president and contacted Danielle again on their comm system.

“Can I get an updated sitrep? Dozens infected here including Liam, myself, and the Chief.” The Chief was the codename they used for the president.

Danielle's voice came back sounding grim. “Tanner, bad news. Naomi, Stephen and Dante are in Boothbay, but they've been detained by law enforcement. “

FIFTY-TWO

Boothbay Harbor, Maine

“Let us through. We're trying to save the life of President Carmichael!” Stephen Shah pleaded with the line of cops who guarded the most direct route down to the waterfront. There were other ways to get to the harbor that the OUTCAST operators could have taken to skirt the law enforcement presence, but none of them would allow them to reach the yacht in time. Instead they had tried to sneak through the line of policemen, each of the three of them carrying one third of the antidote in case only one of them could make it through. But none of them had.

Then they had all been subject to a physical search, and because all of them were found with the same fluid-filled syringes, they were suspected as terrorists. As one cop started to cuff Dante's hands behind his back, the ex-Secret Service agent eyed Shah. They had to do something or the president would die within minutes. Tanner would die. Liam...

As the cop bent down to cinch the cuffs on Dante's wrists, the field operative smashed his elbow into the officer's nose, shattering it into a fountain of blood. Dante took off running down the hill toward the waterfront. Another cop standing next to the fallen one raised his service pistol to shoot, and Shah gave a karate chop to his arm, sending the weapon careening to the ground. "Run, Dante!"

And run he did, maintaining an erratic zig-zag pattern down the hill, a couple of shots from other officers missing wildly. On the way down he paused to roll in front of a tree for cover here, a metal trash can, there. Still, a phalanx of cops took off after him while two more wrestled Shah to the ground. Nay stood cuffed in the hands of a female officer, saying nothing, but observing everything. She remained very calm.

“We're for real,” she said to the cop who had her in custody. “The syringes we carry are full of the antidote that can save the lives of all the people infected by the nerve agent the terrorists used.”

The woman’s reply was icily detached. “Until that can be verified, we have no choice but to detain you.”

Just then a squad car drove up and the uniformed driver jumped out. He walked over to the line of officers. “You have three detainees with chemicals?”

A cop approached him and pointed down the hill, then to Stephen and Naomi.

“I just received verified orders from the Secret Service to not only let them go, but to escort them personally to the president's yacht. Let's move!'

Stephen and Naomi were put into the back of the police car with their backpacks. Stephen wondered for a moment if this was a ploy to get them into the car without a fight, but he figured they wouldn't let them have their bags if that was the case. With sirens and lights on, they barreled down the hill until they saw Dante, sprinting across a walkway to the water's edge. He looked around frantically, as if deciding his next move. He looked back, saw the cop car, then began scanning the water in front of him as though he was planning on diving in.

“Let me talk to him,” Stephen urged the two cops up front, one of whom had picked up the microphone to the squad car's PA system. He stretched the microphone on its cord to the back seat where Shah clutched it.

“Dante! Dante it's us, Stephen and Nay. It's okay! They got the message. They're giving us an escort! Jump in.” Dante began running to the police car.

“How do we get out to the yacht?” Naomi squinted into the sun to look at the majestic vessel still at anchor in the harbor.

“Police boat at a dock up ahead,” the officer driving answered.

“I see the dock but I don't see a boat.” Dante pointed ahead.

The other officer turned around, holding up the radio transmitter. “It's on the way. In fact...” He faced front again and looked out to the right. “...here it comes now.”

A rigid hull inflatable boat with a metal wheelhouse sped toward the dock.

The squad car driver pulled up to the dock and addressed the trio of operators in his backseat. “Go, go, go! They're waiting.”

Stephen had the door open and was outside the car before the officer finished his sentence, with Naomi and Dante close on his heels. Each wore a small backpack. They ran to the dock, arriving just as the boat pulled alongside. It was manned by two officers, one driving and one on deck. The one driving spun it around expertly so that it was next to the dock but facing out ready to take off again.

The deck officer waved them aboard while the boat's engines idled, the water churned to foamy froth by the pilot's skilled maneuvering while he waited for his unexpected passengers to board.

The three OUTCAST operators jumped aboard and the deck officer urged them to grab a handhold as the pilot accelerated. Seconds later they were hydroplaning, the twin two hundred horsepower outboard motors pushing them along at almost sixty miles per hour toward the stricken yacht full of VIPs.

Stephen saw the boat pilot pick up his radio transmitter and say something into it. The engine noise was too loud to let him hear the words, but he guessed he was alerting the yacht's bridge that they were dropping off passengers who would deliver the antidote.

The pilot brought the police craft to the yacht's rear boarding ladder, at the top of which waited a couple of

Secret Service agents. Dante, Naomi and Stephen climbed up onto the yacht.

"Stephen!" Shah heard Tanner's voice and whipped his head to the right.

"Tanner!"

The OUTCAST leader waved a hand. "This way. Hurry!"

He began to run, Dante and Naomi behind him, the Secret Service guys escorting them along the way.

Tanner was waiting in a knot of people, at the center of which was President Carmichael. The leader of the free world knelt on the deck, hunched over like a sick person. And sick he was. Tanner pointed to him. "Him first."

"Do we have a medic?" Stephen ripped off his backpack and unzipped it. He removed one of the syringes—each containing a single human dose according to Jasmijn's final instructions, and held it up.

“We have a ship's doctor,” one of the Secret Service men said, indicating a tall, very harried-looking man with close-cropped black hair, wearing a white doctor's coat. He came forward.

“I can administer the shots,” he said, looking Stephen squarely in the eye. He spoke rapidly but clearly. “I understand time elapsed is critical at this point. We've already lost some people. Any special instructions?” he asked, eyeballing the syringe and tapping it with a finger to eliminate air bubbles.

“Bicep shot,” Stephen returned.

The physician nodded and set a medical bag down next to the POTUS. “Give me space, please.” People backed out of the way as he rolled up the president's sleeve and swabbed it with an antiseptic wipe. He explained what he was doing to the president, but Carmichael was rapidly deteriorating and had no coherent response.

“Hopefully this stuff works,” he said. And then he stuck the hypodermic needle into the arm of the president.

FIFTY-THREE

Boothbay Harbor, Maine

Tanner, Liam, Stephen, Naomi and Dante huddled together watching the president. All around them people were dying or close to it. The sounds of dry heaving rent the air along with the smell of vomit. Multiple people were having seizures while those close to them did their best to provide comfort, knowing they were probably next. President Carmichael's condition seemed to Tanner to be unchanged since receiving the antidote a couple of minutes earlier, but there was no point in waiting to see if the antidote was effective. It was all they had, whether it worked or not.

The OUTCAST team distributed the antidote syringes they had—minus five for themselves— to the Secret Service agents, who wasted no time in shooting themselves with the hopefully life-saving antidote. Then—because we can't help others if we don't help ourselves, kind of like putting the oxygen mask on your kids first in an airplane, they said—they passed out the syringes to the rest of the people aboard the yacht.

Several minutes later one of the president's agents returned from the boat's upper deck and reported that all of the doses had been administered, but that many had already died. Naomi, Stephen and Dante, who had arrived after the cloud of STX had dispersed, reported feeling strange and physically unstable, as if they were about to be sick but weren't yet. But Tanner and Liam were incapacitated. They could still talk and hadn't yet descended into the worst depths of symptoms that STX had to offer, but they now sat on the deck, legs stretched out before them, lacking the energy to stand.

“How's the president?” Tanner asked, eyes looking a bit glazed. He knew that the fate of the president over the next few minutes would mirror his own. Dante looked over at Carmichael, who was now holding his head up. The

POTUS was sort of the canary in the coal mine everyone watched, since it was he who had received the antidote first.

"Looks a little better." Dante sounded a little surprised.

"I feel a little better!" Carmichael announced without warning. Immediately a clutch of agents descended on him, asking him if he was okay. "No really, I feel better," he insisted. "The headache is gone! That damnable headache!"

Soon after, other reports of healing began to trickle in. Headaches subsiding, strength returning, seizures abated...Still, no one wanted to put a hex on things by voicing the hope: it was working.

There were still a lot of dead. Dozens. A couple of more souls succumbed who did not respond at all to the antidote, those who were nearly expired when it was administered.

But overall, the members of OUTCAST could see, the tide was starting to turn. The antidote was working. From beyond the grave, Dr. Jasmijn Rotmensen had made a difference. Within a few minutes, the president was standing and demanding a briefing on the situation in Boothbay in preparation for a live press conference. His people protested the idea, but he brushed them away, insisting that the American people be updated on the developments.

The Secret Service agents were feeling well enough to canvass the yacht from top to bottom in order to ensure there were no terrorists that had somehow snuck aboard, or devices that had been implanted. The barge, meanwhile, had sunk to the bottom of Boothbay Harbor, a stream of bubbles breaking the surface marking its location.

In the midst of it all, Tanner Wilson rose to his feet. He reached out an arm and pulled Liam Reilly to a standing position. Stephen Shah, Naomi Washington and Dante Alvarez crowded around their associates, ready to support them physically should their legs prove unsteady.

But it wasn't necessary.

They stood their ground.

“Remarkable!” Liam said at length. “I was feeling way under the weather for a while there, and now I feel almost fine.”

“Almost fine?” Dante asked, concern creeping into his voice.

“Well yeah, maybe like I have a cold or something, still lingering. But even that feels like it's receding. For a while there...” He looked at Tanner who nodded.

“I didn't think I was going to make it, either.” The leader of OUTCAST looked over at the president, who was busy conferring with his inner circle, and then around at the yacht. Clusters of people gathered in knots, consoling those who had lost loved ones or friends, many of them also marveling at the transformation they'd experienced due to Jasmijn's antidote.

Then he turned back around to his team. "Jasmijn." They shared a moment of silence for the marine scientist who had saved them all at the expense of her own life. Then he placed a call to Danielle. She answered immediately and he updated her on the developments.

"Media reports are just hitting the wires now," she responded. "Ten dead on the Boothbay waterfront walkway, an unknown number on the yacht. All terrorists reported as deceased. Good work, Tanner. Now what?"

The former FBI agent stared out across the water, wondering what other secrets the ocean held. But for now, he had learned enough of them.

"Now we go home."

EPILOGUE

Rabat, Morocco

Mustapha Aziz Samir, the leader of Hofstad, stared out across the Atlantic Ocean from his table at a seaside cafe. He dined alone, preferring solitude after the failure of his pet project, the Poseidon Initiative. It had been a mistake to gamble all of their precious STX on one high-stakes mission. He should have listened to the advisor who had recommended against this course, recommending instead that he hold onto the nerve agent, keeping it in reserve for many years into the future, doling out deadly attacks in fits and starts according to the needs of the organization. But he had disregarded that advice. He had gambled and lost.

Nevertheless, the initiative wasn't a complete failure, he told himself as he watched the pleasure boats come and go from the Bouregreg Marina. Much had been accomplished. The President of the United States of America had been made extremely ill, his nation thrown into a panic as several of his guests aboard his fancy personal yacht were killed. Three other attacks, too. The effort wasn't too shabby, he mused, now watching the gulls vie for table scraps from a family of tourists two tables over.

Even so, his demands had been willfully disregarded. The U.S. embassy in the Hague remained open, never having closed for a single minute. He took consolation in the fact that this decision had cost the blood of American citizens.

And there would be other chances for retribution. Other opportunities for terror.

His server returned. Was he ready to order? He had forgotten to even look at the menu. Samir quickly perused it before handing it to the server with a smile.

"Perfect. I will have the Shellfish Delight."

Read an excerpt from OUTCAST Ops: Game of Drones:

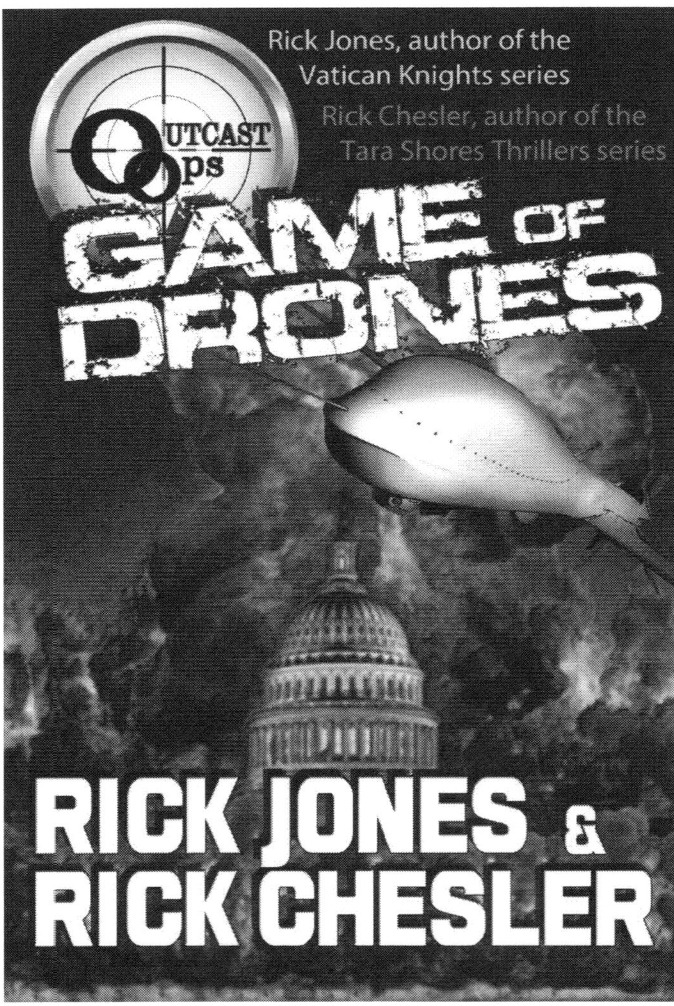

PROLOGUE

Islamabad, Pakistan. Awan Town

North of the Punjab Province

0416 hours

Fourteen members of the Punjab Elite Police Force (PEP) quietly approached a compound southwest of central Islamabad, just inside the sector of Awan Town. A two-story structure located upon a small rise afforded a complete view of the entire estate that was hemmed in by ten-foot walls.

Using darkness as their ally and dressed in black, they wore domed helmets with a collection of gadgetry marching up one side and down the other, including assemblages of night vision goggles (NVG) and thermal ware. Their faceplates were a convexity of opaque plastic, the overall ensembles exuding a 'Robocop' feel replete with custom designed composite shin and forearm guards.

Beneath a crescent moon that cast an eerie glow upon the landscape that was the color of whey, the PEP traveled along the wall's baseline using their NVG scopes to guide them.

When they reached their designated point at the south-side wall, the team leader made a series of predetermined hand gestures to communicate with his unit, mobilizing two members of his team to remove piton guns from their backpacks. They loaded the pitons, already tethered to metal lines, and took aim. They fired off two quick shots—the sounds no louder than a couple of spits—with the sharpened tips embedding deep into the wall's upper reaches.

The team began to scale the lines in coordinated effort. When the first two responders reached the top, they placed mesh-wire tarps over the points of the spikes to blunt them. Once they were up and over, others quickly followed.

As soon as the last man scaled the wall, the team leader examined the facility through the NVG lens of his rifle scope. Along the balconies on the second-tier, guards with assault weapons were stationed as solo or paired teams.

He lowered his scope and signaled his lieutenant: advance the Team Alpha unit under guidance and take out the guards.

Shooting him a thumbs-up, the lieutenant led Team Alpha forward with their weapons at eye level. When they were within range, Alpha Leader lowered his lip mike.

"Team Alpha to Team Bravo, we have four tangos in sight."

"Copy that, Alpha, we see four, too."

"Coordinate termination in thirty," he said.

"In thirty. We copy."

The members of Alpha Team began to acquire assigned targets by centering the guards within the crosshairs of their assault weapons.

"In twenty," whispered Alpha leader.

"*In twenty. We copy.*"

As zero moment approached with the momentum of a bullet train, their orders were clear: *terminate everyone with extreme prejudice excepting the high-value asset.*

"In ten."

"In ten . . ."

The snipers by the wall were scoping the area at ground level for guards walking the perimeter of the residence. So far everything was working to their advantage; the area was clear.

"In five . . . In four . . ."

Adrenaline coursed through their veins like a narcotic, bringing on a dual sensation of euphoric bloodlust for the hunt and the anticipation of mission success.

". . . In three . . ."

". . . In two . . ."

Breaths became measured.

". . . In one . . ."

Fingers began to pull back on the triggers.

". . . Zero."

Suppressed weapons fired in perfect synchronization.

On the balcony where the four hostiles gathered, eruptions of red mist exploded from the chests of two guards who immediately went down as boneless heaps. Before the other two guards could register what happened, bullet holes magically appeared in their foreheads, the shots dropping them just as quickly, the post completely sanitized. As the final body was making its fall—before it *had* a chance to settle upon the balcony floor—the Punjab Elite Police were already on the move to set a perimeter around the residence.

#

Ayman al-Zawahiri was at rest upon a mattress on the floor and reflected, as he usually did on nights that he couldn't sleep, on the glorious past of his younger days.

In 1998 al-Zawahiri was the leading principal of the Egyptian Islamic Jihad. During that year he united with Osama bin Laden, merging their groups to become al-Qaeda. Although he was the leading lieutenant and bin Laden the financier, it was al-Zawahiri who truly governed the forces since he was a man of military sophistication, something bin Laden lacked.

Plans for mass destruction were formulated and missions were carried out all over the planet, the organization depending upon the personal sacrifices of foot soldiers with the promise of Paradise at life's end. As these martyrs came and went and the body count began to rise in the name of Allah, Zawahiri--not Osama bin Laden--became the mastermind behind the war effort of nine-eleven.

With a single attack against American sovereignty, a powerful nation had been brought to its knees. And in the following years during which recuperation moved at a glacial pace, the national psyche remained as fragile as glass. America was no longer invulnerable.

He had never been so proud or vain or self-appreciative as he was on that day. He had become the David to the 'Great Satan's' Goliath. But as he gloated in self-glory, he failed to realize that he had awakened a sleeping giant.

The United States had opened its eyes, stood tall, flexed its muscles, and moved relentlessly through troubled waters like a shark, looking to feed a hunger that could never be satiated. Then, on May 2nd, 2011, after America had trolled the waters long enough, U.S. Special Forces invaded a compound in Abbottabad, Pakistan, killing Osama bin Laden.

It was also the day when Zawahiri discovered that the world—as big as it was—was really too small of a place to hide in. And with a twenty-five million dollar bounty on his head, he went into seclusion in Islamabad, realizing that the United States would not attempt another invasion on Pakistani soil without proper authorization from the country's top principals. Such an incursion would diminish diplomatic ties between the two nations, straining their already tenuous relationship. So he felt safe knowing that no such invite to collar him would be given, especially in the heart of Pakistan.

As he lay there with images of the past parading through his mind's eye, he started when he heard a crash coming from down below. Explosively loud, as though a concussive wave had passed through the house, the ripples shook the walls and floors to the roots of their foundations.

Zawahiri got to his feet and grabbed his gun, an AK-47. He barked commands for his guards to take position along the tops of the stairwells and to 'fight in the name of Allah.'

But Allah would not side with Ayman al-Zawahiri on this night.

#

The front door to the residence appeared incapable of being breached. Made of thick wood pieced together with black bands and rivets, it was like something from medieval times; perhaps it even *was* from medieval times, but the detonation specialist who prepared a partial brick of Semtex could care less. He set the locking mechanism, attached the small detonator, and with a remote the size of a cigarette pack, he flipped the switch.

The door exploded inward as pieces of wood and metal skated across the floor of the residence. Black smoke billowed from the entrance, providing sufficient cover for the PEP teams to press forward with their weapons held at eye level. Within seconds they fanned out, looking for targets.

Insurgent forces on the lower floor took up positions of engagement, but the members of the PEP were too fast, too efficient, their weapons going off with precision shots that killed the insurgents before their bodies hit the ground. Other guerilla forces were dropped immediately as bullets stitched across their chests and abdomens, ejecting gouts of blood in bold arcs and splashes that decorated the walls with gaudy Pollock designs.

When the first level was clear, Team Leader took inventory of his units as they reassembled. Nobody from the PEP had been downed.

He then pointed to the base of each stairwell—there were three altogether—with his fore and middle fingers, directing his team to break up into three separate units and wait for his command.

Once positioned, Alpha Leader spoke through his lip mike. "Flash bangs on five."

"*Flash bangs on five. All units copy.*"

"On four . . . On three . . . On two . . . Engage!"

A series of non-lethal explosions detonated in quick succession as blinding light lit up the entire second level, turning night into day as concussion waves crippled all sense of cognition in those standing at the top. With time-of-opportunity limited to split seconds, the teams rushed up the stairwells with the points of their weapons raised.

#

Al-Zawahiri saw the flash of blinding light filter in from around the seams and cracks of his bedroom door. He held his weapon tight, the mouth of the barrel directed to the door, and waited.

He had heard the volley of gunfire below, the commotion muted behind the closed door. But he knew that the enemy had pushed through his forces and were making their way towards their prized asset.

As everything moved with the slowness of a bad dream, he remembered the moments when he issued a call for suicide bombers, those who were willing to martyr themselves and become legacies. But he did not share that inclination—he did not feel like sacrificing his life for his own cause. So unlike those he called upon to pay the price of admission to Paradise by wearing bomb-laden vests, in the end he wanted to live.

Closing his eyes and praying to Allah for forgiveness with respect to his own cowardice, he listened to the PEP edge closer.

#

The light was blinding. The concussive waves were a powerful blow to the senses of the al-Qaeda forces who lost all capability to coordinate their thoughts. They moved blindly about with their minds and judgment too fractured to make any sense of what was happening.

When the members of the PEP topped the stairs, targets were immediately acquired and brought down, the threat of imminent danger quickly erased. Bullets continued to find their marks, all kill shots, either to the head, heart, or to the center of body mass.

In less than twenty seconds, nearly every room had been cleared. Bodies of al-Qaeda lay everywhere.

The high-valued asset, however, was not among them.

At the end of the hallway stood a single door.

The PEP moved forward with the points of their weapons raised and centered.

Silence, and specifically the element of mystery that came with it, was just as disturbing as the sound of battle. No sound issued from beyond the door. The team leader stood his ground. He set his weapon to grenade mode, aimed, and set off a mortar round. The shell exited the barrel and corkscrewed through the air until it impacted with the door, the resulting explosion decimating it into innumerable shards and splintered pieces.

As a wall of smoke moved about in lazy swirls and eddies, another flash bang was tossed into the room. In the explosion's aftermath, the PEP forces found al-Zawahiri huddled against the corner with his mind in disarray from the grenade, his AK-47 abandoned and lying on the floor in front of him.

This man, once a kingpin of terrorism who sat upon one of the most fearsome thrones in the Middle East, was now in the custody of the Punjab Elite Police Force.

The high-value asset had been attained.

If you enjoy the OUTCAST Ops series, you might also like the Tara Shores Thriller series:

Omnibus edition (3 novels in 1 price-discounted volume):

Read an excerpt from SPLASHDOWN: A Dane and Bones Origins Story, by David Wood and Rick Chesler:

Prologue

July 1543, off the coast of La Florida, New World

Juan Diego de Guerrero emerged from his cabin onto the stern deck of the *Nuestra Señora de la San Pedro* and narrowed his eyes against the driving rain. It was not the precipitation that concerned him, however, but the wind that drove it and the sea's response to that steadily increasing force. He frowned, wiping cold salt spray from his weathered face as he gazed out on the marching waves, a single terrifying word dominating his mind: *Huracán*.

I should have known.

Upon waking with the sunrise he'd been pleased to see that they were beyond sight of land, well underway across the great Atlantic to his Spanish homeland. But even then he'd noticed the unusual conditions —the decreasing interval between swells, the electric tang in the air. Now these were undeniably magnified. It was like the hand of God pulling him back from his goal. Had he done something wrong?

"Captain, I was just coming to find you." Luis López de Olivares, Guerrero's first mate, skidded to a halt on the damp decking. His deeply tanned face was pale, and his calloused fingers worked with nervous energy. "The weather is turning against us." He gave Guerrero a meaningful look, knowing he did not need to finish the thought.

Somewhat of a maverick, Guerrero had been warned about being caught in this part of the world during the summer months. But he had not planned things this way. It had taken him longer than he had anticipated to find what he was looking for and to load it into his ship's hold. Not satisfied with the usual bounty of gold, silver and jade figurines making their way to Europe in a steady stream from the New World, he had meandered much farther south than his contemporaries, in search of ever more exotic treasures and curiosities with which to impress King Charles. Eventually he had come to a southern land known to him only as *Río de la Plata*, where there were rumored to be entire river valleys lined with silver, complete mountain ranges made of the same.

"We will make it." Guerrero stilled his voice to a calm that he did not feel. "We always do."

Olivares turned to look out at the sea. "We shouldn't have traveled so far south. The silver wasn't worth it." The words came out in a low murmur, clearly not intended for Guerrero's ears, but the captain heard.

"It will be all right."

A pang of guilt caused Guerrero to wince. It wasn't prodigious amounts of silver that had drawn Guerrero months' worth of treacherous sailing out of his way. Early reports from his notable predecessors, including Amerigo Vespucci, had spawned provocative talk that Guerrero, then a child dockside laborer, had routinely eavesdropped on in the shadows of Spanish seaports. The explorers' gossip told of a wealth of strange and interesting minerals in addition to silver and gold, some of which had never before been witnessed in all of Europe. At the age of sixteen he would join the King's navy and for a time he forgot about the particulars of the tales of his youth, but still they drove his desire to remain at sea, to explore the world and locate its riches for Spain.

And so it was that decades later, after many false starts, tribulations and general hardships, he came to command the King's vessel, the treasure frigate *San Pedro*. It was also how he'd come to try the patience of his weary crew. Following an arduous coastal voyage, Guerrero's ship had landed at *Rio del Plata*. Guerrero himself spoke to the indigenous tribes who met them on the beach about the minerals he had heard of, and he was introduced in short order to a shaman who claimed that the stones had very special powers, perhaps to a dangerous degree.

The indigenous priest agreed to allow Guerrero's landing party to traverse their territory accompanied by local guides to a distant, rugged site where the natural resources might be excavated, but only under the condition that he first be allowed to bless the entire expedition in an elaborate ritual. To Guerrero, who reflected the widely held sentiment of Europe as a whole, these people were little more than savage heathens prone to the most base superstitions and animal urges, not yet having found the truth of Catholicism.

Olivares turned to face him, straightened his lanky frame, and clenched his fists. "Captain. What *are* those stones?"

Only by sheer force of will did Guerrero maintain his calm. He wondered the same thing, though he was not about to admit it.

He had heard tales of these strange rocks for many years, though, and he thirsted for the chance to finally bring some back to Spain. At the same time, Guerrero knew that the time required for the overland trek would likely put him beyond his safe weather window for the return trip across the Atlantic, but he was on the voyage of a lifetime and it was a chance he was willing to take.

To Guerrero's men, however, the raw ore they painstakingly recovered and transported to the ship's cargo hold proved most unremarkable indeed. From whispered rumors of Guerrero's descriptions, the crew had been expecting some kind of lesser known gemstones—something that looked like rubies, garnets, maybe emeralds. But the rocks were plain-looking by comparison to those usually of value. Nothing they could easily trade in the ports of call for the favors of women and barkeeps. For these drab rocks they had trekked many miles through dank, insect-infested jungles and snake-filled swamps, scrabbled up and down the side of a bleak never-ending mountain of loose shale in order to extract examples of these rarest of New World specimens. A few of the men expressed dissatisfaction at going to such extremes to retrieve minerals not precisely known or valued rather than accepting more of the golden gifts readily offered by the coastal natives.

Guerrero had silenced the most vocal of these dissenters upon return to the ship by having them tied to the mast and whipped until dead while the rest of the crew was rewarded with a wine drenched feast. "Blood shall flow like wine for those who dare speak against his orders," he had shouted over the tortured cries of the condemned. For Guerrero, only absolute authority could command and control such a motley assortment of common men enduring long months at sea. His seafaring career had been long and varied, met overall with mixed success, and he was determined that this was the voyage with which he would finally make a lasting impression on the King.

But now, a sudden and vicious storm stood between him and that opportunity.

Guerrero ignored the question, took a deep breath, and looked down the decks of his hundred-foot-long ship. He was not surprised to see his crew already taking appropriate actions: reefing canvas, securing the cannons and various loose objects on deck, the helmsman adjusting course at the wheel to head them into the waves while barking orders to crew in the rigging.

"Was there something you needed from me, or did you think the middle of a storm was an appropriate time to debate my choice of cargo?"

Duly chastened, Olivares shook his head.

"In that case, resume your duties at once."

Olivares threw up a ragged salute, turned on his heel, and stalked away.

Guerrero clenched his fists. The mate was not wrong. *I should have headed north sooner! Or perhaps if I had made the crossing to Africa and then headed north to*

Europe from there instead of travelling north into the heart of the New World...

But as a wave crashed over the stern deck, the highest on the ship, and he watched a man fall to his death from the crow's nest, he knew that his second-guessing could no longer make a difference. It was a matter of mere hours at most before his ship would be ingested by a hurricane, and with God's blessing they would withstand the storm and be able to limp home. Without it, they would succumb to its fury.

With a last hurried glance at the wind-whipped whitecaps threatening his vessel, Guerrero retreated belowdecks and ran to the cargo hold. His feet sloshed through rank bilge water. He could have assigned crew to do this, but he wanted to personally supervise the securing of his most distinctive gifts. Reaching the wooden crates piled high with ore, he double-secured the ropes lashing the crates to the deck, then added more. He did not wish them to spill over and rip a hole in the hull. Satisfied, he was about to turn on a heel and head back topside when he paused.

Reaching into the nearest crate, he tossed chunks of ore aside until he found a flatter one and removed it. He used the tip of his machete to carve his initials into the rock, slicing a finger once when the rocking of the ship caused the blade to slip, and then thrust it into a pocket of his pantalones.

Were his dead body ever to be brought back to Spain, he desired proof that Juan Diego de Guerrero, the boy who had labored for his entire childhood as a petty dockworker fetching items for sailors, had now retrieved something that would one day light the world on fire.

July 21, 1961, 300 miles off Cape Canaveral, Florida

NASA space capsule *Liberty Bell 7* dangled from its

drogue parachute at an altitude of 1,200 feet. Returning from a successful suborbital flight in a demonstration of emerging United States space power, it was now about to land back on Earth as planned, by splashing down into in the Atlantic Ocean. A small flotilla of support ships and helicopters waited below to retrieve the capsule as soon as it hit the water. Inside the spacecraft, Gus Grissom, among the first wave of a new breed of fliers known as "astronauts," spoke into his radio, his gravelly voice exuding a calm professionalism.

"Atlantic ship Capcom, this is *Liberty Bell 7*, do you read me, over?"

The reply was near instant. "Bell 7, this is Atlantic ship Capcom. I read you loud and clear, over."

"Roger that, Capcom. My rate of descent is twenty-nine feet per second, fuel has been dumped for impact, over."

"Copy that, Bell 7. We are tracking your descent. Everything looks A-okay, over."

For the next few seconds, all eyes on the support ships and aircraft were focused on the falling space capsule. Then the radio channel crackled again.

"Capcom reporting: Splashdown! We have splashdown! Bell 7, a helicopter will reach you in about thirty seconds, over."

The space capsule, shaped roughly like the American iconic symbol for which it was named, complete with a "crack" painted down its side, was about as seaworthy as a cork. It bobbed helplessly in the water, capable of nothing more than drifting until it could be picked up by a helicopter. A tense couple of seconds passed while those listening to the radio frequency waited to see if the astronaut inside the capsule had been knocked around too badly upon hitting the water to reply.

But then Grissom said, "Roger that, 'chute has been jettisoned. I'll be going over my post-flight checklist. As soon as that's done I'll be ready for evac, over."

Broadcast radio commentators intended for audiences listening around the world remarked how thorough and professional Gus Grissom was, that he would rather complete his checklists before leaving the capsule for the comforts of the helicopter and ships even after all he'd endured. The big Huey hovered overhead until they heard Grissom's voice over the communications line once again.

"*Liberty Bell 7* to Capcom. Now prepared for evac, over."

The Huey moved into position over the floating capsule. A cable was lowered from the helicopter.

Suddenly the hatch cover of the spacecraft was seen popping off the craft.

Fitted with explosive bolts for emergency evacuation from the inside, under normal circumstances it was meant to be opened not by the astronaut but by rescue personnel once the capsule had been secured back aboard its transport ship. That ship was aircraft carrier *USS Randolph*, and from its bridge a mission recovery team coordinator frowned beneath a pair of binoculars.

"Grissom's out of the capsule, he's in the water!" he told the radioman, who promptly relayed that message to the pilot of the helicopter, who was told in no uncertain terms to pursue the capsule. Grissom's spacesuit was designed to provide him with flotation, but they had no way of knowing now whether it really worked. What they did know was that without the hatch cover in place, America's space race investment was rapidly flooding with water and would soon be lost to the depths if not secured.

A helicopter crewman descended from the aircraft and connected a cable to the spacecraft. While Grissom floated nearby, buffeted by rotor wash that whipped up the sea surface into a frothy foam, the rescue crew member was winched back into the chopper. The Huey's pilot then managed to lift the capsule a few feet out of the water, but could gain no further altitude, the entire rig slanting dangerously toward the sea.

"Capsule's full of water, we can't lift it!" came the frantic radio transmission to mission support personnel. One more attempt at airlifting the swamped spaceship was made, but to no avail. The laws of physics, to whose mastery the entire mission owed its success to this point, could not be broken. The helicopter could simply not provide enough lift, and the rescue craft itself started to wobble precariously scant feet above the waves.

"Cut the cable, cut the cable!" came the command from Capcom, but the quickness with which the task was carried out made it likely that the helicopter crew hadn't been waiting for orders.

The cable was severed. The capsule dropped back into the sea.

The chopper's pilot, now free of his weighty burden, quickly regained control of the aircraft and maneuvered to pick up the floating astronaut.

Gus Grissom was hauled aboard without further incident, while below them all, *Liberty Bell 7* continued its mission alone to the distant seafloor.

1

April 2, 1999, Monterey, California

U.S. Navy SEAL Dane Maddock tightened his grip on the submersible's control joystick as he eased the *Deep Surveyor III* into a narrow crevice nearly a mile beneath the Pacific. His co-pilot in the two-person craft, fellow SEAL Uriah "Bones" Bonebrake, pointed off to their right where the rock wall of the submarine canyon they'd been following slid past them mere feet away.

"Easy bro, maybe two feet clearance on this side," Bones warned.

"That's more room than I usually have to park at those sleazy clubs you drag me to."

Surprisingly to Dane, Bones remained silent. The six-and-a-half foot tall Cherokee rarely worried about anything, a testament to the fact that he did not consider being a mile underwater in a plastic bubble to be the time or place for levity. Dane cast a sideways glance to Bones' side of their acrylic sphere, where he kept a sharp eye on the irregular canyon wall.

This outing was to be their checkout dive for an intensive program that capped four straight weeks of submersible pilot training. Completing the dive's objective would earn them a new qualification, and Bones in particular was not looking forward to failing.

"Just stay focused, man. This isn't really a course I want to repeat."

Dane looked over at his co-pilot. "You mean you don't think this is fun?"

"Never been this deep in one of these things. Plus, I have to trust your driving." He let out a loud sigh. "I'm sure I'll get used to it sooner or later."

"You wound me. I thought we were like two peas in pod in here!"

"I'd sell all my naked photos of your mom if it would buy me the amount of room a pea must have compared to this. And you've got quite a bit more legroom than me."

Just shy of six feet, Dane did in fact have more space to maneuver within the racks of electronic equipment that guided the craft and allowed it to do useful work. For Bones, on the other hand, although he was, like all SEALs, a superb swimmer, scuba diver and all-around naval warrior, being cramped in the close confines of an underwater vehicle for hours at a time was losing its luster.

Still, he was here for a reason, and that reason was that while Dane had qualified as an ace submersible pilot, Bones had excelled at manipulating the sub's grab-arms and other specialized payload equipment in the simulation testing and training sessions with remotely operated vehicles, or ROVs. Dane had been taken aback when he read the duty assignment roster and saw Bones' name beside his own. The big Indian was always surprising him. Somehow he just kept showing up, which meant that somebody with a higher pay grade than Dane's saw something in the guy. Bones had a certain directness about him, a no-nonsense approach to everyday life situations that sometimes rankled the more reserved Dane, but by now the two had worked together enough that their professionalism had begun to overcome the irritations that initially flared up between them. Most of the time.

"Hey, where you going, Maddock? Our target's down there." Bones pointed down between his feet into the abyss that seemed to stretch below them into Hell itself. Their sonar told them, though, that the canyon's bottom lay "only" another mile deeper. Fortunately to both of them, they were not required to go that far.

"You sure?" Dane manipulated the ship's controls so that they were poised between two rock walls, awaiting confirmation. Bathed in the harsh artificial light of the sub's halogen floodlights, the walls revealed their true colors in a world normally immersed in total blackness.

Strange blue sponges that resembled lichens, vertical fields of white anemones, and myriad other creatures Dane couldn't identify somehow eked out a living down here in this freezing world of immense pressure. But as unique as it was, most of it looked the same to him.

Bones interrupted his thoughts. "In the briefing I was actually awake for, they said the target was 'at lower depth than where the canyon wall convergence narrows to less than three meters.' I did some checking and found that the target usually lives on a flat area. So we go down from here and look for a rocky shelf, I guess."

In response, Dane shot Bones a grudging look of respect and tilted their craft downward, activating the forward thrusters. For all his boisterousness, Bones somehow also found a way to pay attention, no matter how much he pretended otherwise. And theirs was definitely a line of work where not paying attention could get you killed.

They dropped down through the narrow crevice, Dane tweaking the sub's controls to make sure they didn't scrape the walls while Bones directed a movable spotlight to their surroundings while also monitoring their depth and sonar readouts.

"Coming up on something," Dane said, easing back on the thrusters.

"Rocky shelf. This could be it. Look for the... There it is!" Bones adjusted the angle of his high intensity beam until it illuminated a whitish stalk towering perhaps ten feet, its red tip a few feet below their submersible's belly. "Take us down a few feet; then we curve with the wall to the right."

Dane executed the delicate maneuver until they hovered over a flat expanse of rock that reminded him of a stairway landing—a brief interruption of the vertical plunge the canyon took for yet another mile. There, in the center of the platform, grew a massive tubeworm. Pale crabs scuttled out of reach of the craft's floodlights, pouring off the rocky shelf into the water column beneath them like lemmings from a cliff.

"Are we sure this is the right tubeworm?" Dane's careful attention to the controls didn't allow him the luxury of taking in the details of their surroundings to the degree that Bones could.

"Surer than you were about that dude in a dress who hit on you last weekend. I'm looking at the marker right next to it."

Dane took his co-pilot's word that the small cement block that had been previously placed there by their sub instructors lay at the foot of the towering invertebrate.

"Roger that. The marker; not the guy in the dress. And, for the record, it was a girl, she was just..."

"A big, hairy dude?"

Ignoring Bones' jibe, Dane brought their submersible closer to the base of the creature, which swayed slightly with the vehicle's prop-wash.

Bones leaned forward, pressing his head against the sub's acrylic dome as he stared intently at their target. "Okay, stop. I'm within range of the manipulator arm."

Dane let up on the thrusters. "Do your thing."

Clutched in the metal claw at the end of an extensible arm outside the sub was a tubular metal object. Bones delicately pressed buttons that rotated the claw as well as the arm itself in different directions. "I wish we were placing some C4 explosives instead of this boring contraption," he said, referring to the scientific instrumentation package they were supposed to deploy. "That would be much more awesome." He deftly placed the device on the ledge next to the cement marker and released it from the sub's grab arm.

"That's why this is *practice*, Bones. We screw up with this thing and some eggheads don't find out what the temperature variations are down here when that worm farts. Make a mistake with C4 and maybe these canyon walls come..."

A gruff, all-business voice issuing from their communications channel interrupted him. *"Topside to* Deep Surveyor III, *you are ordered to report immediately to Base Command. Proceed to support ship at once, do you copy?"*

Dane looked over at Bones, who was still retracting the now empty manipulator arm back to the sub. When Bones completed that task he looked over at Dane, raising his eyebrows.

Dane said to Bones, "What'd you do, drop the science package over the cliff?"

Bones shook his head and pointed down at the metal cylinder, where a green LED glowed next to the worm. "It's all good."

Dane responded over the radio that he acknowledged the order, then put his hands to work on the sub's controls.

"Let's go find out what they want."

An hour later Dane and Bones strode into the lobby of SEAL Base Command, Monterey Station. Dane addressed a female receptionist in uniform seated behind a horseshoe shaped desk. He started to explain who they were when she waved him down.

"In here now, gentlemen!" a male voice pre-empted from the office, the door to which was open but the man out of sight. The young woman raised an eyebrow and tilted her head in the direction of the office, her meaning clear. *You'd better go.*

Bones gave her his most lascivious smile which she returned before swiveling in her chair to answer a phone call. Dane reached the doorway to Senior Commander Douglas Lawhorne's private office first, where he gave a salute.

"Close the door behind you, and at ease."

As soon as Bones stepped inside, Dane shut the door and then the two of them took seats in front of the commander's desk, which was set off to the left of the well-appointed room. Scale model ships and submarines decorated the walls behind the desk, while the fourth floor floor-to-ceiling windows afforded a magnificent view of Monterey Bay and the waters from which they had just returned. But it wasn't often a newly minted SEAL was summoned directly to a commander's office in the middle of a training exercise, so for the moment Dane refrained from absorbing the atmosphere. He noticed that even Bones, whom he considered a good ADHD candidate, was so far affording the commander his undivided attention.

"Congratulations on earning your Deep Manned Submersible Rating, you two. Well done." Lawhorne's smile did not reach his eyes.

Dane and Bones exchanged quizzical looks that said, *we passed*? But then the commander, a balding man in his early fifties with a chest full of medals, spoke again.

"Your instructor tells me that you both scored highly throughout the exercises. I'm sorry that I don't yet have your detailed evaluations ready for review, or your new pins, but you'll receive them as soon as you get back."

Dane let the obvious question go unspoken, as he felt it was not his place to question a man of the commander's rank unprompted.

"Get back from where?" Bones asked.

Dane did his best to suppress an involuntary cringe. He looked over at his partner in war, who sat casually in his jeans and wool pullover—the same outfit he'd had on in the sub to ward off the chill. A small abalone shell hung around his neck, a nod to the native tribes who once lived in California for whom the shiny-shelled mollusk was an important food source. Dane expected Lawhorne might rebuke Bones for speaking out of turn, but if the officer was irritated he didn't let it show.

"The two of you have been placed on special assignment to the east coast of Florida, effective immediately. That's all I know at this point."

Lawhorne paused to look at his two SEALs as if he expected questions, so Dane ventured, “Pardon me, Sir, but are you going to brief us?”

The man on the other side of the desk shook his head emphatically. “Negative. I am not privy to the details of your assignment because I do not have sufficient clearance.”

Dane’s mouth started to drop open before he pulled it together. Bones also said nothing, an indicator that he too was stunned by the implications of their superior officer’s words.

If *he* didn’t have clearance, then how high-level must this assignment be?

The commander checked his watch. “You board a plane in fifty-three minutes. I’m told you’ll be briefed en route. Get back to your quarters. Pack your bags, wait for ground transport. Dismissed.”

Dane shot to his feet and saluted. Bones ambled up from his chair, saluting with a confused look on his face. Then he said, “Excuse me, Sir, but does this mean we’re going to miss the submersible class graduation party that was supposed to be tonight, or will it be rescheduled?”

Dane rolled his eyes and rubbed his temples.

“Son, you’re going to miss that party but from the way it seems, if you have success on this mission I expect you’ll be coming home to the biggest damn bash you’ve ever had in your life.”

Lawhorne saw the grin forming on Bones’ face and held up a hand before continuing.

“Listen to me. Like I said, I don’t have the details. But this much I do know: your country needs you. Do *not* let it down.”

Printed in Poland
by Amazon Fulfillment
Poland Sp. z o.o., Wrocław

57080650R10264